POINT
OF
FREEDOM

NORDIC LORDS MC BOOK #3

STACEY LYNN

Editing provided by: Amy Jackson Editing

Cover design provided by: QDesign, Amy Queau

Internal formatting provided by: Angela McLaurin, Fictional Formats

POINT
OF
FREEDOM

1

Jules

I should have followed the old adage "Keep your thoughts to yourself."

Had I not, fifteen minutes ago spoken the words "Could this day get any worse?" out loud—if only to myself—I might not have found myself standing in front of the one person who hated me more than he hated anyone else in the entire world.

I spoke those words to the blue sky above me when I found out Jasper Bay High School wasn't going to hire me for their open English teacher position, and I swear God took the challenge, quirked His lips into a smirk, and whispered, "You bet, baby. Buckle up and hold on."

I had thrown that challenge out into the universe and now fate was coming back to kick me right in the butt.

Worse, I had no one else to help me get out of this freaking mess except for Jaden. If he had his choice between helping me and leaving me stranded, Jaden would laugh his ass off while I suffered a slow and painful death.

He had pulled up to the side of the road minutes ago, climbed off his bike, and leaned back against it, his arms crossed over his chest and his feet crossed at the ankles. He hadn't yet removed his sunglasses. The only move he'd made in the last few minutes was to run his hand over his short, cropped blond hair and stare at me with a smirk—daring me to ask him for help.

"Car broke?" he drawled, a sarcastic tilt to his lips.

I glanced at the hood of my car, still smoking, and then to the backseat and Sophie's empty car seat. At least she wasn't around to see us hate each other again.

"Is it that obvious?" I asked. I couldn't help myself.

Jaden brought out a sarcastic side to me more than anyone else. He made my blood boil. I left most encounters with him with my jaw and teeth hurting from clamping my mouth shut so I didn't scream at him.

"I called the garage for help."

Unwrapping his arms from his chest, he pushed off the bike. "Lucky for you I was working at the garage today, then, huh?"

If by 'lucky' he meant 'unluckiest person in the world,' he was correct.

Fate hadn't been on my side for freaking years. Not since my ex-boyfriend, Scratch, died in a motorcycle accident. Not since the life I'd been building in Phoenix ended tits up, and I came back home to avoid the fallout from one more dumbass decision I'd made.

Fate certainly wasn't willing to lend me a hand, since the high school I'd attended at one time wouldn't hire me, even though I knew they had no applicants and I was completely qualified for their teaching position. I suspected this was because when I was twenty-one, I got knocked up by one of the town's bad-ass biker boys.

No one seemed to remember that I loved Scratch more than anything else in the world—except for Sophie now.

No one seemed to care that every time I thought his name, my heart squeezed painfully tight as if being pressed through a paper shredder.

And Jaden, Scratch's brother and the man who blamed me for his brother's death, didn't seem to notice that every single time he stared at me, my heart ached with longing for Scratch. Jaden was almost a mirror image of the man I had loved for as long as I could remember.

His presence made my pulse race—in the best of ways and worst of ways.

Jaden walked around me and popped the hood of my not so old Toyota Camry. Another bloom of smoke wafted out around him.

"When was the last time you changed your oil?"

Um. I shrugged as he glared at me. He'd taken off his sunglasses, folded them, and shoved them into the front of his white T-shirt. "Your transmission fluid?"

My what? "Um."

"Your tires rotated? Your brake fluid?"

"Brakes use fluid?" Seriously? They were brakes… rubber on metal.

I jumped as the loud crashing sound of my hood being slammed shut echoed in the open air. Jaden's boots crunched against the gravel on the side of the road before he stood in front of me.

Glaring at me.

Looking exactly like Scratch on the last night I saw him, when we had argued.

The pressure—the force of Jaden's presence in front of me, with his flared nostrils and narrowed brown eyes—left me gasping for a breath that didn't want to come.

I stumbled back into the side of the car. I inhaled, but my lungs were broken. It stung and burned in my throat and my chest, but all I could do was wheeze in for a breath.

Jaden loomed in closer. He leaned down and glared directly into my wide eyes while I struggled to gain control.

"Are you stupid?"

"No, I'm not stupid," I hissed at him, leaning in. My frustration with Jaden didn't run as deep as his hatred for me. But I wasn't stupid. And I was never again going to let someone talk to me that way.

"I'm a girl. I don't know shit about cars, and no one told me my brakes ran on fluid. I thought they were rubber."

I could have sworn he grinned. But it vanished before the furious glare, which he usually kept on his face in my presence, replaced it.

"Can you fix my car?"

His nose twitched before he finally leaned back. Once he did, I was able to actually breathe again. Damn it. He looked so much like Scratch it was unbelievable.

Some days, when I could catch Jaden at the Nordic Lords clubhouse where he was a member, and he wasn't pissed off I was hanging around... sometimes, I got a profile shot of him and my breath would catch in my throat in the best way possible.

Because those times... it was as if Scratch was still alive. And I could pretend, if only for a moment—until Jaden caught me watching him and vehemence replaced his relaxed look—that Scratch was still alive.

That I hadn't lost the man I loved.

That my daughter hadn't lost her dad before she ever existed.

But then Jaden's brown eyes would darken as black as raging storm waters, dashing my dreams and memories as reality replaced them.

"Jaden?" I asked, because the man was still staring at me. I felt the burn in my sinuses when the sun hit his eyes and his square chin and strong features. "Can you fix my car?"

He looked over my shoulder toward the hood and nodded. "Yeah, in about a week."

My jaw dropped as I sputtered. "A week?"

"Yup. It'll take a while. Can't fix it from here, but by the way the engine's shredded, the oil's probably never been changed and you've done shit to actually care for the thing, I'm guessing it needs a lot of work."

Darn it. How in the hell was I supposed to move and find a job without a car?

"Fine," I muttered, and reached for my phone, digging it out of my purse. As I started sliding through my contacts, a warm hand reached out and covered mine.

I gasped. Not because I was scared of Jaden. But because for six months, no man had touched me and the last time one did, it was done in a way that had made me not want to be touched by anyone.

Also because something strange—and not entirely unwelcome—slithered up the skin on my arm as Jaden's hand clamped down on mine. All the hairs on my arm stood straight up.

"What are you doing?" He growled and I forced my eyes to meet his.

I flinched out of his grasp. Blood drained from my face as he cocked his head and furrowed his brow. He looked back at his hand, which still hovered above mine, before shoving it into his jeans.

I held up my phone. "Calling for a ride."

In one fluid movement he stepped back, reached for his sunglasses, and flicked them back over his eyes. Without seeing the hatred in his eyes, he looked even more like his little brother. My knees went weak. They weren't twins. But they could have been. At only ten months apart in age, they had essentially grown up being treated the exact same. The fact that they looked the exact same, minus their differing eye color, didn't help.

Or they used to.

With Jaden so close to me—and it being so long since any member of the Dillon family had stood so close to me—I could catalogue the slight differences.

A small scar on Jaden's left cheekbone, a slightly crooked nose that said it'd been broken one too many times and not properly reset. Shoulders that were slightly wider than I remembered, and if I did remember correctly, I also had to tilt my neck back a little bit further in order to look directly at him.

Still, I pushed it out of my mind when Jaden cocked his head toward his bike, his teeth clamped together. "Get on the bike."

My head snapped in the direction of the bike and whipped back toward Jaden. He looked more upset about me being on the bike than

I did about wanting to be on it.

"I'll call Olivia."

"You think I want you on the back of my bike?" He leaned down and snarled at me. And swear to God, there was something else I saw in his eyes that I couldn't place... wasn't sure I wanted to place... but it wasn't hate. I just didn't know what it was. "You think I want you—any part of you—touching me or anything that belongs to me? Everything you touch dies."

I gasped, my face paled more than it already had, and my nose began to burn again. Damn it. Screw him! It wasn't my fault, and he would never give me a chance to explain.

"I don't," he finally hissed. "But I'm not the biggest asshole in the world to leave you out here, five miles outside town, stranded. Liv would kick my ass if I left you here. So get your shit and get on my bike."

He reached out and grabbed my phone from me. Shocked at the quickness of his move and lethal expression, I let it slide easily out of my hand.

I opened my mouth to speak and then sighed gratefully as my phone began vibrating in Jaden's large grip. It surprised him enough that he opened his fingers and I snatched it back.

Saved by the buzzer.

I was so thankful for whoever was calling—whoever could come get me—I answered without looking.

That was when I decided Fate was a spiteful bitch.

"You didn't think I wouldn't find you again, did you?"

My skin clammed up instantly, and my knees shook so hard that I leaned against the side of my car before I collapsed.

No way in hell was this happening. Least of all in front of Jaden.

2

Jules

"How'd you get my number?" I asked, watching Jaden. His jaw had gone tight again and I turned away, facing the car.

Based on the mountain of heat coming from behind me, I knew he was watching. I knew Jaden had seen my reaction, and I knew that on some level it had pissed him off.

Not that he'd ever admit it. Especially to me.

"I want my girls back," Rob said. Rob. The man who had smacked me across the face the last time I'd seen him because I was too tired for sex.

Too tired because Sophie had the flu, a temperature of one hundred and three, and I was tired, un-showered, and most of all... not in the mood.

"I told you to leave me alone," I whisper-hissed into the phone.

As soon as the words were out of my mouth, my phone was once again ripped out of my hand and inside Jaden's palm.

His tightened jaw relaxed enough to growl, "Who the fuck is this?"

He did this while keeping his eyes locked on mine. I gaped at my cell phone, which had become a tennis ball being lobbed back and forth between us, and I almost missed it when his eyes narrowed and his knuckles tightened their grip on the phone.

"Stay the fuck away or you'll regret it." He snapped the phone shut and handed it to me. "Who was that asshole?"

My breath was shaky, and my words were most likely completely unbelievable when I said, "No one important."

Jaden leaned in. I caught the faint whiff of stale smoke on his breath. "I thought you weren't a liar."

"I'm not," I snapped right back. "But I'm pretty certain you've made it obvious that my life—and whoever is *in* my life—is none of your damn concern."

He winced slightly as I implied that his niece, Sophie, whom he had yet to bother even saying hello to, wasn't any of his concern. He had made it completely obvious to me and our friends that he wanted nothing to do with me or her. Hell, just weeks ago he had declared his doubt about Sophie being Scratch's.

Although that was stupid. One look at baby photos of Jaden and Scratch would prove Sophie looked exactly like the two of them.

Jaden was in denial. And I was tired of caring about it.

"Get on my bike."

"No." I crossed my arms over my chest and leaned against my car. Between the loss of another job opportunity, the sun beating down on me, and Jaden's mood swings, I felt the beginning twinges of a migraine coming on.

"It's five miles to town, Jules."

I looked around and exhaled. Five miles to town. Seven miles to my home. Sophie would be eating dinner. Then she'd be wondering where I was because I was supposed to be home at least an hour ago, and Sophie always worried about me.

But even with all that, getting on the back of Jaden's bike, putting my arms around him, was bound to be a bad idea. He reminded me enough of Scratch that I'd probably do something like lean in, hold tight, and heaven forbid—enjoy myself.

He also hated me enough that I wouldn't be surprised if he put me on his bike and took a corner too fast on purpose just to fling me off the back.

Besides all that, it was a motorcycle. And it looked exactly like the bike Scratch rode the night he died. And I'd sworn that night—and the next few days afterward when I buried the man I loved, but had to do it at a distance because no one from the club allowed me to get too close—that I would never... *never*... sit on the back of a bike again.

I was a parent and I had to be responsible.

And joyriding on the back of a Harley was *not* responsible.

"I'll walk."

As if he sensed the reason for my indecision, Jaden made the choice for me. He grabbed my hand, pulled me toward the bike, and plopped a helmet on my head before I could argue.

Then I found myself sitting on it, him in front of me, with his back muscles coiled tightly under the familiar Nordic Lords MC leather vest.

Blood pulsed in every pore of my body as I fought the memories of the night the accident happened, the argument Scratch and I'd had, the screams we'd shouted between us, and then the forgiveness... the making up part... the celebrating.

Jaden had to go and open his big mouth and ruin all of it.

"I fucking hate you, Jules, but that doesn't mean I want you dead. Hold the fuck on so we can go."

He revved the engine and started pulling the bike out onto the highway so quickly that I had no other choice except to hang on.

My hands went to his stomach, I closed my eyes, and as we whipped down the highway, going way faster than we needed to, I also felt myself relax and lean into Jade—probably more than I should have.

A smile graced my lips in the wind and open air.

The ride reminded me of how nice it was back when I was really, truly happy.

It reminded me how easy and fun life used to be.

With the wind whipping through my hair, I craved it—the fun and the freedom—because it had been way too long since I'd had either.

I let out a large, shaky exhale as soon as Jaden parked his bike in my parents' driveway. The monstrosity loomed in front of me like a castle. I had loved being the mayor's daughter as a child. Our town was small, but because of that, being the mayor made someone a celebrity. And because of that, I had always been treated like one.

Or a princess, as my dad called me.

Our house even had turrets. They were beautiful, and I had always envied my parents' bedroom, with the rounded sitting area and lofted ceiling.

As a child it was the perfect home to grow up in.

As a teenager, when I'd rebelled by always being by Scratch's side and the rest of the Nordic Lords, I'd embarrassed my family greatly.

Fortunately, they had forgiven me as soon as they laid their eyes on Sophie. She was impossible to not fall in love with, and over the years—even after I moved to Arizona to finish college and start a career—I was grateful for their support.

But now, being back outside their house, with Jaden in particular, the house looked cold and barren.

Or perhaps that was the emotion pouring off Jaden as I pushed off his bike and stood in front of him.

"Thanks," I mumbled. I had no idea what to say to this man who hated me. I couldn't look into eyes so similar to the ones I'd loved and see his hatred for me.

It shot a dull knife into my chest every time it happened.

I turned and began walking toward my front door right as he called my name.

"Yeah?" I asked, looking at him over my shoulder.

His tan hands gripped and twisted on his motorcycle handles. "I didn't expect you to ever come back here."

I sighed. The last thing I wanted was a yelling match in front of my house, where my parents or Sophie could hear. My day had been shitty enough, and exhaustion prevented me from wanting to go another round of battle with Jaden.

The urge to flee inside the walls of my house, protected from his darkened brown eyes, screamed at me.

"Didn't plan on coming back."

Jaden glanced up at my house behind me, and his eyes went blank before he turned them back on me. When he did, a muscle ticked in his cheek. "That phone call. You in some sort of trouble?"

"Nothing I can't handle, Jaden." My hands curled into fists. The last thing I wanted to do was discuss Rob and the disaster that had been. "Thanks for the ride."

His nose wrinkled. "I want to see her."

A warm feeling hit my chest at his words, making me stumble back a step. My head flipped around to the house to see if Sophie could see me. To see if anyone was watching. Thankfully, I didn't see any suspicious fluttering of the sheer window curtains to give away any peering eyes.

Jaden looked down at his boots before he met my eyes. The sincerity, the serious gaze as he hit my eyes, again left me breathless.

Damn it.

I shook the strange thoughts of out my head. All I had ever wanted was Jaden to know her. Countless phone calls after Scratch's funeral to Jaden had gone unreturned. I never even knew if he'd listened to my messages letting him know what happened that night, or that I was pregnant. That I wanted him to know the baby I would have, seeing as how she would be the only family he had left.

But none of that had happened.

Instead, everyone had turned their backs on me. Not that it was surprising: I don't think anyone in the club was fond of the idea of a motorcycle junkie dating the town princess.

"You have seen her." He'd seen her plenty in the last couple of weeks. When he wasn't snarling at me, he completed ignored both of us. The last time being at a party for Ryker and Faith, the same night Olivia and Daemon—the President of the Nordic Lords and good friends of ours—got engaged.

Jaden's jaw clamped together. My pulse began beating faster and hotter under my skin. His hands twisted on the handles, his eyes glanced to the house again. "If she's his, then she's mine."

I bristled at his possessive tone. Not to mention the way his lip curled when he said "if." As if I was still lying about it.

My shoulders wrenched back, my hands flew to my hips. "Scratch was Sophie's dad. And if you think for one single second I'm going to let you be around her, doubting that fact, or being an ass to her like you're being to me, you're wrong."

He threw a leg over his bike and began stalking toward me. "She's my niece, I want to see her." The words fell from his lips as if they'd tripped over barbed wire on the way out of his throat. Between his growled words and his low and threatening voice, it took every ounce of strength I possessed to not cower beneath him.

I wanted him to see her. I wanted Sophie to know her uncle. I wanted her to have the memories of her dad through Jaden's eyes.

Tears pricked my eyes and I sniffed. God, I wanted that for her.

I sniffed again and tried to shake the tears away. "You don't get to be a dick to her."

He nodded once, glanced up at the door behind me, and back to me. When he looked at me, an undecipherable look flew through his eyes before it disappeared. "She could be all I have."

God. Of all the most amazing things the asshole could have said to me, that'd be at the top of the list.

I wanted to give that to him. I had *always* wanted to give that to him.

And with the way he now stood in front of me, fidgeting on his feet, there was no way could I deny him.

I wiped under my nose, hoping my eyes didn't appear as glassy as they felt. "Sure," I said, inhaling deeply. "We'll figure something out."

He seemed to consider that for a moment and then took a step away from me, turning his back to me. "I'll call about your car."

The sudden shift in conversation, the abrupt ending to talk about Sophie, left me reeling.

"Jaden," I called, once he reached his bike. "I want you to see Sophie."

I barely heard the word "soon" fall from his lips before he revved the bike and pulled out of my drive.

I don't know how long I stared at the spot he'd vacated like a hive of wasps were on his ass, but I was still standing there, my head spinning with everything that had happened, when I felt the warmth of my dad's arms curl around my shoulders.

I leaned in, resting my head against his chest.

"I don't see good things for you, sweetie, with that boy back in your life." My dad's warm voice rumbled over me, making me tense.

His grip on my shoulder squeezed and loosened. "I'm not saying that to hurt you, but that boy hasn't been right since Scratch died. He's angry and he's vicious. Not sure it's the best combination for you right now."

I breathed in slowly and exhaled, tears blooming in my eyes all over again. I hadn't spared my parents details when it came to Rob, using my mom's ears as my verbal vomit bucket. I'd unleashed everything I'd been feeling, all the shame for being mixed up with a guy like him in the first place and not being smart enough to realize it.

I blamed the fact that I was a single mom, young, and had always doubted anyone's ability to love me and another man's child.

Rob had faked it real good for a long time. So long that by the time he began showing me who he really was, it took me months to catch up to the fact that he wasn't just having the occasional bad day—he was just really a bad man.

I sniffled again, nodding against my dad's chest, and wrapped my arms around his waist. "I know, Dad. But he has the right know Sophie if he wants to."

He exhaled a breath into the top of my head before his lips pressed my hair. "Sophie's one thing. I have a feeling if he gets to know her, he'll fall in love with her like everyone else does."

I chuckled because he was right. Sophie had a soft voice and a nervous smile, but when you were able to break through that, she poured out her sweet two-year-old love on everyone she met.

"It's your heart I'm worried about."

I choked over my swallow.

Luckily, my dad didn't let me spend too much time wondering what he meant by that, because he let go of me and turned toward the house.

"Your mom's been inside fretting for the last ten minutes. Let's get you some dinner, and you can tell me why you were on that boy's bike in the first place."

It hit me then that was the only thing I heard my dad call Jaden—that boy. He hadn't liked Scratch, mostly because of the motorcycle club he was connected to. But he'd always used his name. Made me wonder, as we walked into my house, why my dad felt the need to distance himself from Jaden in that way.

Was it for his benefit? Or was it for mine?

But then the smell of my mom's beef stroganoff hit my nose—something she was the bomb at making—and Sophie's pudgy feet were trampling down the wood-floored hallway.

The aroma of dinner filled my senses.

Sophie's tight embrace around my hips filled my heart.

And everything about Jaden was completely forgotten.

3

Jaden

The dream—more like a nightmare—pulled me from sleep and left me gasping for breath.

"Fuck."

I sat up in the bed, flung my arm out to the side, and hit a small wall of soft, warm flesh.

Looking over, I grimaced and ran hand over my face and through my blond hair.

"Shit," I muttered when I took in the naked body next to me. The sheet pooled around her waist and her back was to me. I took in the long bleached hair, the curve of her side as it dipped to her waist and rose by her hip.

Shayla? Shania? Shit. Did it matter who she was? My head pounded, the vicious remnants of a night spent at the club, trying to forget. Fuck, I was trying to forget everything last night.

"Hey." I pushed on her hip, rocking her gently.

The club bunny groaned, draped an arm over her eyes, and rolled to her back.

"Time to go."

"Five more minutes," she mumbled and drew the sheet over her chest. Which sucked, because I couldn't remember the chick's name, but I had a vivid memory of sucking on those tits of hers. They were the only nice-looking thing about her—probably because she paid for them.

I shoved her hip harder to make my point. "I ain't a fuckin' hotel bellboy and this isn't your wake up call, bitch. Get up and get the hell out of my bed."

She rolled over and opened an eye. Her quick intake of breath, her smeared mascara, and the way she grabbed the sides of her head, all told me her night had been as rough as mine.

I blamed Jules for my night. She was always fucking with my head—more so now that she was back in town with her little girl, Sophie.

Damn. Had I really told her I wanted to see Sophie?

"Get out," I repeated to the woman as she sat up and groaned in pain.

"Chill out, Jaden, I'm goin'."

I flung my own covers off, saw my dick hard and pressed against my lower stomach.

Fuck. What I wanted was to wrap my hand around it and take care of business. Instead, I saw the club bunny look at me with a hungry glint in her eye.

"Get out." If I didn't remember fucking her the first time, I wasn't going to refresh my memory with another lousy lay.

She raised a brow and stood from the bed, now clothed in a black thong. The sight did nothing for me, and my hard-on began to soften. What in the hell was I thinking, taking her to bed? She was just a used club bunny, someone who hung around and flung her pussy for free.

My kind of girl, normally.

Yesterday's trip with Jules, her arms wrapped around me tightly on the bike, squeezing close to me, and the light that hit her pale blue eyes –

What the fuck?

I growled, frustrated and pissed at myself for going there in my thoughts about Jules. Again.

My brother's girl.

The girl who was responsible for taking the last family member I had.

Screw her.

Screw the club bunny—Shayna! That was it. The name written in glitter across her tank top probably helped.

"See you around?" she asked, one eyebrow raised.

"Not likely," I muttered as I hauled ass to the bathroom. I needed a shower, a good jack-off, and a beating in the ring outside to expel the leftover alcohol from my system.

Maybe then I'd forget the dream.

Maybe then I'd forget the screams I heard in my ears every time I imagined or dreamed about the night my brother crashed his bike, racing like hell from—or toward—who the hell knew what.

And maybe, once I finally took care of business, I'd forget that every single damn time I'd closed my eyes in the last few weeks, all I saw was Jules's eyes staring back at me.

Begging me… pleading with me… to forgive her.

And then I'd forget the dream where I threw my arms around her, dug my fingers into her scalp, and kissed the ever-loving shit out of her before screwing her like an animal, where the only sound in the air was her screaming my name as I made her come.

The water beat down on my back and shoulders. The heat stung my skin as it rolled down my chest. I closed my eyes, gripping my dick, pulling and tugging with a force harder than necessary.

I couldn't fucking help it. Jules had messed with my head as a teenager, but I had let all that shit go when she'd chosen Scratch. I hadn't ever liked it, and found it easier to pretend I hated her. That had become even easier when he'd died and she'd taken off after cheating on him.

"Fuck," I groaned, my release building. My orgasm coiled in my tight balls, right before I released into my hand. Cream from my dick spurted out on the wall and in my fingers as I continued tugging, wringing every last miserable ounce of pleasure from my body all by myself.

I didn't want my hand.

I wanted Jules. I wanted her legs wrapped around my waist as I pounded into her. I wanted to take out my hatred of her, my anger with her, by releasing my orgasm inside of her, leaving her bruised for days so she'd remember who it was that left her feeling that way.

Wanting her made me hate her—mostly because it had never been right to want her in the first place when she belonged to my brother. It certainly hadn't been right to want her when she cheated on him. And it definitely wasn't right to want her now—not when she was raising my brother's kid, back in town and back in my life, fuckin' with my head all over again.

Wanting Jules had fucked up my life, taken the most important person from me.

It was safer to keep hating her.

So why the fuck I'd told her I wanted to know and see Sophie, I still had no damn idea.

"Bet that was fun, yesterday." Daemon grinned at me, fists raised in the middle of the ring.

The asshole was taunting me, dancing lighter on his feet than he should have been able to, because the dude was not a boxer.

I'd kick his ass regardless of him being our Club President—or my best friend.

I swung and got blocked by his forearm. "You're a dick."

He grinned, took a step back. "So how'd Jules look, standing outside her car in the hot sun, sweat all over her body?"

"I'm tellin' Liv you're checking out other women."

We dodged and weaved around the ring, blocking more shots than hitting our targets, mostly because we boxed and fought every day and knew each other's moves better than we knew our own.

He ducked under my right hook, but I anticipated it, and as he moved, my left leg kicked out, swooped under his right leg, and his ass landed on the mat with a groan.

I smirked, leaning over him. "You want more?"

His gloved hand hit my knee. "Get the hell away from me. Don't you have a car to fix?"

I looked up, a growl escaping my lips as I saw Jules's Camry gleaming in the sun.

Brakes use fluid? Jesus. Stupid girls needed men in their lives—to take care of cars, at the very least. Although I had bit back a grin when she'd said it.

But it was her false innocence that had left me clenching my fists and my jaw. Fuck her. Fuck her car. She ruined everything she came near—why would a car be any different?

"Hey, dick."

I snapped my eyes to Daemon, his hair pulled into a ponytail at the base of his neck and his blue eyes fixed on mine.

He began unwrapping the tape from his hands. "I know this shit is hard for you, but don't fuck her over."

I pressed my gloved hands together, my neck more stiff from the statement than the beating I just took. "Quit worryin' about it." I turned, ripping off the gloves and the tape.

"The thing is," he started, and my jaw instantly clenched. Very little pissed me off with Daemon, but talking about Jules was always the best way to do it. "You screw over Jules and we lose Sophie."

Sophie. My niece. Fuck. I would have been an idiot to not recognize the resemblance to Scratch. Yet when I first saw Jules and Sophie together, the shock of her having a kid, all I could think about was all the messages she'd left after my brother had died. The texts begging me to call her. The voice messages that, in my rage to blame her for his death, I'd deleted without listening to.

It wasn't the first day I'd wondered if I should have listened to them.

I shook it off. Daemon knew. Daemon always knew how I'd wanted her—lost her to my brother and manned up and put it behind me.

You tried to. Shit.

"I took her home and asked to see the kid, all right?"

Daemon nodded. His throat bobbed when he swallowed and his arms crossed over his chest. "Good."

Shitty. Painful. Able to rip open every fucking painful scar that I'd been able to lance with violence, drink, and women over the last few years is what it was. 'Good' would never be a word I used to describe it.

My nose twitched and I spit into a bucket outside the ring. I needed a drink. Something to numb the constant ache I'd felt ever since I saw Jules standing in Daemon's house months ago.

I turned to Daemon and our eyes met, his narrowed and cautioning. Mine, fuck. I closed my eyes, pulled in a deep breath.

"We done?"

A muscle tic in his jaw confirmed it.

"Later, then." I lifted a hand, climbed through the ropes of the boxing ring, and took off for the garage.

As I began digging through her engine, cleaning it, repairing every damn thing she hadn't put the effort into maintaining in the last few years—from the carburetor to the filter to all the fluid—I couldn't stop thinking about her.

Her hips.

Her lips.

Her soft fucking blue eyes that seemed so damn scared of me, yet hopeful at the same time. Like I had the damn power to offer her absolution. Forgiveness for all her sins and her wrongs.

Fuck if I did.

If anything, losing Scratch—the last remaining member of my blood family—had taught me that I wasn't shit. I didn't have shit to give to anyone. Least of all some kid related to me.

Or her mom.

4

Jules

I clung to Faith's hand. I couldn't believe it as I gaped at the beautiful diamond on her finger. Tears swelled in my eyes as I recalled how just months ago, she'd called me back to Jasper Bay when she couldn't be there for our friend, Olivia, who had just been shot. Instead, Faith was trapped in her own hell, being owned as a prostitute for a rival club, the Black Death. But Daemon and Ryker Knight—brothers, and apparently awesome lovers and men—had rescued them both.

I brushed away happy tears with one hand, squeezed her hand tighter with my other. "I'm so happy for you."

"Thanks, sweetie." Faith wrapped her arms around me, hugging me as tightly as I embraced her. She was engaged to a man she had loved her entire life. I couldn't be happier. "Your time will come again."

That same soft spear of pain delved deep inside my chest at the thought. I pulled back, smiling and brushing away tears, but they were no longer just happy ones. But who was I to ruin the party the club was having in celebration of Faith and Ryker getting engaged?

Not only that, but for now, the club was safe. The Black Death had been vanquished from town and nothing could hurt them.

"Come on." Faith tugged my hand, pulling me toward the bar.

"You're not allowed to be sad at my party."

"I'm not sad." The slight catch in my throat was a dead giveaway of my lie. Faith flashed me a knowing glance and slid a shot glass in front of me.

"Thanks, Tripp." Faith nodded toward the guy behind the bar. He was older than us, but not by much, based on the fine wrinkles around his lips, eyes, and across his forehead.

He paused to nod his full, slightly peppered hair in my direction.

Inconsequential.

That was how I felt whenever I stepped into the club. An outsider, regardless that I'd borne a girl of one of their own. The stigma of what I'd done—or what they believed I'd done—years ago settled like a weight in my gut, leaving me ten pounds heavier every time I was around the Nordic Lords.

At one time it'd been different.

Everything had been different. I had never had their respect, but I'd had their acceptance. Those days were long gone now, though, and it wasn't the first time I'd been around this group of crazy, rowdy, oftentimes law-breaking men and wondered what in the hell I was doing back in Jasper Bay.

"Hey." Faith nudged my side with her elbow and I blinked out of my thoughts. "It's okay to have a hard time being back here, you know."

I eyed her warily, waiting to see if she'd bring up Scratch or the accident—or Sophie, for that matter. When I saw understanding in her softened eyes and slightly downturned smile, I leaned in and rested my head against her shoulder.

Faith knew how I felt maybe more than anyone: she'd grown up in this club, but after her dad turned on the men, her mom sold her to a rival club in order to pay for her own drug supply. Faith spent years living a hell I wouldn't wish upon my worst enemy. She had only been back in the club for the last few months, and yet seemed so completely in love with Ryker, not only her one-time ex-fiancé, but they'd been reunited and tonight was about celebrating them becoming engaged again.

If anyone knew how it felt to walk through the doors to the Nordic Lords' Clubhouse with a weight on their shoulders, it was Faith.

I sipped my beer slowly, tipping the bottom of the bottle back and forth on the bar top, and scanned the small gathering room.

Cue balls slamming into their intended targets echoed above the old-school rock music pouring from the speakers hanging in the corners of the room.

Men cheered. They slung their beer. They kissed their women—or whoever was available—but what always surprised me the most being around these men was the freedom, the easy living despite their hardened lives and sometimes lack of morals.

Their women were loud and crass. The men loved it.

No one seemed as if they gave a shit about anything else in their lives except for what was in this room. My parents had never understood how their lifestyle had appealed to me when I was young. They never understood how someone who had been raised in my lifestyle would risk throwing it away for someone like Scratch.

We had been young teenagers when we started dating, and he had died three years ago. But we had a kind of love that, even as much as my parents tried to fight me about, I knew would last forever. Being in this room of loud voices and huge amounts of love reminded me of the reason I had loved it here so much when I was young. It reminded me why I had loved being with Scratch, Olivia, and Faith.

Here, I was free. I was free to screw up without condemnation. I was free to explore and do whatever I wanted, and most of all, I was free to be me without the stress of wondering who would tell my parents.

A slow smile tugged at the edges of my lips.

"Come on," I finally said. I slammed down my beer, threw back a shot of vodka, and grabbed Faith's hand. "Let's party."

She raised her glass, threw her long black hair over her shoulder, and laughed. "You're on."

I dragged her over to Olivia where she immediately threw her arms around me and Faith. In the background, Daemon and Ryker froze their gazes to their women. Their eyes raked down Olivia's and Faith's bodies. The heat from their men almost left me feeling as if I was watching a ménage I hadn't been invited to. Heat stained my cheeks.

"Drink up!" Olivia declared.

Another drink was placed into my palm from out of nowhere, and I raised my glass in celebration.

"Congratulations to Faith and Ryker!" I shouted. Men joined in with the whoops and hollers of the answering shouts, and I watched as Ryker wrapped his tanned arm around Faith's shoulder, pulled her close, and kissed her obscenely.

And I got lost. I got lost in the sounds, in the excitement, in the free liquor, and in the freedom of being able to live in the moment for the first time in months—possibly years.

My head and my stomach swam with warmth from the booze.

My smile grew larger with each passing shot someone handed to me.

I danced on tables with Olivia and sang off-key with my arms wrapped around Faith.

Then, out of the corner of my eye, I caught Jaden.

His scowl permanently fixed, like it always was in my presence, directly on me.

I swayed on the coffee table where Faith and I stood, and grabbed onto her forearms.

"You okay?" she asked, laughter ringing loud and clear in her slightly drunken voice. Faith rarely drank, and never got drunk, but apparently I wasn't the only one letting go tonight.

I forced my eyes off Jaden, pulling them as if I had to drag them through sludge or quicksand. He sucked me in with his darkened gaze and pulled me in further by looking so much like his brother.

My breath caught in my throat and I stepped off the table, crashing into a half-naked couple sprawled on the loveseat.

"Sorry, Jimmy," I mumbled, reaching out to steady myself.

"Johnny."

"Whatever." They were twins, and no one in the club could tell them apart. I didn't feel bad about it as the full force of my drunkenness hit me.

My stomach flipped from overindulging, and feeling Jaden's eyes still on me, I needed air. I needed space and I needed to breathe.

Rushing out the door of the clubhouse on unsteady feet, I pushed open the front door and gasped for breath.

Fall was settling in and the chilled burst of breeze blew through my thin shirt and shorts. My hands dropped to my knees and I breathed in the cool, crisp air.

"You okay?"

I lifted my head toward the masculine voice and slowly stood up. A man I'd met only a few times stood in front of me, head cocked to the side with his brightly inked arms crossed over his chest.

"I'm good, Finn."

"Where's Sophie?"

I took in Finn's scowl, his heavy accent, and the tic in his jaw. Exhaustion and excess beer poured through my veins.

"At my parents'," I said, brushing a few stray blond hair strands out of my face. "Why?"

His nose twitched. "Wondering why you're here and not with her." He shrugged, as if he hadn't been completely offensive.

My ire increased instantly. "I'm not allowed to have a night out?" I asked and leaned in. Screw him. Screw all of the men and people in general who judged me. I was a damn good mom and Sophie didn't want for anything. I busted my ass to see that all her needs were met before I attended to mine.

And damn it, I was twenty-four with an almost three-year-old. It was okay for me to have a night out.

The door behind me opened and I felt the brush of heat, heard the music pour outside, and inhaled a whiff of the familiar cologne that smelled oh so damn good.

I closed my eyes and sighed. "Shit."

"What's going on?" Jaden asked, looking eerily similar to Finn in scowl and annoyance.

"Nothing." I stood up, rolled my shoulders back, and went for my phone, because no way in hell was I okay to drive anywhere.

Finn turned his eyes to Jaden. "Just seeing if she was okay. What are you doing out here?"

If I wasn't mistaken, Finn's lip twitched slightly. I preferred when he was being silent and sullen. Talking wasn't a trait I liked in him—not when he was judging me.

Jaden glanced back and forth between us and I took a step away from him. He'd unleash his assholery upon me quicker than Finn could, for certain. A muscle in his neck popped and pulsed.

"Heading home."

"Funny," Finn said, a grin spreading wide. "Jules was just saying she needed a ride."

What? "I didn't—"

"Thought I'd take her. We were just getting ready to head out."

My eyeballs almost exploded as Finn moved toward me and reached his hand out. "Ready to go?"

"I—" I had no words. For the first time in my life, I was stunned speechless.

"I got her."

My head snapped to Jaden so quick I felt the sting of whiplash.

"Really? She's closer to my place." If possible, Finn's smile grew wider. Oh hell, he was goading Jaden. Pointless pursuit, truly. There was nothing to goad Jaden over—especially when it came to me.

"I've got a ride."

Both men turned and looked at me. Finn smiled, Jaden scowled.

Typical.

"Who?" Jaden asked, walking toward me.

On instinct, I took a step back. Who? How in the hell should I know?

Heat suffused my cheeks and I prayed like hell he couldn't see it. I had always been a miserable liar.

"Uh." My eyes darted to the sides and all around as I tried to think of someone who could come get me. Someone other than my parents. When I didn't immediately come up with an answer, Jaden stepped up.

"Let's go." He spun a set of keys around his index finger, catching them in his grip.

"I'm fine."

From behind me, I heard the door to the club open and close again. My head snapped around, searching for Finn, but he was gone. Bastard.

I fought against the urge to run into the clubhouse just to kick him in the nuts. What in the hell was his problem?

I didn't have time to think about it because I had larger problems—mostly in the shape and size of a six-foot-and-then-some muscled, angry biker towering over me.

"You got a man?" he asked, and stalked toward me, closing the expanse between us in three quick strides. I didn't answer at first, mostly because I hadn't been able to function clearly around Jaden ever since that damn bike ride with him almost a week ago. He was so much like Scratch, yet so different.

"You know I don't," I muttered, heat returning to my cheeks. I turned to look away from him, too afraid of what he'd see in my eyes. Too afraid of what I'd feel if I looked at him anymore. Damn it.

Coming back to Jasper Bay was about Sophie being with her uncle and me being free of dickhead Rob. Not feeling all swoony and stupid around Jaden.

"I know," he clipped. Our feet were so close together the tips of our shoes almost touched. "'Cuz if you had one, he wouldn't let you be around men like us. And if he was a stupid man who let you do stupid shit like that, he'd certainly be around to take you home when you drank too much, so you're not left wandering drunk around town."

I squeezed my eyes close, searched for a quip or a smartass answer behind my closed and darkened eyelids, and still I came up empty.

Although the parking lot felt like it was beginning to spin when I opened my eyes.

Crap. I was wasted.

"Shit," Jaden muttered, making a decision I couldn't understand. He grabbed my wrist and pulled me toward a truck. As he opened the door, I took in his tapping, booted foot on the pavement. "Get in."

I looked at his boot, dragged my eyes slowly up to the high bench seat in the old truck I knew he'd had forever. It felt like a long way up as I swayed on my feet.

"I think I need a ladder," I admitted. My eyes closed and my head tipped back.

"Shit." Next thing I knew, two large and searing hot hands were wrapped around my waist and I was dropped into the bench seat. He pointed a finger at me when I dragged my unfocused eyes to him. "Don't fuckin' puke in my truck."

Well, I hadn't considered that… but now that he mentioned it.

The last thing I remembered was the rumbling and shaking of his engine as he pulled out of the clubhouse parking lot.

Then everything went black.

5
Jaden

Jules's soft snoring fell from her slightly parted lips as I pulled my truck into my apartment complex and slammed the shifter into park. I turned to her, glaring at her because I couldn't help the whirlwind of shit I felt every time I looked at her.

Her sleeping in my truck, making it reek of her sweet perfume that burned my nose on every inhale, left me on edge.

"Shit," I murmured, and scrubbed a hand down my face.

Why had I brought her to my own damn house? I should have dropped her passed-out ass on the doorstep to the precious mayor's house and been done with it.

I had been halfway to her parents' home when I thought of what would happen if her parents saw her in this state. Would it hurt my chances of seeing Sophie? Not that I should have given a shit. Or understood why I suddenly cared so much about getting to know the little girl. I'd ignored both of them for weeks.

Now she was sitting in my truck, and I was the one taking care of her while she looked so damn innocent and fragile, curled into a ball, her bare feet propped up on the seat next to her, and her head resting against the doorframe.

"Fuck it." I climbed out of the cab of my truck and slammed my door. My hands balled into fists at my side as I walked around the back of the tailgate, the entire time keeping my eyes narrowed on the sleepy drunk. I flung open her door, almost wanting her to fall out and land flat on her ass.

That'd teach her for getting too drunk to control herself. And for letting me put her in my truck.

Her head dipped and bobbed from the sudden movement and I found myself unbuckling her and scooping her up before she could fall, all thoughts of seeing her with road rash down the sides of her cheeks forgotten.

Jules settled in my arms as soon as I began carrying her up the stairs to the second-level, outside entrance. My place was shit—mostly because I barely spent time there. Also because no one else ever came to my place. Finally because I didn't have anyone who gave a shit about nice crap in my life, ever.

Walking into it with Jules cradled in my arms, her body singeing my chest with an uncomfortable heat, had me taking a quick glance around my bare walls, the stained carpet that'd been that way since before I moved in, and the chipped linoleum flooring and countertop.

I dropped her on my bed as if she'd burned me, and scrubbed my arms to be free from her smell and her touch.

She wasn't even awake.

A slight moan escaped her pink lips and my hands flew to my hips as I stared at her, hovering over her like a fucking creeper.

The sound went straight from her lips to my gut and my lip twisted in disgust.

Disgust because she was Jules: my brother's killer. If not intentionally, certainly unintentionally. She might not have shoved his bike onto the patch of black ice that left his wheels spinning out of control, but if she wouldn't have cheated on him, he wouldn't have been at her place arguing with her that night.

"Fuck," I groaned.

The sound reverberated against my stained white walls and Jules opened her eyes.

"Jaden?" Her voice was dry as she croaked.

"What?" I growled.

She sat up, slowly pushing herself off the bed, and dropped her head into the palm of one of her hands. "Where am I?"

I turned around, not wanting to see her looking so damn miserable in my bed while I had some strange, alien urge to actually fucking *help* her.

What the hell?

"My house."

"Why?"

I glared at her over my shoulder. Her small hand brushed the blond hair out of her eyes as her head lobbed to the side and then back.

"You want Sophie to see you looking this shitty?" I stalked out of the room and stomped across the worn gray carpet before she could say anything else.

In the kitchen, I braced my fists over the edge of the counter and tried to slow my racing heart. My pulse thundered in my ears as if I was underwater, and my heart pounded against my chest.

For a second, until I thought of Scratch, there had been a moment when I'd actually *liked* seeing Jules in my messed bed, lying across the tangled sheets in a pair of short shorts riding up high on her thighs, and the hint of her bra peeking out over the edge of her tank top.

"Get your shit together, asshole."

I blinked, erasing the image, and reached for a bottle of pain pills. I filled a glass of water and took it back to my bedroom.

When I hit the door, I heard the water running from the bathroom. My eyes darted between the closed door, the hint of light shining under the door, and the pain pills in my hand.

My hand squeezed around them before I finally dropped

everything on the cracked table next to my nightstand. Water splashed over the rim of the cup. I should have cleaned it up, but I didn't.

Drop the shit and get out. Let her pass out, and take her home in the morning.

I spun on my heels, intent on listening to my conscience's advice, when the door opened.

I froze on my feet as Jules braced herself against the doorway. Her skin looked pale green as the light from the bathroom shone behind her. And she looked so damn small.

Small enough that if I were to wrap my hands around her waist, I knew my fingers would touch. She looked fragile. Breakable.

For the first time in years, I didn't want to be the one doing the breaking.

"You okay?" I asked, moving toward her.

She shook her head and frowned. "I feel like shit," she mumbled, and pushed off the doorframe. The small movement left her wobbling on her feet.

And before I knew it, my hand clamped around her wrist to steady her. One of her hands grabbed onto my bicep.

Heat zapped up to my elbow like I'd banged it on the doorframe. But I hadn't. The heat was coming from her touching my skin. I fought a snarl and my hands turned into fists again. Every muscle in my arm coiled tight with the tension.

I tried to shake her off but her fingers curled around me like a damn vise grip.

I couldn't pry her off. I was stuck, looming over her small, thin frame when her eyes slowly pulled to mine.

And I didn't hate it as much as I thought I would.

Or wanted to.

Fuck.

Her lips parted as she sucked in a small breath. She swayed slightly and her head tilted to the right. She looked at me as if she was examining every feature of my face, and for some dumbass reason, I fucking let her.

She didn't seem to care that I was scowling down at her, my eyes narrowed on her, wanting her to just pass the fuck out so I didn't have to see the slight glaze in her blue eyes.

Her free hand raised up and gently ran down my jaw.

I twitched from the sudden, but soft, and—fucking hell—sweet as sin contact of her skin willingly on mine.

I swallowed, felt every movement of my Adam's apple bob up and down with the thick movement.

"You look just like him."

I sniffed, my nostrils flared, but still, that damn warm contact on my jaw running slowly across my skin had me frozen in place, my hand still holding onto hers as she just... fucking... watched me.

Her hand fell back down to her side.

"But angrier."

My shoulders tightened—from her perusal or the lack of contact, who the hell knew.

Her eyes rolled into her head and her head dipped again. Shit. She was still wasted. My hands gripped her shoulders and I ignored the blast it sent to my dick.

I walked her to the bed, intent on ignoring the words she'd spoken, the way she'd so easily compared me to Scott—or Scratch to everyone but me, and probably her at one time.

She shifted once we reached the bed.

"Lay down." She closed her eyes and opened them. I moved to push her down but she let out a tiny moan and I couldn't move.

I couldn't let go. Somehow she'd super-glued me to her. Damn sneaky bitch.

"Jaden?" My name rolled off her lips, smacking me against my chest.

"What?"

She sniffed. Fuck, if she cried I'd be pissed. "I miss him. All the damn time. And you look so much like him."

She shook her head and my fingers dug into her shoulders.

I bent over her, glared right into her eyes—the only damn thing different about Scratch and I besides our personalities. He'd always been happier than I could ever fake it.

"I'm not him." I enunciated the words so she'd be fucking clear on who was standing in front of her, who had their hands on her, and who—for some Goddamned unknown reason—fucking wanted her.

"I know that."

"Do you?" I leaned in closer.

She moved toward me, her breath and lips so close to mine I could practically taste her. The warmth of her breath skated across my skin as I pulled her close.

Jesus. Was I going to fucking do this? Kiss this woman? My head told me to stop, to—for once in my life—do the right damn thing and walk away before I went too far and couldn't take it back.

My other head—the one screaming in pain against my zipper—reared forward.

"Jules." I didn't know if it was a growl or a whisper. But damn it, I'd always wanted her. "You want this?"

She nodded and her lips parted. "Jaden..." Her voice trailed off as she swallowed.

And then she burped.

I flinched from the smell... the thick hint of bile and... *fuck*. Vomit.

She lurched toward me right as I scooped her in my arms. I'd barely got her flung over the toilet as she began filling it with rejected liquor.

I plugged my throat with my tongue, keeping the nasty odor from making me gag. But then I did the fucking strangest thing. I held her hair. I rubbed her back through the soft cotton tank top.

When she was done, I washed her face with a warm washcloth and carried her back to bed.

She said nothing, except letting out the occasional moan of pain. My dick didn't understand the difference. It stayed permanently hard until I'd tucked her under my damn comforter. I even fucking straightened it.

My head spun in confusion. I didn't take care of people. That wasn't me.

And yeah, she wouldn't remember it in the morning. She most likely wouldn't remember how I was a breath away from kissing her, probably pushing her into my bed and doing a fuck of a lot more than kissing.

And after I'd taken off my jeans and clothes and grabbed a blanket and plopped down on my couch—I couldn't fucking figure out why that pissed me off so much.

6
Jules

I had never felt incredibly talented at anything in life. Sure I'd gotten a college degree, been able to successfully raise and care for my daughter on my own. But other than doing what I had to do, because I didn't have any other options, there was never anything I could do in my life that made me special. Nothing unique about me at all.

Except for the one thing my college roommates had always given me shit for—the talent of being able to drink as much as I wanted, and—even if I threw up or passed out—never forget anything.

As I woke up in the morning, my head thumping from the slight pain of a hangover, I loathed the damn talent. It was suddenly my curse.

I rolled over on the soft pillow that I knew didn't belong to me and inhaled deeply. I breathed in the scent of Jaden's shampoo, a lingering cologne smell, and even the slight smell of his sweat.

Which should have been disgusting.

But I had the unfortunate ability to remember what it felt like when his hands curled into the backs of my shoulders as he stared at me with something much different than pure hatred. I remembered the way I'd moved closer to him—wanting to feel his thick, full lips capture mine.

And I remembered the tender way he'd rubbed my black, cleaned my face, and held my hair back in one of his large hands while I'd puked my inner organs into his toilet.

I closed my eyes, feeling a burn in the back of my eyes and my sinuses as I tried to wipe the memory away.

It shouldn't have happened.

Jaden was probably wasted—probably saw me as nothing more than the club bunnies he normally took to bed. If we were sober, there was no way he would have ever looked at me like that.

I breathed deep and exhaled slowly, relishing the last moment I'd have in his bed in probably ever, before I climbed out from under the warm sheets. After a quick trip to the bathroom where I scrubbed my teeth with toothpaste and a finger, and fixed my stringy hair as best I could, I leaned close to the mirror.

"Forget about it and get the hell out of here."

My reflection blinked and nodded in agreement. That was the best part of talking to myself in the bathroom—the person I talked to always agreed with me.

I crept slowly out of the bathroom, intent on sneaking out, and calling Liv—or hell, even my dad if I had to—once I was outside. I didn't remember where Jaden lived, but Jasper Bay was a small town and I could figure it out.

My bare feet trudged softly down his small hall. The last thing I wanted was to wake Jaden up. If I knew him at all, he'd be pissed about last night, too.

I wanted to disappear with only the warm memory flooding my belly of what his hands felt like on my skin, and not the angry scowl I was sure I'd get from him.

Spying my purse on the table, I grabbed it quickly, careful to make sure the metal buckles didn't clink-clank on his glass tabletop.

I made the horrible mistake of turning around, trying to search for my flip-flops when I saw Jaden.

He lay sprawled out on the couch, a thick, black blanket pooling at his waist and only covering his bottom half. One leg cocked to the side so I could see a flash of his knee and lower leg. But on top? Nothing covered him. Not even a shirt.

One of his hands fell down his side, his hand cupping his groin, with the other arm flung over his eyes.

I closed my eyes, blinking slowly, as I took in the muscular man. His corded arms and thick biceps. His chest and abs that were thick and muscular, but not chiseled like a model. Instead, he was thick and strong and tough in a way that showed he'd earned his toughness by fighting and hard living—not lifting weights in the gym and surviving on asparagus and chicken.

He lived hard.

He probably fucked hard.

Oh God. What the hell are you doing?

Drool pooled at the edges of my mouth as I stared at him in the early morning daylight. So early that I could tell through the cheap, dusty blinds that the sun was just starting to come up. The small glimpse of light was enough for me to know that he might look like Scratch…

But he didn't.

He was hard and defined and rough and angry in a way that was uniquely him.

I licked my lips, tried to turn around and search for my damn shoes. I had to get out of there. Quickly.

But when I did, my hip bumped his table and I let out a quiet curse, biting my lip to keep from swearing louder.

"Your shoes are in the truck."

Crap. I'd woken the beast. A shiver of fear ran down my spine and I straightened up, keeping my back to him.

"You hear me?" His voice was thick and gravelly from sleep, but the creak in the floor told me he was headed my way.

Oh shit.

I nodded, staring at my purse in my hands. "Okay," I finally muttered. I cleared my throat, feeling a golf ball stuck deep inside. "Thanks, then."

A jingle of keys behind me had me snapping my head in his direction.

Which was a mistake. Huge mistake. My eyes flew wide and heat burst on every visible part of my skin.

Damn it. He was so…

Hell. Jaden was just a god. A big, angry, lumbering, pissed-off god most of the time. But that didn't change the way a heated desire instantly flooded my body and pooled in my lower stomach as I took in his large, sleepy, and sexy-as-hell body in one quick glance.

And shit. He was hard. A thick bulge was obvious through his white boxer briefs.

I immediately looked away and began fumbling in my purse. Liv. Dad. Hell, I'd call Satan and sell my soul if the Devil would get me out of this apartment in five seconds.

"Jules."

My fingers curled around my phone and I pressed it to my chest.

Jaden said my name again, but it wasn't in the typical growl I'd become so accustomed to.

"What?" I asked, looking over my shoulder. My eyes stayed frozen on his, too afraid of what would happen to my cheeks if I looked further south again.

His head cocked to the side and he ran a hand through his hair. His lips curled and then he sighed. "Give me five minutes and I'll get you home."

I swallowed again. No way was I spending the morning in his truck. Me and him and a cramped space with his hair messed from sleep equaled nothing good.

"I'll call Liv. And I need to get home, I'm sure my parents are worried."

His nose wrinkled and damn it, when he turned, I glanced down. *Oh, holy hell.*

I glanced away but not before I saw a smirk fill his lips. Sexy lips. Swollen, sleepy lips I wanted to –

Shut up!

"I sent your parents a text last night saying you were staying at Liv's. They won't be worried."

My jaw dropped as I caught his boxer-clad ass turning and walking down the hall.

"Five fucking minutes, Jules. We got shit to talk about, and if you sneak out on me I'm going to be pissed." His voice rang from down the hall, and something about knowing he was in the room—his room—where I'd just been sent a swirl of lust to the apex of my thighs.

"What else is new?" I snapped, because shoot—I'd lost control of my emotions and my tongue around him.

A low, rumbling laugh was all I got in response. It vibrated off the walls of hallway, where I stood frozen, and straight to my groin.

Jaden could laugh?

"You were wasted last night." The tight grip of his hands on the steering wheel belied the nonchalance of his words.

I moved my eyes from his scarred knuckles and stared straight out the window. The bright sunshine blared into my brain, reminding me of the exact words he spoke.

"Shouldn't do that shit at the club."

No shit? I pressed my lips together to prevent the words from escaping. Jaden had been strange ever since I heard that foreign laughing sound in his room. When he'd come out, dressed in his usual jeans and T-shirt and thrown his leather cut on with the Nordic Lords MC logo, he hadn't said anything. But he stood close to me, held the door for me, and practically escorted me out to his truck.

I'd stayed silent, unnerved. I almost wanted to elbow him in the gut just to hear him swear at me. Maybe that would make everything that almost happened last night finally dissipate from my memory.

Sitting with him in his truck again, inhaling the stench of stale smoke and his damn cologne, wasn't helping that mission one single bit.

"I was fine," I said, when I finally remembered he'd said something to me.

"Lot of men in that room wouldn't have cared if you were too drunk, Jules. We're not good men."

I closed my eyes, and the vision of his lips moving close to mine flashed. I fought the urge to call him out, too afraid to start a conversation I was in no hurry to jump into.

When I didn't answer, Jaden sighed as if exasperated with me.

Finally, we were back to normal. I almost smiled.

"My car almost done?" I asked. "I need it this week."

The simple question made him curse. The tires squealed in the truck as he jacked the wheel harshly to the left.

Tires spun and I slammed my shoulder into the side window as I reached for the oh-shit handle.

"What the hell?" I screamed as he righted the truck, now driving in the complete opposite direction of my parents' house.

"Fuck." He glanced at me, watched me rubbing my shoulder and scowled. "Finished it yesterday, forgot to tell you."

My lips twisted in pain. My brain still spun in a circle inside my head, rattling against my skull. I needed painkillers. And a nap. Possibly a new brain.

He glanced at me still rubbing my shoulder. "Sorry."

He muttered the word so softly I almost missed it.

The quick change in direction, the softness in his voice, left me reeling.

"What do you need it for?"

"Huh?" I frowned.

He rolled his eyes and his grip on the steering wheel tightened. "Your car. What do you need it for?"

"Oh." I fidgeted with my hair, tucking it behind my ears. "Um, I'm moving next weekend."

"What?" He hissed it at me like he was pissed. Then he growled. "Where?"

Somehow, the angry scowl back in place and the curl of his lips comforted me. I knew how to handle a pissed-off Jaden.

I frowned and rubbed my forehead. "Uh… just to the east side of town. I found a place for me and Sophie to move into."

"Oh." His wrists cracked as he twisted his hands around the leather steering wheel again.

My frown stayed in place and my eyebrows pulled in as I sat in the cab, watching him but trying not to. His moods not only gave me whiplash, but even snapping at me, he was still being nicer.

Weird. Too weird. I didn't know what to do make of it, but sitting in his cab as we headed toward the club, I decided I liked it. A lot.

We were quiet until we reached the club, me thinking of not only Jaden, but the new job I was starting a salon in a couple of weeks. I'd met the three silliest and kindest women last week when Liv and Faith and I were getting pedicures. They were sisters, and a bit flaky, but kind and sweet and had offered me a job on the spot.

It wasn't a teaching position, but it'd pay the bills. Plus they promised me time off to do some substitute work if it became available.

There was no way I could say no. Getting free haircuts and highlights and pedicures was a huge signing bonus. But I needed to move and get Sophie settled into her new daycare before I could start work.

"When are you moving?"

The suddenness of his question had me snapping my head in his direction, and I realized we'd pulled into the clubhouse parking lot.

"Next Friday."

Jaden opened the door and climbed out. "I'll get men to help."

I hopped out of the truck and met him at the front. "Not necessary. But thanks."

Jaden spun on his heels, and in an instant I found myself plastered against the front of his truck—a wall of hot metal behind me... a wall of hot, angry Jaden in front of me.

He towered over me and I leaned back, tilting my chin to look at him.

His lips pulled into a thin line. "Said I'd get fuckin' men to help you, Jules."

Oh God. He smelled delicious. I couldn't think as his hands went to the hood of his truck at the outside edges of my shoulders. My eyes darted to both of them, back and forth. His hands were so close to being where they'd been on me—just inches from my skin, like last night.

My belly fluttered and I pressed my thighs together.

"Okay." Jaden nice didn't compute in my beer-addled brain. But who was I to turn down free help?

I swallowed slowly, trying to maintain composure and not do something asinine. Like wrap my arms around his waist and pull him to me.

"Can I get my car now?" I looked over his shoulder, unable to stare into his brown eyes. They'd probably set me on fire.

"We gonna talk about last night?"

I choked. "Last night?"

Jaden let out a quiet, rumbling laugh. It sounded foreign. And sexy.

I licked my lips.

"Last night. Me bringing you to my place. Taking care of you –"

"Thanks for holding my hair," I cut him off. I didn't want to know where he was going. I wanted to pretend it didn't happen. Or pretend it *had* happened so I would know what his lips felt like.

But this was Jaden. He hated me. Had always hated me. He never thought I was good enough for Scratch and never wanted me around. Whatever almost happened last night would have been a huge mistake.

"That was nice of you," I continued, not giving him a chance to talk. "And I appreciate that. And the pills. And... whatever else." I waved a hand in the air and kept babbling. "So thanks for that and for the offer to help me move. But I don't think that's a good idea. It was a moment of weakness on my part... you, me, drunk... looking like Scratch... I just... I wanted him back."

His nose twitched and he loomed in. "You wanted Scratch last night?"

I nodded. I knew I'd gone too far, said something that had slow burning waves of hot lava rolling off his shoulders and shooting daggers out of his eyes, but I couldn't shut up. "Yeah, and I just got you confused with him. Wanted it to be him, not you. Won't happen again."

I blinked. And hell, I should have shut up.

Because Jaden leaned down and brushed his lips across my jaw and... oh, shit. My entire body trembled underneath him.

"You didn't want him. You wanted me, and we both know it. You wanted the bad brother last night, Jules. Let's not fuckin' lie about it. And you know what else?"

I couldn't think. Couldn't speak. All I could do was swallow. A whimper escaped my lips as his hips pressed into me.

Oh, God. I tried glancing around the parking lot, but it was early and no one was around. No one could help me.

No one would see this.

Thank God.

"Asked you a question, Jules."

"What else?" I croaked. Heat burned my cheeks, from lust and embarrassment. My body betrayed my senses.

"I would have given it to you last night. Anything you wanted, you turned those lying innocent eyes on me and I would have fucked you so hard you'd forget all about Scratch."

"That's…" I swallowed and his lips grazed the hollow of my throat. "That's an asshole thing to say, Jaden."

"I know." He pulled away, our noses almost touching, our harsh breathing mingling together. "Good thing in the light of day I remember what a selfish, lying killer you are, isn't it?"

His eyes hardened on me until all I saw was black coal for eyes and venomous rage flashing from them.

He pushed off me and began walking away. "Your fucking car is over there, unlocked."

Tears pooled and spilled from my eyes as he disappeared. I took in his tightly clenched fists, the way he cracked his neck from side to side, and right before he walked through the clubhouse door I watched how he froze, as if he wanted to turn back around. Then his hands ran through his hair and he slammed the door open, vanishing behind.

I stayed outside, plastered against the grill of the truck, gasping for breath long after he was gone.

It took me forever to calm down. Longer to have my heart rate return to normal and for my mind to stop swirling in confusion.

I'd felt his hunger for me. Hard not to when his thick erection was pressed against my thigh.

I also still felt his hatred for me pouring off him.

I shook my head and headed toward my car on shaking feet.

Jaden was trouble. He hated me, even if his body wanted me.

Going through with any of it would lead to trouble. And I'd had enough trouble, enough violence, and enough anger in my life over the last few years to know it'd be smarter to say the hell away from anything to do with Jaden.

By the time I pulled my car into my parents' driveway, I'd sufficiently convinced myself of all of it.

He could see Sophie, but Jaden and I? We'd never happen. It'd be the worst possible decision I could make. And I'd made plenty.

7
Jules

"Hey, Mom." I brushed my lips against my mom's cheek as she sat at the kitchen table, drinking her morning cup of coffee.

"Rough night?" she asked, not looking up from reading the morning newspaper.

Rough night. Rough morning. Rough four years. You name it, I had lived it.

I needed to shower, wash the stench of vomit and beer and Jaden off me, but there were priorities.

Namely, coffee. Helping myself to a cup, I ignored the tinge of disappointment in her question.

Sighing, my mom pushed off the kitchen table and walked toward me at the counter. My hand began shaking as I poured sugar into my mug.

"Not sure you staying out to get wasted is the best thing you can do for your daughter, honey."

I brought the mug to my lips and took my first swallow. "Won't happen again." I took the disappointment and disapproval in her eyes because she was right. I never behaved like I had last night, always trying to be the best example for Sophie to follow.

But wasn't I allowed a small amount of fun in my life?

My mom sighed again and fixed her already perfectly done hair. It matched mine except hers had a few noticeable wisps of gray at the temples. For being almost fifty, my mom still looked amazing. Taller than me, but just as thin. Her light brown eyes looked at me sadly as I stood under her gaze.

"I know you've had it rough, Jules. I'm just not sure being back here, around all those people, is best for you."

My fingers gripped my mug tighter. I knew they hated my friends when I was younger. But what my parents never understood was that Liv and Faith liked me for me, not because of something I could give them or buy for them, like all the other girls in Jasper Bay. I'd never fit in with them and their desires to leave for big cities with their big city dreams.

Even unlike Liv and Faith, I'd always loved the small town feel of Jasper Bay. I enjoyed the quietness and the familiarity. I liked smiling and waving at people I passed on the streets, having known them since I was pushed around town in a stroller.

"Are you saying I should have stayed in Phoenix?" With Rob, a civil engineer who had more money than sense, and more anger and beatings than either of the latter?

My unasked question earned me a frown.

"Never." She pulled me into a hug. I moved my coffee mug to the counter to prevent it sloshing on either of us. "I know what losing Scratch did to you, and I know how much you still miss him. Your dad and I just worry about you, that's all."

I let go of the mug and wrapped my arms around her waist. "Thanks, Mom."

And I meant it. They might not have liked Scratch, but as soon as I found out I was pregnant, they'd supported me one hundred percent, sometimes flying down to Phoenix while I took my college finals just to give me more time to study.

I'd accomplished a lot at my young age. I was still figuring life out, but I also knew, regardless of bad decisions and poor planning, that my parents would always be there for me.

Her shoulders heaved a heavy breath. "And I also know it's okay for you to be young and do things like party all night long. Being a mom doesn't mean you have to end your life. But I'd hate to see you make the same mistakes again, finding a man who isn't worthy of you just because you're fighting against the memory of him."

I squeezed my eyes closed. She didn't have to mention any names about men not being worthy of me. Rob and Jaden fell through her lips unspoken. But it wasn't fair to compare one to the other at all.

Jaden might hate me, but I seriously doubted he'd slap me around. Which didn't matter anyway, seeing as how the fire that had burned through his eyes as he'd stared me at this morning pretty much sealed the deal on anything happening with us.

Not that I'd thought of those dark brown inferno eyes on my drive home.

Or anytime I blinked.

"I'll be smart, Mom. Promise."

She huffed into my hair. "You always are."

Her arms dropped from my waist and I went back to my coffee, intent on moving on from the conversation, but I couldn't.

"Mom?" I called to her as she was headed out the door. "He wants to see Sophie."

My mom spun elegantly on her high-heeled shoes, her khaki-colored linen pants swaying with the movement. She opened her mouth and then closed it. I could practically see gears turning in her head as she debated what to say. She slowly licked her lips and nodded once. "Probably be a good idea, seeing as she's all he could have for family."

As she left, blowing me a kiss before she headed up the stairs to do who-knows-what, I grinned into my mug. My parents didn't like Jaden—certainly didn't like the Nordic Lords and anything they stood for—but to them, all of that was inconsequential when it came to family.

Same as my reaction to Jaden.

I had to figure out how to push it aside so he could meet Sophie and spend time with her.

If only that was as easily done as it was to think it.

"You got this?" one of the girls asked.

I had stopped into Bella Salon, where I would begin working next week, to pick up paperwork.

I flipped through the W-4 information and other files before I bit my bottom lip. "Yeah, um…"

"Cassie," she filled in for me.

"Thanks." Blush spread to my cheeks. They all looked so similar it was hard to tell them apart even though Cassie, the girl talking to me, was the big sister. "I'll get it, I swear."

Cassie simply smiled and fluffed her long blond hair. They were all model-tall, thin, and smiled more than anyone I knew.

"Not a problem. We're used to it. Can I give you some help?"

I sighed, grateful. "Yes, please."

Cassie laughed, showing a full mouth of straight white teeth. "Callie, cutting the hair right now? Always wears a ring on the middle finger of her left hand. And Cammie has a soft spot for kids, obviously."

I turned my head and watched Cammie brushing Sophie's blond pigtails, pretending to cut them. I didn't know what they were saying, but both of them had been full of giggles for the last ten minutes since we'd arrived. It probably wasn't good form to bring a kid to work, but since I was just picking up paperwork, I didn't think it'd be an issue.

Neither did Cammie, who had swooped Sophie into her arms and set her in a beauty chair immediately. They hadn't stopped giggling since.

"You don't like kids?" I asked Callie once her client had gone up to the register to pay Cassie. Huh. Maybe I'd figure them out easily enough. Cassie preferred working behind the counter, that much I figured out quickly.

Callie leaned in and crinkled her lips. "They're always sticky."

"No kidding," I said laughing.

"Ticky hands! Ticky hands!" Sophie clapped and repeated the words as if she thought it was hilarious.

Callie shot me a look of mock disgust as she headed toward the back. "See what I mean?"

"Ignore her. She's kidding." Cammie winked and picked up Sophie from the chair, setting her on her little pudgy feet.

"No worries. Thanks for letting me come in today and get that paperwork out of the way."

Callie smiled and waved me away, handing a sucker to Sophie, who shot her a full grin.

"How about we go to the park and get some ice cream? See how sticky we can make those hands of yours?"

Sophie clapped her hands. "Ticky hands! Ticky hands!"

Callie and I both laughed and said our goodbyes, and I ushered Sophie out the door.

Working at Bella Salon would not have been my first choice. But the girls were friendly, and clearly had no problems with Sophie. My smile was wide and genuine as we walked down the street to Jasper Bay's ice cream parlor. It was a small-town place, typical of the quaintness of Jasper Bay and the things I loved about my town, complete with thirty flavors.

Since fall would be coming soon, and the brutality of living through a northern winter was licking at our heels, Sophie and I took the time to enjoy our Mackinac Island Fudge ice cream cones sitting outside.

It dribbled down her chin and all over her fingers, but she didn't care as she licked it away. Her napkins were never used, regardless of my gentle reminders. I figured her tongue worked just as well, so I let her be.

Occasionally, people from town stopped by and said hello. They welcomed us back as if we'd never left, and it wasn't long before I was certain that Sophie had charmed every single visitor.

With the ice cream done, I cleaned her with a wet wipe and we hauled it to the park, taking turns skipping and chasing each other for the three blocks it took to get there.

I loved the enormous wooden park. The park had been redone in the years I'd been gone, and now a giant wooden pirate ship took the place of the rusty metal swings I'd grown up on.

Sophie seemed to enjoy it too, as she dashed in and out of all the hidey-holes, laughing with glee. I let her have her fun while I took a spot on a nearby park bench, careful to keep an eye on her.

I was resting my head back, enjoying the feel of the warm sun without the typical humidity that accompanied a Minnesota summer, when my phone buzzed in my hand.

My pulse increased as soon as I saw Rob's name flash across the screen. My eyes darted to Sophie, ensuring she was safe—something I did on instinct in the few times I'd had contact with him after the last time I saw him.

I froze, unable to answer the phone while it vibrated in my hand, and heaved a sigh of relief when it stopped.

"Sophie!" I called and waved her over. "We need to go!"

He might have been a country away from us, but I wasn't taking chances. Suddenly, being in the open space left me feeling vulnerable.

"No, Mama!"

I moved to run after her, to pick her up and carry her the short walk to my car if need be, when my phone began buzzing in my hand again. My fingers instantly clenched around it and I heaved a sigh. While keeping an eye on Sophie disappearing into another hiding place, I let her have her fun and answered the phone.

"What do you want, Rob?" My voice was tight with anger and fear. Why he couldn't leave me alone and find another unsuspecting fool in the greater metropolis of Phoenix, I had no clue.

"Already told you. Want my girls back." His smooth voice sent chills down my spine. I had been fooled by his gelled hair, his attractive smile, and his designer clothes. Looking for someone completely opposite of anything that reminded me of Scratch had led me directly into Rob's arms when I had gone out one night with some co-workers.

He fooled me good.

But he wouldn't again.

"We're not your girls," I hissed into the phone, and sank into a park bench. In the background, I heard the distinct rumbling of motorcycles and turned my head.

My eyes widened as Jaden and two other men pulled into parking lot at the park. Their engines idled but I could practically feel the vibrations of their bikes rumbling across the ground straight toward me.

"Want to tell me who the guy was who threatened me last week? He'll be sorry he did."

I snorted. I almost laughed. Somehow, seeing three Nordic Lords perched on their Harleys mere yards from me had me feeling safer than I had in years.

Rob couldn't fuck with me here.

"Move on from us, Rob. We're never coming back to Phoenix, and I would think you'd have found someone else to slap around by now."

He sighed and his voice softened. I'd been fooled by that sound so many times. I could see his frown and the way he'd run his hands through his hair, begging me to forgive him. "I know, baby," he crooned. Disgust swirled in my gut. "It was just a hard day at work, but I swear to you, come home to me and let me love you the way I always did and everything will be different."

I laughed. I couldn't help it. Sophie squealed on a playground ten feet from me, sliding down a slide, and off to the side, I saw Jaden headed toward us. The men he was with had turned off their bikes, but still sat on them.

Sophie was safe. I was safe.

Rob could go to hell.

"Different than what?" I asked, gaining courage to speak things to him I wouldn't have dared do in person. "Different than the time you left bruises on my arm? Or my cheek? What about the time you bruised my ribs?"

"Jules," he growled. I was goading him, I knew it. "I'll come and get you if I have to."

But as Jaden drew closer, I couldn't stop myself either. Straightening my shoulders, I gripped my phone tighter and stared directly into Jaden's eyes, his jaw tightly clenched, scowl securely fixed, and his hands loosely at his sides.

Dangerous hands. Hands that I had no doubt had killed people far more dangerous than Rob.

"Go to hell, Rob. We wouldn't go anywhere with you ever again, and if you do try to come here, you'll be the only one regretting anything."

I hung up and dropped the phone into my purse right as Jaden reached me.

8

Jaden

Jules had been ignoring me. At least it felt that way. And the fact that I felt anything when it came to Jules pissed me the fuck off. So when Tripp, Jimmy, and I were flying through town on our way to the garage to get work done and I saw her sitting on the park bench, I didn't think.

I pulled over. What had me fuming with rage was the way her face looked when her phone rang and she answered it.

The way she curled into herself as she began speaking. I couldn't hear her, but I saw her mouth moving and I saw the way she tightened her shoulders. I was moving off my bike, telling Tripp and Jimmy to stay the fuck still, before I cared about why I was moving.

Or wanting to help her. *Again.*

But I also saw the way she took me in as I walked toward her, her eyes quickly scanning my body as if I had something she needed. And maybe I did. My hardening dick certainly liked the idea of that.

I only caught the name 'Rob' rolling off her lips before red began flashing at the outer edges of my vision.

That asshole was still bothering her?

"Who the fuck was that?" I nodded at the phone in her hand as she tried sliding it into her purse. "That the same guy who called you last week?"

Jules wrinkled her nose and her eyes darted to Sophie.

"Answer me."

Her head snapped to mine and her eyes narrowed. "Pardon me?"

I grinned. Her formal question made me smile in spite of my annoyance over the fact that she hadn't called for me to see Sophie and the simmering rage over some asshole bothering her.

And when in the hell was the last time I did that?

"The dick on the phone. That the same guy from the other day?"

She blew out a breath, as if annoyed with me. Fuck that. If anyone had any right to be pissed, it was me. I was still pissed at the way she'd thrown Scratch's name last weekend when all I'd wanted to do was haul her ass into my room at the club. Fuck the fact she'd been with my brother. Fuck the fact I hated her and blamed her for his death. I'd spent twenty minutes with her heating up the cab of my truck with her own nervousness, and by the time we'd pulled into the club, I was boiling with need.

Even the club bunnies hadn't helped during the week. For the first time since I'd joined the club and the men had let me have free rein on the free pussy, I hadn't wanted it. Even Shania, or Shayla, or who-the-fuck-ever, with her perfect tits. They weren't so perfect anymore. They were too big. Too fake. I suddenly found myself craving the small handfuls that had been in my bed.

And that pissed me off, too.

"Fine," she huffed. "Yes, it was him. And no, it's not a big deal. Just my ex, who won't leave me alone. Happy now?"

Her hip cocked to the side and her hand clamped down on it. Jules trying to be a spitfire almost made me grin again. Then I caught a flash of bright pink in the distance and my skin paled.

"What the fuck? You let her do that shit?"

Jules snapped her head over her shoulder and laughed quietly. "That? She's fine."

Fuck if she was fine. The pipsqueak had to be fifteen feet in the air, scaling a fake rock wall. She could fall and break something. Or die.

My feet moved quickly toward Sophie while Jules followed me.

"She's fine, Jaden. Sophie climbs like this all the time. Been doing it since she could walk at ten months and she's never been hurt. I swear she's part monkey."

I didn't care.

When I caught Sophie, my hands wrapped around her waist and I set her on the ground.

She looked up at me with wide, blue eyes and quickly hid behind Jules.

Typical reaction for whenever she caught me staring at her.

"She could be hurt." That shit couldn't be natural.

Jules laughed again. When I pulled my eyes from Sophie hiding behind her legs, she bit her bottom lip and shook her head. "Part monkey, I swear it. She'll be fine. She just has an unnatural love for heights and all things dangerous."

Like her dad. Shit. Scratch had been the same way. The daredevil between the two of us. Laying out his first dirt bike when he was six, scratched from toe to ear, and didn't give a shit. He just got back on the bike and rode again. He crashed so many fuckin' bikes in his lifetime, always laying them out trying to do crazy shit. He was always scratched up. Hence the nickname. The guy was almost always bleeding and scabbed over from some idiotic maneuver he hadn't accomplished.

I blinked my eyes and my hands flew to my hips. *Shit.*

When I opened them, Jules was smiling at me softly. I ignored the glazed, teary-eyed look in her eyes as if she knew exactly what I was remembering.

"I Tophee."

I looked down at the blond head of curls secured into pigtails, peeking out behind Jules's leg.

That innocent look. Those huge blue eyes. My breath caught in my throat. Fucking hell, chop the long hair and it was my brother in pint-sized form staring back at me.

I squatted down to her level and reached out my hand. She put hers in my palm instantly. So damn trusting.

"Jaden," I told her as her little pudgy palm warmed mine. Something foreign crept up my arm, slithered into my chest, and squeezed into my heart. I flinched from the alien heat invading my body as I stared into eyes that looked so damn similar to Scratch's.

My head dropped as realization struck me. My head might not know what the hell to do about Jules, but Scratch would kick my ass and put a bullet in me if he saw me treating his kid the way I had been.

Jules's hand came down slowly, her fingers gliding down Sophie's neck as we had our first conversation without any words. She hid behind her mom's legs, so similar to the way I first met her weeks ago, and yet so different now.

This was my chance to not fuck it up this time.

I swallowed, felt my Adam's apple bob slowly as I said, "I'm your uncle."

A strangled choke fell from Jules's lips above us, but I didn't look.

"Uncah Jaden." Sophie's lips pressed together into a pout and she frowned, as if testing the words on her lips for the first time and unsure of what they meant.

That made two of us.

I had never had to take care of anyone. Ever since my parents were killed in a shoot-out with a rival club when Scratch and I were just kids. Switch, my parent's friend and a member of the club, took us in with his old lady, Marie, and raised us. Scratch had rolled with life, even then. I'd never had the freedom he did. Never felt the way he did. I was always more serious. More angry.

Something like recognition flashed in the half-pint's eyes and she smiled. "You yuv my dad."

A thickness exploded in my throat and I pushed it back. Jules's hand tightened its grip on the back of her daughter's head.

I dropped Sophie's hand and stood up, my knees cracking as I pushed up from the squatting position.

"Yeah." It was all I could choke out over the tightness clawing at me from the inside out. Loved her dad. Shit. I'd been an asshole. I probably deserved the bullet Scratch would have leveled at me if he were still alive.

I caught Jules's eyes staring me with wonder, and possibly fear.

"You movin' tomorrow?" I asked her, needing desperately to change the subject.

Her eyes widened fractionally before she understood and let me have it. "Yeah. Movers are coming at nine o'clock."

I felt the pull of my eyebrows. "Thought I told you the men from the club would take care of that."

She fidgeted on her feet, not looking at me. The way she avoided me rankled me and a muscle ticked in my jaw. "We don't have a lot of stuff, so it's not necessary."

I glared at her, took a small step closer until there were only inches separating us. I jumped as Sophie's hand brushed against my denim-clad legs, and I looked down at her.

She looked up and grinned.

I scowled back at Jules and nodded my head in Sophie's direction. "Club takes care of its own."

How in the hell did all that change so quickly?

"Tomorrow." I pointed at her, removing Sophie's grip from my jeans.

Then I got the fuck away from them as fast as I could.

My skin itched with the need to do something stupid like haul Sophie into my arms, press her cheek against my chest and never let go, all while I devoured Jules's parted and shocked lips with my tongue.

9

Jules

"Not sure why they're here helping. We already had everything set up."

I rolled my eyes, keeping my back to my dad as we watched ten men from the Nordic Lords load up the small moving truck I'd rented for the day. When I moved back to Jasper Bay, I had everything shipped to my parents' house and it had been stacked in their garage for the last six weeks, still packed up.

Moving would be easy, since besides some clothes and toys, I hadn't unpacked a single box.

I still didn't understand either, fully. But I couldn't forget the determination in Jaden's stare when he swore the club took care of their own. He hadn't been talking about me; I knew that. Watching him acknowledge Sophie for the very first time, finally getting over whatever shit he believed in his head about her not belonging to Scratch, had my heart unwittingly softening toward him.

Gawking at the men from the living room window in my parents' house, the warmth of my dad's love behind me, left my head reeling. Every warning my dad had spoken in my direction for the last twenty-four hours about me and Sophie getting entangled in "Nordic Life" rolled off my back, completely forgotten.

Jaden's corded arms, muscles bulging from the heavy lifting, left my body wanting to become completely entangled.

I sighed, rubbed a hand across my forehead, and turned from the window. "I'm going to find Sophie."

"Jules." My name left my dad's mouth on a heavy, defeated sigh. As if he already knew the decision I'd made about what I wanted.

"Don't say it."

"Just… be careful."

I swallowed the lump in my throat and nodded once before I left the room.

I found Sophie outside, playing with two baby dolls, pretending to rock and feed them both while she sat on the front porch. Her feet were too short to touch the next step down so her flip-flop covered feet swung lazily back and forth.

I smiled at the tiny amounts of hot pink polish on her toes.

Plopping down next to her on the front stoop, I ran a hand through her hair and pulled her in for a quick kiss.

"Hey, pumpkin."

"Who dat?" She barely looked up as one of her fingers pointed at the men in general.

"Those men were friends with your daddy."

I had never hidden Sophie's dad from her. She had a scrapbook of photos of us together and some of just Scratch that we looked at every night before she went to bed. But still the mention of him always made me catch my breath.

"What dat?" she asked again, pointing at the motorcycles that lined the street at the end of my parents' driveway. They were parked as bikers always did it: bikes backed up the curb at an angle, ready to make a quick getaway if necessary.

"Motorcycles," I told her. "Black and silver, right?"

"Scary." She pouted her lips at me and shook her head slightly. I frowned, looking down at her, not understanding why she said that. It wasn't the first time she'd been around the men. We'd been to several parties where she had seen the bikes and the rough partying of the men who owned them.

"Why?"

She dropped her dolls and pressed her palms to her ears. "Dey loud."

I chuckled softly. "Yeah, they are."

We sat quietly for several minutes, Sophie playing with her dolls, me watching the men trudge up and down the ramp to the moving truck.

I tried to pull my eyes off Jaden as he and Ryker carried my couch up the ramp, but my eyes froze on him. And his arms. The way they flexed and tightened as he lifted the couch told me it was heavy, but the two men carried half of the large sectional as if it was a box of pillows.

On their way back out of the truck, the men now empty-handed, Jaden paused and wiped the back of his hand across his forehead. His eyes closed as he inhaled a deep breath and tilted his head toward the sun.

It wasn't hot out. It actually felt perfectly cool—the best kind of day for moving. But then again, I'd been banished from helping as soon as the group of bossy bikers had shown up at my house, and I wasn't the one moving boxes and furniture wearing jeans and long shirts and leather vests.

When his head dipped down, he turned and our gazes met.

I tried to pull away, to focus on Sophie playing next to me, but everything else faded away as Jaden jumped off the back of the truck and began walking toward me. Or us.

Jesus. He probably just wants to say hi to Sophie.

He stopped at the bottom of the cement steps, his shadow falling over us. I instantly felt cool from the loss of the sunlight. Or maybe it was the way his eyes were fixed on mine.

I still hadn't been able to pull my eyes from his. Stupid, I was becoming.

"We're almost done."

I stood up, brushed my sweaty, clammy hands down my thighs and cursed myself. Sweaty, nervous hands for Jaden? It was the epitome of ridiculousness.

"Okay, thanks." I nodded and stood up straight. Even two stairs up from Jaden, I was barely at eye level. Had he grown since the park yesterday? His broad shoulders certainly seemed wider and stronger when his hands when to his hips and he tilted his head.

His eyebrows pulled in and he flashed me a look that screamed impatience. What had I done to annoy him now?

"We need your address."

Oh. "Right." I rattled it off, Jaden staring at me the entire time, and then he nodded.

"Got it. Are you going to follow us?"

Follow a caravan of bikers and a moving truck through town like some sort of parade? Seemed a bit too attention-inducing.

"We'll be right behind you." I nodded my head toward Sophie. "I have to finish getting some of her things packed. So, I'm um…" Why was my heart pounding wildly against my chest? I had no idea, but I couldn't calm it and I didn't want Jaden to see how much his closeness affected me. "I'm going to go do that."

I turned to move, completely forgetting about Sophie sitting at my feet, and barely missed stepping on her fingers.

"Sorry, pumpkin."

"It's otay. I not hurt." She didn't stop trying to feed her baby doll from a plastic bottle at my apology.

My hand gripped the handle and I froze as he called my name.

"Yeah?" I turned and looked at him over my shoulder. Which was stupid. I should have known better than to look directly at him. All hard lines and angry scowls—

And a damn smirk on his lips that told me he knew exactly what I was feeling.

Crap.

He stuck out his hand, wiggled his fingers. "I need the key."

"Key?"

He huffed. "To your apartment? Pretty sure you don't want us busting the door down."

Oh. "Right. I'll be right back."

He nodded and looked away, breaking whatever he'd spell he put on me. I flung myself into my parents' house, slamming the door behind me. My back pressed against the wood, cooling my overheated skin.

Hell. Instant attraction to Jaden like that could only mean trouble.

From the kitchen, I saw my mom's head dart through the doorway and I felt busted—as if she just caught me making out with Jaden outside the front door, late for curfew.

"Hey," I said when I hit the kitchen, immediately reaching for my purse. With trembling fingers, I began twisting one of my new apartment keys off the ring. As I was doing it, I took off another and slid it to my mom on the kitchen counter. I had no idea why I needed six keys for an apartment with one door.

"Jules."

I closed my eyes. That voice. The warning in it told me she knew exactly what I'd been doing with my back pressed against the door.

Fighting foolishness.

"Yeah?" I sighed. I couldn't even bring myself to look at her.

Her sigh in response equaled mine in frustration and fear. "Be careful."

I swallowed my nerves and nodded. "I will. And we're only just across of town when you want to see Sophie."

My mom grinned.

I leaned in and kissed her cheek.

"I'm still willing to babysit for you."

"I know. But the agreement was I moved back and we were on our own. Like it should be."

Her warm palms came out and cupped my cheeks as she pulled me in and pressed her lips against my forehead. "I know, but you know where we are if you need us."

"Of course," I muttered and stepped back. "I need get back out there."

I hurried out of the kitchen, away from her worrisome and loving eyes, and flung open the front door to the house. My breath got caught in my throat and I choked when I saw Jaden.

Big, scary-ass, angry and scowling Jaden, rocking a baby doll wrapped in a pink blanket and feeding the plastic, squished face a bottle of fake juice.

I snorted. My fingers flew to my mouth, but based on the warning look he shot me, he totally heard me.

"Don't start."

I grinned. I couldn't help it. Sophie was practically sitting in his lap, feeding her own baby doll, and Jaden in his leather cut, mimicking her actions was too…

Perfect.

I grabbed my phone out of my pocket and caught Jaden's glare.

"Don't even think about it."

Oh, I was thinking about it, all right. And doing it, too. I raised my phone and shouted, "Say cheese!"

Sophie's head rose up and Jaden's face turned purple. "Cheese!"

I snapped. Then I snapped four more times before Jaden launched himself off the stoop and stole my phone.

"It was cute." I grinned, ignoring the fluttering in my belly from his closeness and the smell of his sweat. "Except for your purple face."

He scowled. Typical. "Not funny."

"Two minutes and she's got you covered in pink. It *is* funny."

He flicked his head back to Sophie and sighed. His head dropped like he'd been completely defeated. When he looked back at me, a look flashed across his entire face that almost left my knees buckling in shock.

Endearing. All of his harsh features softened in a way that left me breathless and unmoving.

I shook my head, snapping myself out of it. Life was so much easier when, even still attractive, Jaden was pissed at me.

I held out my key, gripping the small end of it with my thumb and finger. "Here."

Jaden blinked, saw the key, and reached for it. Except his entire fist closed around it, including my fingers, and he tugged.

Hard.

I stumbled right into his chest. The only thing between us was our hands.

"Delete the photos." He frowned.

I smiled and hoped like hell he couldn't feel the thundering in my chest. I could barely hear him over the storm raging in my ears.

"No way in hell."

His hand tightened and his nostrils flared.

"Jules."

I grinned wider and arched a brow. "Jaden."

"No one sees that shit."

I could agree to that. Mostly. "No one but her. She'll love them."

His hand released mine as if I'd made him remember something. My hand, empty of the key and his warmth, prickled. I rubbed it against my thigh to erase the odd feeling.

"Next time, though, smile." I darted around him, scooped up Sophie and her dolls while completely avoiding Jaden, and hauled my butt inside.

By the time I'd packed our clothes and the rest of her dolls, I hadn't yet gotten to and loaded up my car. The men were long gone, and it was just me and now sleepy Sophie making the quick trek across town to our new house.

10

Jules

"Wow!" I exclaimed right as Olivia launched her arms around my shoulders. "You guys move fast."

Olivia pulled back and grinned. "The guys are doing it all, but Faith and I thought we'd stay after they were done unloading and help you unpack."

Perfect. I grinned and looked at the truck, half empty. Jaden, Daemon, and the rest of the men couldn't have been there for longer than thirty minutes. They'd be done in no time at all.

"Awesome," I told Olivia, and opened Sophie's door to unbuckle her from her car seat.

"Home?" she asked, her eyes moving to the apartment building in front of us.

It wasn't much, but the two-bedroom place would be good for us. Simple, not fancy, but close to a daycare center and town so we could walk in the summer if we wanted. It even had a pool in the courtyard out back, with a small grouping of picnic tables and outdoor grills for the summer.

I nodded and reached under arms. "Home." Patting her gently on her bottom, I scooted her toward Faith's arms. "The men are still unpacking so stay out of the way, but you can go check out your new room."

Faith grinned and scooped her up. "We'll be inside."

"Thanks, Faith!" I called after her. She flashed me a smile over her shoulder.

"What else are friends for, than to be your little bitches on moving day!"

"Little ears!" I jumped at the masculine shout.

I laughed as Ryker stood at the top of the stairway, hands curled over the railing, and smiling down at us. When he caught up to Faith on the stairs, his hand cradled the back of her head and he pulled her in for a quick but scorching kiss.

"Come on." I linked my arm through Olivia's and pulled her toward my new house—a home where Sophie was meeting the men who knew her dad. A home where I was once again close to my parents. A home that was safe and far away from Rob. It almost felt too good to be true. "Help me unpack."

"Your wish is my command."

I shoved my hip into hers as I laughed. "Shut up, twerp."

"You got shit in your car?" Daemon asked when he hit the bottom stairs.

"Yeah, some clothes and toys. Oh, and a cooler full of beer for you."

Daemon nodded, heading toward my car. "Fuckin' sweet."

Olivia laughed and shook her head. "Men."

We hit the front door of my new apartment right as the twins set half of my sectional couch down in the living room. When they saw us walk in, one of them pointed at the couch.

"This okay here?"

I took in the small room and the corner where my television would go. "It's good, thanks, Jimmy."

He flashed me a grin filled with a small amount of shock. I shook my head. "The rest of these idiots might not be able to tell you apart, but I can." I pointed my finger at his cheek. "You have a freckle next to your nose."

He almost looked bashful as he rubbed the side of the nose. "Right."

"You didn't tell us apart the other night." Johnny grinned and stood in front of me, arms crossed over his chest, flirtatious smile in place.

Silly boy. He was too young for me, and too skinny. I also knew that when he and his brother were together, they couldn't focus on crap. The fact that they'd hauled my couch inside without breaking it was a miracle.

"You had some chick's face smashed to yours and my vision was blurry from beer."

He took a step forward, flirtatious grin widening. "Jealous?"

I winked and moved to the side as Daemon came in, setting the cooler on the floor.

"Drink up!" he shouted, grabbed a beer and turned back outside.

"Back the fuck up, Jimmy."

I jumped from the harshness of the masculine voice. When I looked over my shoulder, Jaden stood in the doorway, three heavy boxes of plates and pans in his arms.

Damn.

"Johnny," I corrected him and rolled my eyes to Johnny. "They'll figure it out."

Johnny's eyes dropped from mine and he headed back outside. Jaden moved around him until he stood next to me in the kitchen and slid the boxes onto the counter.

I instantly felt caged-in by the heat pouring off him—not only from the outside, but from his anger.

Inwardly, I rolled my eyes. Fortunately I had the sense not to do it directly at him.

With one hand on top of the boxes, he leaned in, towering over me. Sweat beaded along his hairline and glistened across the top of his eyebrows. His brown eyes deepened and narrowed.

My hands balled into fists to prevent me from reaching out and running a finger across his skin to remove the sweat beads.

That'd be gross.

But I still had some undeniable urge to lean in and lick his skin. My cheeks warmed at the thought and I looked away.

"Don't fuckin' flirt with the men."

My eyes widened. "What?"

"You heard me."

My nose twitched and I scowled. "I wasn't flirting."

"Not what it looked like to me."

"Then maybe," I said, leaning up on my toes so I could glare at him more closely, "you should get your eyes checked. I was being nice. There's a difference."

"Not when you're one of us and we freely take any available woman we want—and some that aren't." He grinned in satisfaction. Whether at the fact he'd fucked a married woman, I didn't know. I didn't want to find out, either.

I did know that he smelled good. Really good. Sweat with cologne and pure, raging masculinity. I leaned in further, inhaling his scent while trying to stay pissed.

"You're an asshole. And I don't know why you care who I flirt with anyway."

"Don't push me, Jules." His breath was heavy and thick. My brain instantly fogged, taking me back to the day he'd plastered me against his truck and ran his lips over my skin.

A low hum escaped my throat and Jaden's hand instantly went to the back of my neck.

"You want this?" he growled. His grip on my neck tightened and my eyes widened as he held me firmly in place.

I tried to shake my head but could barely move.

He sneered. "I think you do."

God, yes. "Go to hell." My words lacked impact due to the needy, breathy tone of my voice. And the fact I was lying.

"If I go… I'm meeting you there." His lips crashed into me and I gasped, instantly opening my mouth in shock. He pressed against me, pulled me to him by his grip on the back of my neck until my chest brushed against his.

Fire exploded in my veins and on my skin. It flared out from my pores until my own body felt covered in heat, completely consumed.

The kiss wasn't nice. It was angry, and I could feel the battle and the rage within Jaden seeping into my mouth as his tongue devoured me. Our mouths dueled in an intense fight. Fighting for what, I didn't know.

Our attraction to one another?

The fact that I was in love with Scratch but wanted Jaden, too?

The fact that he hated me?

I didn't question it. I just leaned in, pressed up further on my toes until I was as close to Jaden as I could get. He swallowed my next moan and my hand came up, holding myself to him by wrapping my small fingers around his bicep.

"Oh! Crap!"

Olivia's voice slowly broke through the lustful fog of Jaden's kiss.

His hand immediately fell from my neck and he pushed me back. I stumbled into the counter behind me, bracing myself while trying to regain control of my breathing and my brain.

"Sorry!" I caught her grin before she covered her mouth and fled from the room.

My eyes widened as I took in the room—men walking in and out of the hallway and doorway, everyone averting their eyes away from my kitchen.

Where Jaden and I had just been making out. Blood rushed from my brain, and my skin cooled as it paled. What in the hell had I just done?

"Oh my God." I turned around, slammed my elbows on the countertop, and dropped my head into my hands.

No answer came. Jaden certainly didn't say anything to make me feel better about the fact that half his club had just seen us making out like horny teenagers. I felt the heat from his stare and his body leave the room, along with the soft thuds of his booted feet when he walked away from me.

Hours later, I stood in the center of my new living room surveying the small but newly decorated space. My hands on my hips, I spun in a slow circle and smiled.

"I can't believe we've unpacked it all."

Faith raised a bottle of water and tipped it in my direction. "Place looks great, and it's perfect for you and Sophie."

I exhaled slowly, feeling the tension and stress from a full day's work leave my body. My L-shaped sectional fit perfectly into the living room, leaving just enough space for a bookshelf full of Sophie's toys, hidden in baskets on the shelves, and my TV stand.

We'd unpacked every single box, with Daemon, Ryker, and Jaden insisting on not leaving until everything had been emptied, and the cardboard broken down and thrown in the dumpster outside. Ryker had even found my pink-handled hammer and hung various artwork and picture frames we found as we unpacked.

It felt like home and I hadn't even spent the night there yet— although Sophie had crashed two hours earlier, and had fallen asleep easily enough in her new room with her old Cinderella bedspread and various other movie posters of her favorite characters on the walls.

I felt like crashing, too. But the men still had boxes to take to the dumpster, and no way was I getting ready for bed with Jaden anywhere near me.

My body still hadn't fully cooled from his maddening touch earlier.

Olivia snickered from her sprawled-out view on the couch.

"So how was he?" She smirked and took a quick sip of her red wine. *My* red wine. I wanted to snatch it out of her cute little hands and dump it over her head.

"Shut up."

She raised an eyebrow. "That good, huh?"

Goodness. Better. Between the roughness of his hand on my neck and the way his tongue plundered my mouth, I'd be feeling and tasting that kiss for days.

I shook my head, wanting to forget it. It was a mistake and shouldn't have happened.

I couldn't control my body's reaction to Jaden. His domineering kiss earlier told me he felt the same. But that didn't mean we were good for one another.

Hell, we didn't even *like* each other.

And there was still too much he didn't know—didn't want to know.

"I don't know what happened," I explained as I headed to the kitchen for a new wine glass. "But it won't again. I guarantee it."

Faith snorted and looked at me doubtfully. "Sure, sweetie."

I bared my teeth at her.

She threw her head back and laughed. "You're not scaring me."

"No matter," I said. My skin crawled with pleasurable memories as I set the wine glass on the counter and poured the wine. I stood in the exact spot where Jaden had taken me earlier.

Possessed me. Consumed me enough to make me forget we had been in a room with a dozen other people.

I tipped the glass to my lips as I heard the guys hitting the top stair, their stomping boots echoing along the outside wooden floor until they reached my door. Daemon and Ryker entered first, Jaden behind them.

He hadn't looked at me since he'd walked away from me. Six hours of unpacking, unloading, and cleaning my apartment, and he hadn't left or spared me a glance. When he'd left the kitchen earlier, I didn't expect to see him come back at all.

But there he was, standing just inside my doorway.

"Let's go, ladies," Ryker said, and waved his arm toward Faith and Olivia on the couch.

Both of them shot me a grin as they crawled off the couch. They wrapped their arms around me as the three of us embraced.

"Give me all the details tomorrow," Olivia whispered.

"Oh, God. I hate you, but thank you for the help today."

"Be careful," Faith said.

When they dropped their arms, I shook my head, knowing my cheeks were already flushed. They both had knowing looks on their faces.

I mouthed "*I hate you*" to both of them before they turned, met their men in the entryway, and were escorted down the stairs.

Jaden still hadn't looked at me. He stood like a sentry posting guard until the light clicking of the door shutting behind him had us both snapping our heads in the direction of the door.

We were in my new house.

Completely alone.

My legs trembled with nerves as I sipped my wine, pretending Jaden's presence didn't affect me.

That I didn't want him to wrap his hand around my neck again, pull me in and ravage me—

"That shouldn't have happened."

But then he spoke and I remembered he hated me.

But it didn't change the fact I still wanted him.

Crap.

11

Jaden

Her blue eyes felt like they burned my skin. Kissing her earlier had been one of my bigger fuck-ups.

Unfortunately, my dick still thought the idea was wonderful. I would have adjusted myself if Jules wasn't staring directly at me.

I didn't even have an excuse to offer her as I stood just inside her doorway, eyebrows pulled in and my lips pressed into a thin line. Mostly because I still didn't understand what had happened.

I hated this woman. At least I wanted to. Somewhere along the way I'd begun admitting to myself that I didn't despise her as much as I declared to.

But what had happened earlier in her kitchen, in a room surrounded by a dozen Nordic Lords and her two friends—not to mention Sophie?

I had no excuse.

Lust hijacked my common sense.

Jules blinked at me and looked away—probably because I was staring at her like an asshole and hadn't moved since the door closed.

I couldn't remember if I'd said anything, or just thought it. For safety's sake, I repeated myself. "That shouldn't have happened."

"I agree."

Her quick response rattled me. Pissed me off somehow. Which was dumb: it *had* been a mistake. And just in case I hadn't been clear before, I planned on it now.

"I don't like you."

Her lips twitched, like she wanted to argue with me but thought better of it. Shame. My body buzzed with adrenaline and needed a fight—or a different kind of outlet—in order to erase the energy flooding my veins.

"I'm well aware of your misplaced hatred of me, thanks."

Misplaced? Who the hell was she kidding?

My feet moved forward until I stood on the other side of the counter, palms splayed flat on it and my arms locked straight.

"You kiddin' me?" I practically snarled it at her. I wanted her to fear me. Because damn it, regardless of how fucking cute she looked in her short shorts that showed her toned, tanned skin, I still blamed her.

Jules stared back, unblinking and unmoving except for the slow tilt of her wine glass to her lips. She sighed as she set the glass back down on the counter. "Aren't you ever going to ask me about the truth? Don't you want to know it?"

"I know the truth."

"You know what you saw. And what you saw was bullshit."

I glared at her, kept glaring as anger began making my skin boil. Screw her.

Not a bad idea.

Jesus. I couldn't even be angry with her for seconds without my blood flowing to my hardened dick.

This was stupid and pointless. There was nothing she could ever say that would make me think differently about her role in Scratch's death.

But hell if she didn't look sexy as fuck, her tiny little body and her wide blue eyes shooting off confidence and anger in equal measure.

I pushed off the counter, intent on leaving, because I was two seconds away from wanting to hit something or fuck her. Throwing her against a wall in her new apartment would probably not be the best way to end the night.

I'd find a different outlet.

But then she called my name and I looked at her over my shoulder. I watched her as she walked toward me, arms crossed over her chest, sly grin on her face.

When she reached me, she rested one shoulder against the wall.

"What?"

"You can be pissed at me all you want, take out your anger and shit on me. That's fine." She shrugged like she meant it. The fact that she didn't care what I thought of her anymore had me grinding my teeth together. "But don't take it out on Sophie."

"Wasn't planning on it." Because damn it, the kid was cute as fuck. Ten minutes in her room earlier, helping unpack her dolls and books, and I could admit that at the very least. Besides, Scratch would want me in her life—and if she wasn't a pain in her ass like her mom, I could do that for him.

"But maybe you should consider one thing before you start spouting your bullshit at me again." She arched an eyebrow.

I almost felt like I'd been caught in some kind of trap with the way she grinned at me. I couldn't help it. I took the bait.

"What's that?" One edge of my lip lifted into a sneer and I faced her, almost mirroring her pose.

"You should consider your own role in that night. If you would have kept your mouth shut, not told him what you *thought* you saw, then Scratch wouldn't have been pissed. Wouldn't have rushed to my place, and he wouldn't –"

"You're blaming *me*?" My eyes flew wide open at her accusation and I moved.

I was standing in front of her, arms caging her to the wall that her back was now pressed against. My chest heaved with bated breath.

Her wide eyes matched mine and she inhaled a quick gasp.

"No." She shook her head. Her blond hair skimmed against my thumbs next to her head, and I had to close my eyes. How could I want her so badly when I was still so pissed at her? "I'm saying it was an accident, and neither of us are to blame, Jaden. You just won't accept that yet."

I blew out a breath—of frustration with the way her scent scrambled my brain, regret because it wasn't the first time I'd thought the same damn thing, and anger because *she* was the one pointing it out to me.

"I saw you." Each word I formed fell from lips with punctuated precision. "You'd been avoiding the club all week long and weren't returning Scratch's phone calls, and then I fucking saw you at that ritzy fuckin' restaurant, all wrapped around another guy. He was going crazy, wondering what he did to piss you off, and you were out fucking around with another guy."

Water pooled in her eyes. I didn't have the time to feel like shit for my harsh words. My nerves were strung too tight as I replayed the memory of that night in my head: Jules throwing her head back and laughing, reaching out and clasping some douche-nugget's hand. All while Scratch was at the club, working double-time at the garage, because she hadn't seen him or called him or answered a fucking phone in call in a week.

He'd been a wreck *before* I'd caught her cheating.

"Jaden."

I blinked, watched her wipe away the tears slowly tumbling down her cheek. My gut churned with more regret. "I had found out earlier that week I was pregnant and I was avoiding Scratch because I couldn't figure out how to tell him. I was scared he'd walk away, scared he'd be pissed. I was so terrified that my entire life was about to change and I couldn't figure out how to handle it yet."

She sniffed, wiped more tears away, and my hands finally fell from the wall to my hips. The sound of my jaw cracking and her sniffling echoed in the small space.

"And that guy was someone my parents wanted me to entertain for the weekend. Mike was the governor's son and they were in the area working on his next election campaign. It was dinner and a favor to my parents. That was it, I swear it."

I pinched the bridge of my nose with my thumb and finger, eyes closed because I couldn't look at her and see any more damn tears. Couldn't see her when I could see her pulse jumping in the hollow of her throat, and her full lips still looked swollen from our earlier kiss.

Maybe that one was my imagination. I just knew I hadn't been able to stop staring at her pink, full lips while she talked.

"Fuck."

She sniffed again. "I loved him, Jaden. I loved him more than anything and I would never do that to him."

The sincerity in her pained voice pinched something inside my chest. Compassion? Understanding?

Hell, was I even capable of feeling those things? I certainly hadn't ever before.

Her hand reached out and wrapped around my forearm. The small contact singed my skin and my lips curled up on end. I couldn't take my eyes off her hand or the way her fingers were so small they didn't wrap fully around my arm.

"Jaden."

I pulled my eyes to her. Her tears were gone, only the slight trail of stained makeup and red veins in her eyes remained.

"I'm sorry he's gone, but it's not my fault. And it's not yours. It just is."

My nostrils flared as I took her in. Her breathing came in quick, small pants. My eyes trailed across her face, down her neck to her chest, and back to her hand on my arm.

I didn't even want to shake it off this time.

Something about Jules had gripped me—always gripped me— and yeah, I knew she wasn't fully responsible for Scratch's death. Hell, it wasn't the first time he'd crashed a bike, either. More like the twentieth.

But I had needed someone to blame, and Jules was the easiest target.

Staring at her now, watching her pulse thrum against her sensitive skin, I couldn't remember what we'd just been talking about. I knew it'd been huge. A game changer, possibly.

But all I could see was the girl in front of me that I'd wanted before.

And now I had a chance. Even if I did want her to stop it.

"Jules." I growled her name, showing my barely there restraint, and leaned in. I took one small step and watched her back arch against the wall.

Jesus. Did she want this? She couldn't.

"Tell me to stop."

My free hand came up and moved back to the wall where it'd been before. This time, my thumb played with her soft hair that was there, enjoying the feel of her and the way the small movement flickered a slight trace of her shampoo into the air.

I heard her swallow. Saw her open her mouth to speak and close it.

Then she licked her lips—and I was done for.

12
Jules

"Stop."

I blinked, stared straight into Jaden's eyes—that were mere inches from mine—and sucked in as much oxygen as I could. It wasn't much.

I dropped my hand to my side as his eyebrows pulled in. I couldn't do this. Not tonight… probably not *any* night, but certainly not after we'd just been talking about Scratch.

The similarities were endless, and even as I began crying, all I wanted was for Jaden to wrap his arms around me, offering me the comfort I so desperately needed whenever I thought about the night Scratch died.

God, it was so stupid: a night filled with immaturity and accusations, and none of it ever should have happened. And I couldn't stand there, pressed against a wall with Jaden standing so close, and not think of his brother.

That wasn't what I wanted to be on my mind when—*if*—anything ever happened with Jaden. I'd want it be about us. Not that there would be an 'us.'

"You need to go." My words lacked conviction and Jaden noticed.

Whatever lustful emotion he felt seemed to increase, radiating off him as he moved closer. I felt his desire for me pulse against my skin before he even touched me.

Jaden brought his nose down, rubbed it along the length of mine, and inhaled a deep breath. How could his lungs work? Mine felt frozen in carbonite.

But his touch felt incredible. Stupid of me to let him to get so close, but I was past the point of pushing him away. I couldn't think straight. His breath on my skin and his darkened eyes stole my sense.

"You don't want me to go, and I don't really think you want me to stop." As he spoke, his lips skimmed my cheek back to my ear, and then he bit.

"God." I mewled right into his ear. With his weight on me, his strong, muscled presence surrounding me, all rational thought fled my brain, leaving me unable to think.

I wanted to wrap my hands around his arms and pull him until his chest fell against mine. My hardened nipples needed the relief of pressure against them.

"Jaden," I moaned. My hips shifted against him as his mouth trailed down the side of my neck.

He hadn't made a sound. Just moved. Slowly. Tenderly.

I didn't want him tender. My brain swirled with lust as his mouth pressed against the hollow of my collarbone.

His erection pressed against my stomach.

"I don't think you want me to go, Jules. I think you want me to make you come."

I did. It'd been too long since a man went gentle on me. Years. Since Scratch. God knows Rob never did.

Shit.

"Jaden." I tugged on his hair, tried to pull him away, but he didn't falter in his ministrations.

His tongue licked my skin as his hands went to my waist and under my shirt.

"We need to stop."

"No fuckin' way," he growled, right as his hand reach my bra.

I succumbed. I gave in to the temptation, the heated feel of his callused skin along my sensitive stomach, and let go.

My hands moved to his shirt, pushing off his leather vest and frantically clawing at the hem of his shirt. He took in my sudden movements, the way my hands tangled in the soft cotton, as I rolled my hips into his.

God, he was hot. Sweaty and burning my fingertips as I finally found his skin. My hands trailed up his abdomen, taking his shirt with them while I felt the muscles under my touch.

Not rippled.

But strong. Fierce. Powerful.

"Jesus, Jules," he groaned as if in pain when I lifted his shirt to his shoulders. He ripped it over his head, separating from me, and panted.

His eyes wild, his breathing heavy—he looked as crazed as he'd made me feel.

"Want to hear you come," he growled, right before his lips smashed into mine.

My head hit the wall behind me as his hands went back to my shirt. This time he ripped it over my head and pulled the cups of my bra down.

His mouth was there. His hands were everywhere. The weight of him pressing against me had me feeling the rough texture of the wall as it abraded my bare skin.

"Shit," he muttered, pulling a nipple into his mouth again.

I moaned. My fingers flew to the back of his head, holding him there because I needed it.

I held him there, needing relief. I needed it fast and hard in a way I knew only he could give me.

Because this wouldn't be nice. There was too much between us— too much anger and hatred and distrust for this moment to be anything except a good, hard and fast fuck.

I'd never wanted anything more.

He bit my nipple and I cried out. Pain mixed with pleasure and I knew he was just getting warmed up.

Then his hands were at my shorts. He ripped off the button, yanking my shorts apart without giving a shit about my zipper.

I gasped when he dropped to his knees in front of me.

"Jaden?"

Ebony burned in his eyes he looked up at me.

I caught a quick flash of regret right before he pulled down my underwear and pushed two fingers into me.

Hard.

I jolted onto my tiptoes but one of his hands gripped my hip, stopping my escape from the sudden, and completely welcome, invasion.

"Jaden," I cried. My hands gripped his hair. I didn't know what else to do with them besides claw at his shoulders as his fingers moved inside me. Pushing and pulling. Pressing against the perfect spot. "Oh my God."

"Shit, that's hot." He glanced up at me again before his mouth followed his fingers.

I pressed the palm of my hand against my mouth to keep quiet.

His tongue flicked my clit before his mouth took the place of his fingers. Then both hands were on my hips, lifting me.

He held me against the wall, pulling my legs over his shoulders all while his mouth never stopped moving against my pussy.

"Oh fuck, yeah," he muttered, his mouth still on me. "Taste so fucking good."

And I had nothing to hold onto as I shamelessly shifted my hips against his mouth. My head fell against the wall and my feet locked together behind his shoulders.

I was completely at Jaden's mercy. My fingers clawed the wall, fighting for purchase as my orgasm hit me.

I shattered. Into a thousand jagged pieces. Everything I had been exploded from the inside out while he continued licking and fucking me with his tongue. His fingers squeezed into my hips, pressing me against the wall, and my heels dug into his back as my core pulsed around his thick, unrelenting tongue.

I cried out in pleasure, having long forgotten the need to be quiet, all while Jaden slowed his ministrations.

"Beautiful." He slowly moved my legs off his shoulders and back to the floor. My knees almost buckled but he held onto my hips until I was steady.

His head rested against my stomach while I struggled to catch my breath and reality fell down on my shoulders.

"Oh my God," I exhaled. I closed my eyes, my heart beating in my ears. And I couldn't look at him.

I didn't want to know what he would see when he looked at me.

"Mommy!"

My eyes flew open and my beating heart fell to my knees.

"Oh fuck," I whispered.

Jaden's head snapped up, looking directly at my widened, fear-stricken eyes. He jumped to his feet like I'd burned him.

Reality snapped me back to the present like a stretched rubber band as I frantically reached for my underwear and a shirt.

It wasn't until I threw one on that I realized it hit me mid-thigh and it was Jaden's.

"Fuck," Jaden growled. His head fell to his hands and he scrubbed his face.

"Damn it." I didn't have time to say anything else as Sophie let out another scream for me.

I left him standing in my entryway, staring at my back while I hurried to Sophie's room, wearing Jaden's top.

Shit. Shit. Shit.

When I entered her doorway she was sitting up, rubbing her closed eyes with tightly wound fists. Her hair was sweaty and matted to her head.

I brushed it off her forehead as soon as I reached her bed.

"Hey, pumpkin." My pulse beat in my ears. What kind of mother was I to have sex in the living area where Sophie could see? "You okay?"

Oh my God. Had she heard us? Heard me? Shame pooled in my belly.

"Bad dream," she sobbed, her arms wrapping around my waist as she pulled herself close. My arms squeezed her in return.

"Tell me about it."

Her forehead rubbed against mine. "Forgot."

I chuckled softly as my hands continued brushing out her hair, calming her down until her breathing settled and she fell back asleep. My heart beat rapidly against my chest as I held her sleeping form pressed against me.

I could have left within minutes… possibly seconds. But I hadn't yet heard the door close so I didn't know if Jaden had left or was still in my apartment.

Another round with him, alone, seemed like a bad idea.

What in the hell had I just done, throwing myself at Jaden like a club bunny?

Rob's voice whispered in my head: *Whore. Always such a dirty whore.*

For the second time that night, tears pooled in my eyes and fell down my cheeks.

"She all right?"

"Jesus." My hand flew to my chest. I took in the darkened shadow in the doorway and exhaled. "You scared me. I thought you'd left."

He pushed off the doorframe and entered Sophie's room. My arm wrapped around her waist and squeezed her tighter.

He was too quiet as he walked right up to us, only visible by the pale lamp lit next to Sophie's bed, I couldn't make out any features other than his furrowed eyebrows. Only in his jeans, the button undone—I couldn't help but look.

When he reached us, he hesitantly reached out a hand and ran it down Sophie's hair like I had been doing before he scared the crap out of me. I watched his hand move, fingers curling slightly through her locks before he dropped them at the end. The move was so tender, so gentle—and so unlike the Jaden I was familiar with. I felt my breath catch in my throat when he pulled his hand back and shoved it into the pocket of his jeans.

"Wanted to make sure she was okay."

Why? I wanted to ask, but didn't. Jaden look confused enough, and I didn't think he'd answer anyway.

"She's fine," I whispered and laid her down gently in her bed. "Just a bad dream, but she'll be okay now."

Something caught his eye and I followed his movement. The catch in my breath grew three times larger when he reached out and picked up a photo album. On the front cover was a photo of me and Scratch, right after my high school graduation.

His muscled arms showed beneath a T-shirt that he'd ripped the sleeves off of. One of his arms was wrapped around my neck, pulling me into his side as he planted a kiss on my cheek. My face was all squished up, but even with his lips on my skin, he was partly smiling.

I loved it.

I loved showing the album to Sophie every day. Loved it even more when I would catch her in her room, playing with her dolls, and wander over and talk to the photos of Scratch.

Seeing Jaden holding the small album in his large hands sent a jolt of something through me—something that I couldn't name, but I didn't hate it. Wasn't sure I liked it, either.

"I made that for her," I whispered, standing from the bed and wiping my hands down my thighs. Why was I sweating? "Always wanted her to know him."

I fought the tears that still wanted to fall. One crying session in front of Jaden was enough for the day. Especially after that orgasm I still hadn't fully recovered from.

Silently, he flipped through the pages—quickly, as if he didn't want to truly see them but couldn't put the book down until he'd seen every one. His eyes narrowed and his jaw clenched several times before he set the book down.

He stared at it, shoving his hands back into his pockets. I wasn't sure what to say—what I could say—so I stayed silent.

"Scratch." His quiet voice was dry—tortured, almost. His head snapped to mine and his eyes roamed my face. He shook his head, blinked. "Fucking hell."

Before I could ask what he meant, he was out the door of Sophie's room, the front door to my apartment slamming closed.

I jolted from the shock, the angry way he'd speared me with his eyes right before he swore, and realized my body was trembling as I stood frozen to the carpet, long after Jaden was gone.

And I was still wearing his T-shirt.

13

Jaden

Never in my life did I feel freer than when I was on my bike, the brothers in my club surrounding me, and the open highway in front of us.

What had tainted that slightly, in the last few months, was a deal Daemon had made on behalf of the club to begin running drugs for Sporelli, a Mafia family out of Chicago. Men never wanted to be indebted to anyone, but when Sporelli approached Daemon over the summer, he couldn't say no.

We'd originally planned to work with a rival club, Black Death, when they discovered Sporelli had been trying to take over the ports in Jasper Bay to increase their drug shipments into international waters and west of the Mississippi. Water made for easy transport. We'd been on board with the plan with Black Death once they agreed they'd give up Faith, who they'd bought and forced into their prostitution business. But then Sporelli let Daemon know that Olivia's dad, Bull Masters—former President of the Nordic Lords and now buried six feet under—had been the one who'd had Olivia's mom shot and killed five years ago. That night had changed everything for a lot of us.

Olivia had left town, escaped the club life that had turned their back on her while she was mourning the loss of her mom and recovering from a bullet wound. Ryker had shown up minutes after it happened, hadn't been able to catch the guy, and because of a misunderstanding with Faith,—he'd taken off to New Orleans.

But when Sporelli told us that Bull had planned that hit, everything changed again.

Daemon took his side in a shootout against Black Death. Ryker came back and took out Bull, and now we were stuck, trying to figure out how in the fuck we were going to get out from under our agreement with Sporelli with none of our club members dying while we did it.

Unfortunately, I could barely think of all that bullshit as we caravanned south down I-35 headed toward Minneapolis. Daemon, Switch, and Tripp were in the front of a semi-truck loaded with smack and cocaine. Finn and I were behind the truck, with five other men behind us and another semi—a decoy.

When it came to drug runs, we'd separate as soon as we got close to the city. Made it more dangerous to risk being separated and having our group of men split in two, but five and six men with a truck was less suspicious than a dozen.

Fortunately for us, new runs meant little suspicions with local police. In a few weeks—as drugs began hitting the streets in increasing measure—that's when shit would get more difficult.

By then I hoped like fuck Daemon had a plan to deal with Sporellis.

But even that wasn't on my mind too much as the wind whipped across my skin and leathers, chilling me slightly in the cool night air.

My head was still wrapped up in Jules—the way her pussy felt on my tongue and around my fingers as she came so hard I almost came in my jeans. Damn it. It'd been a mistake. Something I couldn't undo.

Wasn't even sure I wanted to take it back.

But mostly I kept thinking of that damn photo album loaded with pictures of my brother. Him smiling. Growling. On his bike. In the hospital with road rash. But in almost all of them, in the dim light in Sophie's room, I could see the peace and happiness radiating out of his fucking blue eyes.

Eyes that looked at Jules like she was his queen.

I couldn't have felt like a bigger asshole. There were a lot of shitty things I'd done in my life. A lot of shit I wouldn't risk confessing. A lot of guilt and a lot of anger had been vanquished at the expense of others—their blood and their lives I had on my hands.

But fucking my brother's girl just because she made my dick hard?

That had to be the biggest betrayal. Even in his death.

But it didn't mean I could shake her from my head either.

Lights from the city shone in our future. In front of the first semi, Daemon raised his hand in a circular motion.

We stayed in formation as we took the previously discussed exits. Daemon, Switch, Finn, Johnny, and I followed the first loaded semi while the rest of the men took off with the decoy, heading slightly west and on a more direct route to the drop-off point at a lot between Minneapolis and St. Paul.

Assuming everything went according to plan, we'd see them again in thirty minutes.

My adrenaline began spiking at the mission. I hated this shit—the drugs and our new alliance—but nothing made me more focused than a job that could go bad real quick.

We might just be bikers to some—dirty men who drank beer and partied hard and revved our mean engines just to piss off the suburbanites.

But we'd seen shit no one else had. We lived in a world of our own making, and it wasn't all pretty or easy.

With Finn next to me, I caught him looking at me, head bobbing trying to get my attention.

I spared him a glance, keeping the truck and men in front of us in my line of vision when I turned my head.

From next to me, the crazy fucker smiled wide.

"Asshole!" I shouted over the rushing wind and noise of our engines.

Finn just raised a brow and nodded again, then paid attention to the road. He was a quiet son of a bitch, not speaking unless necessary, but holy damn if he wasn't smart.

Always taking shit in, he had a sixth sense when shit was going to get bad.

If Finn was smiling, everything would be fine.

I sighed, twisted my hands on the rubber grips beneath my gloved palms. A slight rumble of disappointment ran through me at the thought.

A part of me loved the fight, loved the danger and the wildness. And with the frustration and tension between me and Jules, I needed some way to get rid of it.

Putting a bullet in Sporelli would work just fine.

Erik Sporelli met us at the loading dock as soon as we rolled in.

Ryker and the rest of our men were standing across from him when we pulled in. All eyes turned to us as the truck was parked and we climbed off our bikes.

Following Daemon, I stayed a slight distance back, scanning the area while keeping my eyes peeled for hidden men.

I didn't see them. Didn't mean they weren't there; just sneaky fuckers. No way in hell would a Sporelli be at a meet alone with ten men who'd easily gut him and bury him.

Based on Ryker's scowl, I figured he was thinking the same thing. He probably should have been grateful to the younger Sporelli in front of us. They'd found Faith and took her to safety in Minneapolis when Black Death kidnapped her after a showdown at Sturgis Rally during the summer. Ryker had gone ballistic when he'd seen her—seen how much she'd been hurt at Black Death hands.

But if it hadn't been for Sporelli and their underground contacts, she could have been worse.

Ryker might have wanted to thank Erik for that, but he was also holding a grudge—not only because we were under Sporelli's eye right now, but because he'd seen Faith naked.

Naked and beaten, but naked all the same.

"It's all here," Daemon said, once hellos had been exchanged. I barely spared Sporelli a nod as he took in the truck.

He cocked a half grin. "Mind if I check?"

Daemon glanced around, probably thinking the same thing I had been. Where were his men? "Where are they?"

"They're around." He waved his hand dismissively, proving what I figured.

They *were* sneaky bastards, hiding under the cover of darkness just in case shit went bad. We couldn't take out Sporelli if we wanted to—not without knowing where the enemy was.

With a slightly clenched jaw, Daemon waved his arm out. The rest of us took a step back as Sporelli passed us.

As his hand hit the metal handle, Sporelli glanced back with a smart-ass grin. "Anything gonna blow up?"

Daemon's lip twitched. "Not today."

A slight glare of warning flashed in Sporelli's eyes before he turned to the truck. The loud banging of metal on metal vibrated in the open air as the door lifted. A slight increase in the tension prickling the air had me looking around.

Sure enough, I had no clue where they came from, but over a dozen armed men stepped from the shadows, surrounding us and the truck.

Muscles I didn't know existed coiled tight in my back and shoulders. I looked to Daemon.

He had his hands loosely held at his sides, but I took in the tightness around his eyes and lips. With a slight shake of his head, he silently told the rest of us to remain calm.

Once Sporelli moved inside the truck, his men closed the space around us and entered with him. Several stood guard at our backs while he inspected each crate we'd delivered.

"Looks good," he finally said, jumping out of his truck like he was in jeans instead of his flashy Italian suit. "We'll contact you when there's more coming. Probably next month."

Daemon's upper lip curled and his hands tightened. "Lotta product you're moving."

Sporelli grinned, flashed a smile with sparkling white teeth that I'm sure got him laid nightly. "Yes, well, there's a lot of land that's demanding the product." He shook Daemon's hand, and continued. "Don't worry, we'll keep you busy."

I thought I heard Daemon growl his disgust and frustration, but Sporelli didn't seem to mind.

"See ya around, Daemon."

We stood still until Sporelli and his men had left, waited a few minutes even longer after we knew we were alone before Daemon threw his hands through his hair and cursed.

"Fucking shit!"

"Don't know how much longer we can run this shit, Daemon," Ryker said, stepping up to him.

"No shit?"

"Settle," Switch said, stepping between the brothers, who looked ready to throw down. Personally, I wanted to sit back and watch it happen. Maybe join the brawl. A fight between brothers might not get too heated, but it'd be good for the tightness in my chest. "We'll figure shit out, but we got a ride home to do. Stow your shit until we're at the club with your women and a drink."

Both Ryker and Daemon smiled immediately. Ah, hell: pussy and beer.

Sounded good to me.

Except it made me think of Jules again. I still had the taste of her pussy on my tongue. And I knew I could never have it again.

14

Jules

She's only two. She's only two.

I repeated the silent mantra while I watched my daughter thrash and roll on the grass lawn outside our apartment. The mom in me knew—*knew*—she'd been through a lot of changes in the last few weeks and was having a difficult time adjusting. A move across the country, moving in with grandparents, and now another new place to call home.

She'd been trying my sanity since she'd woken up at five o'clock this morning, though. At seven, I was ready to call a redo and put us both back to bed. I would have, too, if I wasn't supposed to be starting my new job at Bella Salon this morning.

Now, at eight, as I watched her throw her hundredth tantrum of the morning, I was done.

I wanted to haul ass back to the apartment, gulp a glass of wine in hopes it refueled my patience.

I put my hands on my hips and watched her silently. It was generally the fastest way—let the loud tantrum run its course and we'd be on our way—but she'd been at this for what felt like hours now, and I had neighbors to worry about. Last thing I wanted was us getting evicted in our first week due to my daughter's shrill, ear-piercing screams.

Maybe I should buy my neighbors some ear plugs.

"Enough." I used my mom voice to no avail. Granted, my mom voice wasn't very stern. I hadn't yet mastered the serious look and quick, snapping words my mom had always used on me. But my gentler approach seemed to work with Sophie most of the time.

Again, she screamed louder.

I reached down and scooped her up just as the loud and familiar rumbling of a truck engine filled the air. I watched as Jaden pulled into a spot four spaces down.

With Sophie in my arms, I burrowed her crying, tear-stained face into my shoulder and walked to the truck right as Jaden climbed out.

Ignoring the way my pulse automatically increased as he met me on the sidewalk, I frowned.

He stared at me with blank eyes, showing no emotion of what had passed between us just nights ago.

"What are you doing here?"

He ignored me and pointed to Sophie. "What's wrong with her?"

A heavy weight hit my gut, but I pushed past it. I didn't have the time to deal with him, our epic mistake, or the way my thighs were already clenching together as Jaden moved closer to me. Us.

"She doesn't want to go to her new daycare." Shuffling her weight onto my other hip, I readjusted my purse and Sophie's diaper bag. "And I'm late for work."

"No mommy work!"

I flinched from her screeching sound and tried to protect her flailing feet from smacking into my hips. "You'll be fine," I cooed.

Jaden took a step forward, his lips pressed together. "Hey, Soph."

Her little head snapped up and she smiled in a way that was completely opposite from the way she'd looked at me all morning. A small bite of jealousy niggled at me. She'd smile for Jaden and not me?

"Uncah Jaden!" Her arms unlatched from my neck and she

launched herself into his arms.

He exhaled an "oomph" at her quick and unexpected impact as her monkey legs wrapped around his waist.

"Hi!"

"You givin' your mom a hard time?"

Her little face scrunched up. "No daycare."

"She'll be fine," I said, swiping hair out of my face and tucking it behind my ear. I took a moment and reveled in the way Sophie looked tangled around Jaden's body and in his arms. He held her like he'd been holding her for years. Like he'd never hated her on the spot. "She never wants to go to daycare, but she's fine within minutes."

Jaden looked at me, glanced at Sophie's brightly lit face, and back to me. "I can take her."

"Uh. No?"

"What do you mean, no?" The familiarity in the tightness of his angry eyes filled me with a normalcy I could almost live with. "You said I could see her."

I rubbed my hand across my forehead, pressed my fingertips into my temples to relieve the beginning thumps of a stress headache. "Because," I sighed. "She needs routine and familiarity—it's the quickest way to get her to adjust. You can see her later if you want."

His lips twitched and he pressed them together. "Can't she start that shit tomorrow?"

"Stuff."

"Huh?" He frowned.

"Don't swear around her."

He huffed a quick laugh. "Babe. You want her around bikers? She'll hear that crap."

"Stuff," I hissed at him. But my belly flipped at 'babe.' It was condescending and said mockingly, but by the way my lower stomach warmed and pulsed with heat, my body didn't seem to mind.

"Whatever," he mumbled. His fingers threaded through Sophie's hair as she reached out and cupped Jaden's cheek with her small hand.

"I see Uncah Jaden," she said, pulling on his cheek so his eyes were inches from hers. She grinned.

I melted into the concrete.

"Where will you take her?" I relented, giving in way too easily.

Jaden grinned. "Thought I'd show her around the club and the garage. Olivia will be there."

That helped. At least Olivia would know what to do with Sophie if she freaked out.

I sighed. "Fine, but only today. Tomorrow she goes to daycare. And make sure you call me if you need anything."

Jaden licked his lips and nodded. My eyes stared at his tongue darting out, slowly swiping his bottom lip.

I bit back a groan. God. What was wrong with me?

"Let me get her car seat." I spun on my heels, hurrying to my car and away from the way he made me feel.

I had to stop doing that. Nothing would happen with Jaden ever again.

My hands sweated as I climbed around the confusing contraption, unlocking the safety harness from the backseat of my Camry. By the time I was done, I'd scratched the belt hooks against my knuckles and I was so flustered that my hair had become matted against my forehead.

Awesome. Because showing up at a salon with the Barbie triplets looking like a hot mess made a great first impression.

Jaden watched me haul the car seat into his truck, and I explained how to buckle it in properly so Sophie would be safe. I was pretty certain his eyes rolled a few times.

"There." I pushed her diaper bag into his chest. His hands reached out and clasped it. "Extra clothes, wipes, snacks, whatever you need is in there. If you need help, ask Liv or call me."

"I've got this, Jules."

"Yeah?" I arched a brow. "You spent a lot of time around kids?"

"No, but I'm not an idiot." His teeth ground together, making a scratching sound. I looked at Sophie, buckled into the front seat of his cab truck, happily swinging her feet back and forth and sucking her thumb while cuddling her pink elephant blanket.

She looked so small in the huge truck and a tingle of nerves went down my spine.

"Be careful with her," I said, turning to Jaden. My fingers trembled as I closed her door. "She's all I have." Damn it. Leaving Sophie at daycare was hard enough on me. Leaving her with Jaden was terrifying. Not because I thought something bad would happen, but because I'd wanted this for months.

For years. My greatest wish—for Sophie to know Scratch's family—was finally happening.

I sniffed, regaining control. "What will you do with her?"

He shrugged. "Who knows? Maybe I'll take her to the garage and teach her how to change oil and brake fluid—that kind of shit."

He smiled mockingly.

I ignored the way it made my pulse flutter. "Stuff."

He grinned. "That too."

I rolled my eyes as he headed around the front of the truck. He hit the hood twice, gaining Sophie's attention from the inside, and flashed her a wink.

Damn him. When had he become so freaking nice?

My first morning at Bella Salon went uneventfully. The hardest part was telling the three girls apart, but after taking Cammie's advice, mentally cataloguing what each girl was wearing as soon as they said hello, I didn't screw up a name once.

Mondays were apparently slow mornings, and I had hated that part—only because it left me too much time to think of Jaden. The way he'd been so gentle with Sophie this morning.

The way he *hadn't* been gentle with me—

I shook the thought out of my head as I rang up a customer and checked out.

I'd already called the garage four times that morning, and each time Olivia had laughingly answered that Sophie was doing just fine. That men from the club seemed enthralled with her and she wasn't getting in anyone's way. Mostly she just clung to Jaden's leg while he worked.

Which had settled my nerves. Somewhat.

"Here you go," I said to Mrs. Claviss, and handed her the receipt. I knew her from my childhood, and she'd always been kind to me. She and my mom had been friends since I learned how to crawl. I was pretty sure her visit was my mom's doing, considering she'd shown up looking perfect already.

"Take care, Jules, and I'm glad you're home. I bet your mom is, too."

I smiled politely. "Of course. And it's great to be home again."

She waved me goodbye as Cassie walked up next to me with a supply of hair products to restock on the shelves.

"She seems nice," she said. "How do you know her?"

I began placing shampoo on a shelf. "She's been friends with my mom forever. Runs the Sunday school class at my parents' church."

"Is there anyone in this town who isn't friendly? I feel like everyone we've met has been incredibly nice."

My mind instantly saw Jaden's hardened eyes and clenched fists.

"Most of them are." I resisted the urge to press my palms against my cheeks to see if they were as hot as they felt.

"All right. Well, you can take off whenever you're done with this. Have a good day!"

I watched her practically skip to the back of the salon, and shook my head, smiling. They were always so cheerful. Maybe I should bring Jaden in here, and see if their cheerfulness would rub off on him.

The thought made me snort out loud as I finished with the products.

"See you girls tomorrow!" I said after I clocked out and had said my goodbyes. One final phone call to Olivia had told me that yes, Sophie was still fine. Jaden was apparently inside the clubhouse with her, getting her a snack, and everything was just fine.

I hung up on her after she told me to stop worrying.

But I took her advice and decided to see how Faith was doing. After she and Ryker had hooked up, she'd taken Olivia's old job working at Gunner's tattoo shop. It was just two blocks away, on the same street as Bella Salon.

In truth, everything in Jasper Bay was two blocks away from each other.

I smiled as I entered GetInked2 and saw Faith ringing up a costumer at the counter. The customer, a young girl who barely looked eighteen, had a white patch at the back of her neck—evidence of her new ink.

"Hey, Faith."

She looked up, pushed her black hair over her ear, and grinned. "Hey! Just a second." She turned back to the customer, reviewed the aftercare instruction sheet, and once the girl was gone, turned her attention on me. "What are you doing here?"

"Just got off work, was wondering if you'd want to grab a late lunch if you haven't eaten yet."

"You bet. Let me go to the back and tell Gunner real quick."

I waited, my fingers tapping mindlessly on the glass countertop, and surveyed the piercings. They'd always fascinated me and made me feel icky at the same time. The good girl in me couldn't understand how someone would mutilate their body so permanently. Or why they'd want to stretch their earlobes. What would those people look like when they were eighty and had quarter-sized holes in their lobes?

But another part of me—a part that had loved the freedom of being with Scratch—found something adventurous about being pierced in a place no one could see. I'd never wanted my eyebrow or lip pierced. Or my belly button—that seemed too cliché for a girl to do.

But other body parts?

A small, thrilling buzz danced along my skin and heated my cheeks at the thought.

"Ready?" Faith asked, snapping me out of my jewelry perusal. She grinned. "See something you want?"

Uh. "No," I mumbled, chewing on my thumbnail.

Faith noticed the nervous gesture. "What do you want?" she asked, walking behind the counter. She set her purse down on the glass countertop and pulled out a small ring of miniature keys. "Gunner has a slow day, he could do something."

Gunner? See my nipples? I licked my lips nervously.

Faith chucked softly. "C'mon Jules, you're staring at this stuff like you're having some fantasy."

And I was. The way Jaden bit my nipple… what would he do if he saw a metal loop around it? I squeezed my eyes closed. It wouldn't happen again.

Whatever we'd done had been a mistake.

"I'd pay a thousand dollars right now to know what you're thinking about."

My eyes snapped open and I was met with Faith's wide grin. Her crystal clear blue eyes sparkled.

"Um. I've always wondered about what that would be like."

Heat suffused my cheeks as I tapped on the glass, giving in—not that I'd do it, but I could at least admit my curiosity to Faith. She'd never judge.

She peered down and saw the small metal ring with the light blue jewel centered on it.

Her eyes widened with glee. "Your nipples?" she whispered before her mouth spread into a full grin. Her mouth opened like she wanted to squeal.

I flinched in anticipation.

"Oh my gosh, you have to! You absolutely have to do it. It'd be so cute. So naughty under all your sweet girliness."

"No way." I shook my head and took a step back. "It's just a thought… a curiosity. I could never do it."

Faith clapped her hands together. "But it'd be so awesome. And the little jewel matches your eyes. You have *got* to do this!"

Nerves bubbled from my throat into a pathetic laugh. It wasn't very long ago that Faith had been under a heavy weight of her life with Black Death. The fact that she was now smiling and laughing so freely spoke volumes of the healing she'd done in the last few months— physically and emotionally.

I almost didn't want to make her disappointed by saying no.

But that'd be idiotic. Who pierces their nipples just to make one of their best friends happy?

I shook my head again. "No way, Faith. Let's just do lunch."

She pressed her lips together into a pout. "Not unless you do this."

"You're blackmailing me for lunch in exchange for nipple piercing?"

"Who wants their nips pierced?"

I snapped my head to the left. Gunner walked out of the hallway, a smirk on his lips as he stared at my chest.

"Gross, Gunner."

"Sorry." He wiggled his eyebrows. "I hear nipple talk and I have to look."

My eyes flashed Faith. "And he's the guy you want to do this to me?"

Faith grinned and shrugged. "Come on. You know you want to."

"All the cool kids are doing it," I responded sarcastically.

But darn it—I felt the pull toward doing something crazy. I felt myself giving in and heard Faith squeal when she noticed my resistance fading.

"Yay!" Her feet moved so quickly she practically jumped over the counter before she grabbed my hand. "Gunner, quick! Before she changes her mind."

"On it," he mumbled, and went to the back.

"Why does this seem so important to you?" I asked Faith as I allowed her to pull me toward one of the chairs. The ink stations were set up behind a half-wall on the back side of the counter. You couldn't see people getting work done from the front entryway, but you could hear the buzz of the needles when you walked in if a client was there.

Now, there was only the sound of Thirty Seconds to Mars blaring through the speakers and my heart pounding in my ears.

She shrugged and shoved me into a chair. "Because you're always so serious, and I know you have a ton on your lap with moving back and Sophie and being a single mom. But I also want you to remember to have some fun every once in a while, like you used to. And besides, no one would see this, so it's like your own naughty secret." She stopped, waggled her eyebrow. "And I bet Jaden would freaking love it."

My cheeks boiled with heat and I choked. "Jaden? Nothing would happen with him."

Liar, liar, pants on fire.

Faith snorted. "Right. Like nothing happened on Friday?"

She was referring to the kiss. I knew that.

Yet it didn't stop me from remembering the way he'd dropped to his knees in front of me, propped my thighs on his shoulders, and then ate me like a man starving.

"Oh my God," she gasped and fell into a swiveling stool next to the chair. "Something *did* happen. You have to tell me." She clasped her hands together, pleading.

"Nothing," I choked out. "Nothing happened."

"Liar, but I'll let it slide. You two will figure out your crap eventually."

I scowled—wondered how it'd become so obvious to other people that we, in fact, did have 'crap to settle,' as she so eloquently put it.

But then Gunner was back. Faith jumped out of her chair. "I'll go get the jewelry!"

Gunner shook his head. "You sure you want to do this?"

I stared at his hands while he tugged on rubber gloves. Then he pulled out some metal gun thing, a thick metal spike. Might be an exaggeration, but I knew that metal needle was going to be shot through my sensitive nipples.

They hardened beneath my bra at the thought. My body tingled with anticipation.

I wouldn't admit it, but Faith was right. Even though nothing would happen again with Jaden. I still wondered, what would he *do* if he saw my pierced nipples?

The corners of my lips lifted into a grin.

"Yeah." I cleared my throat. "I'm ready."

15

Jaden

"What dat?" Sophie's grease-smudged finger pointed under the hood of the car I was currently working on.

"Filter," I replied. Who knew a kid could ask so many questions? She'd been full of them all day long, pointing her fingers and scrunching her eyebrows toward everything that caught her attention.

If she didn't have a grease smudge across her forehead and down her right cheek, it might have gotten annoying. But damned if I didn't think Sophie's unending questions were the cutest thing. It helped that her huge blue eyes had the same fascinated curiosity that Scratch's always did.

She'd peppered me with questions about tools, cars, men, the clubhouse, and the outdoor gun range for the last six hours. Yet some strange part of me took some pride in being the one to answer them.

As if her blue eyes looked at me with trust, and each question I answered, every small explanation I gave, only increased her trust in me.

I hoped like hell I didn't fuck that up. If Scratch couldn't be here to take care of his kid, that job became mine. And as the morning and afternoon wore on, Sophie staying either close to me or keeping her eyes on me when another brother came and pulled her away, I began feeling the weight of that job.

It unsettled something inside me, being responsible for someone so small.

Made me realize how big of a job Jules had had over the last two years.

Made me pissed she hadn't tried harder to tell me about the kid. More pissed at myself that I knew I wouldn't have taken the time to listen.

My hand slipped as I tightened the bolt on the gasket case.

"Fuck!"

I pulled my hand back, saw the blood already pouring from the knuckles on my right hand, and cursed again.

I grabbed the first thing I saw—a dirty rag at the edge of the hood—and wrapped it up.

Sophie pouted. "You otay?"

I hissed in a breath. I'd be fine, but scratching skin off your knuckles hurt like a bitch. "Fine."

"You tay bad word."

I snorted. "Yeah, half-pint. Get used to it."

I turned, searching for a clean rag or something to stop the bleeding, when Sophie jumped off the stool I had perched her on so she could watch me work.

"Mommy!"

I found a clean rag, dropped the dirty one in the trash, and rewrapped my hand.

Sophie was halfway to the parking lot by the time I caught up to her, and Jules was just parking her car.

When she opened her door, Sophie threw her arms around Jules's thighs and squeezed tight.

I paused in my step, something thick lodged in my throat as Jules's smile increased until it reached ear to ear. She reached down and picked Sophie up, planting her on her hip.

Her smile disappeared and I watched her wince, but it disappeared before the blonde duo crossed the parking lot.

"Hey," I said. Red smudges appeared on her cheeks and I frowned. "What's going on?"

She shook her head, pulled her eyes to the sky before bringing them back to me.

"Nothing," she said.

Bullshit, I thought.

"How was Sophie today?"

I looked at the half-pint, my new nickname for her, and shook my head with a grin. "She talks a lot."

Jules laughed. Damned if that sound didn't spark something to life in my crotch. I clutched my injured hand tighter.

"Yeah, kids do that. Sorry."

I shrugged. "No need. She learned a lot, guys played with her some, and she helped me work."

Jules wiped at the grease lining Sophie's cheek. "I can see that."

"Uncah Jaden tay bad word."

I feigned a growl at Sophie for blowing my cover. "Weren't supposed to tell on me." I looked at Jules unashamed. "Told you it'd happen."

She looked at the bloody rag on my hand. "What happened?"

"Nothing." *Wanna kiss it and make it better?* I squeezed my hand harder and mentally kicked my own ass. "It'll be fine."

I should have left—turned heel and walked away, found a bandage for my hand. But I couldn't. Something about Jules pulled me in, just like always. Something indescribable.

Heat pulsed between us.

A thick silence fell around us as Sophie wiggled on her mom's hips. Jules winced when Sophie gripped her shirt as she set the girl on her feet. She took off like a shot toward Switch.

Who knew that fuckin' guy could be so good with kids? Watching him crouch down, lift Sophie, and throw her in the air so high her squeals lit up the parking lot still shocked the hell out of me—even if it was the tenth time he'd done that.

Something about Jules wasn't right. She was keeping something from me. It wasn't my right to ask, but something in me demanded to know.

"What's wrong?"

She cleared her throat and looked away, her eyes focused on Sophie with Switch. "Nothing."

Liar.

Loudly, the door to the garage office slammed against the outside wall and Liv poked her head through the doorway. "Julianna McAllister! Get your ass in here and show me your tits!"

Jules's cheeks burst into flames.

Her head dropped, and she muttered, "Oh, God."

I spoke before I could stop myself, taking a step toward her at the same time. "Why does she want to see your tits, Jules?"

My eyes settled on them like they were homing beacons.

There was only reason—

My dick hardened instantly, as if it was trying to force its way out of my zipper.

"You naughty, naughty girl," I smirked, my eyes regretfully raising to hers. "You got pierced?"

"No." Her red cheeks belied her words.

The thought of metal strung through nipples my mouth couldn't get enough of just nights ago was enough for me to want to blow my load. A barbell? A ring? Something with a sparkling jewel my teeth could bite down and tug—

Fuck. I adjusted my dick. I didn't care that Jules saw my hand go to my jeans, either. I fuckin' ate it up.

"I'll show you mine if you show me yours." My voice was heavy with sudden need.

"You're not pierced."

I arched an eyebrow. "You sure?" She licked her lips.

I almost came in my pants at the thought of what I suddenly wanted her tongue doing. Like tracing my piercing at the tip of my dick. Then her eyes dropped to my denim-covered crotch. Again.

Yes, my dick shouted.

A low, hungry sound escaped her throat.

"Jules!"

I looked up, growling at Liv in frustration when she screamed again.

"Liv needs me." She turned, hurried off without looking back before I could tell her that I needed her.

But as I watched her tight ass disappear into the office, I couldn't exactly figure out what I needed her for.

Something told me it wasn't just to play a sweaty game of hide-and-seek the apadravya.

"Talk to him," Daemon said. His eyes were on mine, mine were on his, but I didn't hear a damn thing he said. I just saw his lips moving silently.

Because hours later, my dick was still hard and my brain was still thinking *nipples, nipples, nipples. Jules has pierced nipples.*

Fuck.

I scrubbed my hand down my face. "What?"

Daemon slammed his fist into the table. "What the hell's wrong with you?"

Ryker laughed across the table from me. He leaned back in his chair, crossed his arms over his chest, and grinned. "I know."

I growled at him. "Don't fuckin' say it."

"What am I missing?" Daemon's eyes darted between the two of us. "And what in the hell does it have to do with Sporelli."

I glared at Ryker. "Nothing."

He laughed. A full, throw-your-head-back kind of laugh that got the attention of the rest of the men around the table. They all stared at him.

Daemon focused on me. "Then talk to the damn chief."

Hell. I hated that pot-bellied asshole. He'd been in the club's pocket for years, but using him seemed like a pussy way to go about fixing all this crap with Sporelli.

"Fine," I muttered, and then another thought occurred to me. "We ever figure out how they seem to know everything that happens around here before we do?"

Sporelli's knowledge of life in Jasper Bay had eaten at me for weeks. They knew where Faith was before we could find her, and they'd been in town—and responsible for—when Olivia had been shot a couple months back. They'd actually been the ones to do the shooting, although the target had been her ex-boyfriend.

"I'm on it," said Xbox, our resident computer hacker. The guy was thin and sleek, and I swore when he wasn't on his bike he didn't do anything except fuck with computers. He had at least a dozen in his room at the club and never allowed anyone else in there. "Pretty sure someone in town is feeding them information."

"A plant?" My eyes narrowed and my hands balled into fists. Based on a quick glance around the table, I wasn't the only one who tensed with fury at the idea of someone from our town—one we bled to keep safe—narcing on us.

"Figure it out faster," Daemon sneered at Xbox. Then he slammed the gavel down on the wood table, effectively putting an end to our meeting.

As we walked into the club, Daemon smacked a hand on my shoulder. "You need to hit the ring?"

He grinned. Letting him try to beat the shit out of me held a certain appeal. Maybe he'd knock some damn sense back into me.

"Nah, I'm all right."

Daemon shoved me. Hard. I turned around and scowled at him

over my shoulder. It lacked heat, though, and Daemon knew it. We'd been friends far too long for him to fall for my shit.

"Tough shit. Maybe I need it."

"Yeah?" I asked, wicked grin on my face. "Regretting the decision to get hitched already?"

Daemon growled and swung at me. We were in the middle of the clubhouse but he didn't give a shit. Men turned and cheered as we squared off.

"Yeah? You looked real good playing the daddy role today."

He wiped the smirk off my face with one damn sentence. Everything stopped. I didn't even see Daemon's fist heading at my chin until pain blared through my jaw and I dropped to the ground.

Daddy? I wasn't a fucking dad. Didn't ever want to be one, either. Cold tendrils wrapped around my heart and squeezed until I was able to shake off the sting of Daemon's punch. But he'd already done what I needed him to do: knock sense back into me.

My parents died when Scratch and I were little, and after Scratch died, I had vowed to never get close to anyone besides the brothers in my club again—and even they were kept at a distance.

There was no point in trying—or wanting—to have anything do with Jules or Sophie again. I didn't have anything to give them. Nothing to give a woman besides a good, hard and fast fuck that left her legs shaking for days.

And I certainly didn't have shit to give a little girl who needed a dad to help raise her. That man would never be me, and I was fooling myself for thinking otherwise.

By the time Daemon wrapped his arm around my shoulder and yanked me into the ring so we could finish sparring, the cold tendrils and had turned my veins to ice.

I needed to stay far away from Sophie and Jules.

It was the best thing for everyone.

16

Jules

Two weeks went by and Sophie and I were starting to feel settled in our new home. She'd quit having nightmares at night, which told me she had adjusted to not only our new apartment, but also her new daycare. She cried the first few times I dropped her off into the hands of Shelly, a sweet lady old enough to be my grandma. Shelly didn't seem to mind Sophie's tears as she scooped her up and got her settled at one of the art stations in the brightly lit and decorated room for two- and three-year-olds.

Sophie had yelled for Jaden. Wanted her "Uncah" the first week I dropped her off, and I gritted my teeth every time she clung to me, wrapping her feet around my back and her hands around my neck.

It took everything inside me not to snap. Because fuck him.

I didn't know what game he was playing—or what game he'd started playing but had just as quickly decided wasn't worth the waste of his time.

In two weeks, we hadn't heard from him. No sudden showing up, wanting to see Sophie, or take her to the garage. And when we stopped by to see Faith or Olivia, Jaden was somehow always missing.

And everyone seemed to notice. Shifty eyes were cast in my

114

direction from club members I didn't know well—even if they all had seemed to sweep Sophie into the fold, treating her as if she belonged to all of them.

But the distance toward me was palpable. It came from everyone besides Daemon and Ryker. And Pappy.

God, he smelled bad. The man was old, skinny, looked as if he could keel over and bite the dust at any minute and *no one* talked to him—no one but me and Faith, and we always had. The man didn't understand anything about personal hygiene, but he had wisdom growing out of his ears. When I talked to him, it always made me sad that no one seemed to take him seriously. I didn't know much about him except that he'd been old when the club began way back when Daemon's parents were young and single. But Pappy told incredible stories of growing up in the South, and he'd seen a ton of crap during then. He'd served in the military, and the stories he told from the times he'd been activated made me teary-eyed, even if the stories were thirty plus years old.

So when Sophie and I went to the club, I would huddle in the corner with Pappy and try my hardest to listen to his stories, all while keeping one eye trained on Sophie and pretending my other eye wasn't focused on the doorway, hoping for Jaden to walk through.

I couldn't stop thinking about him.

He was everywhere and nowhere.

Our last conversation, the salacious look in his eye as he questioned me about getting my nipples pierced, reverberated through my head all day and most of the night.

I woke up with nipples tingling, a pressure between my thighs, and nothing I did relieved it. Nothing was as good as the night Jaden had propped me against the wall over his shoulders and taken me.

I doubted anything would feel as good as that ever again.

And I hated Jaden for giving that to me, teasing me, weaseling his way into my life and Sophie's heart, only to vanish just as quickly as he came.

"Hey."

I closed my eyes, rubbed my fingers against my temple, before I focused on Callie.

I could easily tell them apart now. Two weeks of working in the salon, every day, and the three sisters no longer looked the same.

"Sorry, Callie."

Her smile was wide and genuine, just like always. Callie's smile was the widest out of the three of them, and always quickest to appear.

"You okay? You look like you were lost inside your head." Her eyes lost their sparkle and I knew what she was thinking: *Again.*

"Yeah, I'm okay, just upset about losing that substitute job this week."

Which was a lie, but Callie didn't seem to notice. I hadn't gotten a substitute job that I'd heard about from the gossip at Bella Salon. One of the elementary teachers said their fourth grade English teacher was going on a six-week maternity leave.

I'd called the school immediately, and been turned down.

I'd been pissed, mostly because I knew there was a cloud over me that came in the form of a Nordic Lords Viking skull and crossbones logo. Yet I'd been relieved, too.

I was starting to like the salon. The girls were fabulous. The pay was decent, enough for Sophie and me to live on. They loved Sophie. Sophie loved them. And no one cared if I took off early or brought Sophie in on nights the salon was open late.

It was perfect for me.

But I hated all the lying I was doing lately—lying to myself and to Sophie. Every lie that fell easily off my tongue ate a larger whole in my gut. I told myself it was necessary: Sophie didn't need her heartbroken any more than Jaden had already managed to do, so I made my excuses of him being busy when she didn't see him. Ignored the way she talked about him as if the four hours they spent together at the garage were the most important four hours she'd ever had in her entire life. Maybe it was. More than once she'd mentioned how Jaden looked just like "picture daddy."

My heart had shattered into a thousand jagged pieces when she put the two together.

I wanted to take each jagged, broken piece and shove it into Jaden's chest so he would grasp the magnitude of the shit he'd pulled on her.

I was saved from having to explain myself further when the bell rang, and Callie's next client walked in. I was even more thankful when the phone rang and I got out of my own head.

"Bella Salon, this is Jules, how can I help you?" I greeted the caller in the perkiest voice I could muster.

The hairs on the back of my neck prickled as I was met with silence. But it wasn't just silence; a thick, steady breathing came through the phone.

My grip tightened on the phone and I frowned. "Hello?"

"Oh, Jules, this is too easy."

The prickles on my neck traveled down my spine and arms. Every hair on my body stood on end. The low, calm laugh rumbled through the phone until I thought I was going to vomit.

Then the phone disconnected.

Rob.

Damn it. My whole body shuddered and I dropped the phone. My knees went shaky and weak and I fell back into the counter behind me.

"Jules? You okay?"

I looked up, saw Cammie watching me with narrowed eyes. Concerned eyes. God.

Oxygen left my lungs in a heavy breath. I couldn't suck it back in. My lungs stopped working, my vision blurred, and I shook my head.

"I need Sophie," I said, and collapsed to my knees.

I heard the chaos around me, but I was lost inside myself as I tried gasping for breath.

Because it was Rob. And he not only found my new cell phone, but he knew exactly where I was and where I worked. And how in the hell could he have eyes on me when he was all the way in Phoenix?

"Oh God," I muttered, and dropped my head into my hands. I willed myself to get moving, and with shaking hands I found my cell phone. It took three tries for me to unlock my phone before Cassie sidled up next to me and pressed a warm washcloth to my forehead. "Callie went to get Sophie. We'll bring her here."

I shook my head. That wouldn't work. If Rob had eyes on me, he could have eyes on Sophie.

"I have to go." I stood up, frantically dug through my purse for my keys when Cassie squeezed my arms. "I have to call Daemon."

I needed the men. They'd know how to find Rob.

Cassie squeezed my arm. "Okay, I'll do that."

I heard her on the phone muttering something, and by the time she hung up I had my keys in my hand and my breath breathing at marathon speed, but I could walk. Hopefully I could drive.

"Liv?"

Cassie bit her tongue. "Um, no. Daemon answered."

I nodded. "Better, then. I'm sorry, but I need to go."

"Jules," she said, gripping my wrist. "Callie's on her way to get Sophie. Take a minute and sit down. Relax. You want to be calm when they get back here and wait for Daemon and whoever else comes with them. Do you want to tell me what's going on?"

I shook my head. The words wouldn't come, because I hadn't told anyone about Rob besides my parents.

Rob sounded different. He sounded pleased. His greasy, slick voice had chuckled with pleasure. He hadn't been tightly wound and threatening, like the times I'd picked up before when he'd called.

Today… his voice had been smooth. Confident.

Full of victory.

"Oh God." The floor fell from beneath my feet. I stared at Cassie, her eyes wide with fear. It in no way matched the terror rolling through me. "He's got her."

17

Jaden

"Jaden! Fuckin' bike! Now!"

I snapped my head up from under the hood of the '78 Camaro I was working on. She was a work of art: all original interior with new, slick black paint job. The engine was still shit, but another week and my brothers in the club and I would have it back to running perfectly.

"Finn!" he shouted, and waved his hands toward every other club member who was in the parking lot, hanging out by the boxing ring. Six men snapped their heads toward their Prez. We all moved instantly. "Let's go!"

Daemon's loud insistence had me moving without thinking. When a brother—especially the President—yelled like that, you did what you were told.

"What is it?" I asked as we climbed on our bikes.

"Jules and Sophie."

He speared me with a glance, told me in completely unspoken words as we peeled out of the garage what a dumbass I'd been being for the last two weeks.

It was his fuckin' fault—throwing the daddy word at my feet to get a rise out of me.

119

The only thing that had swelled that day was the black eye I'd given him in the ring.

But the pounding I'd taken in return hadn't stopped that word from taking up residence in my head: Dad. Daddy. Father. Responsible.

That wasn't me. It had been Scratch. And Sophie would always be his. Even if he never saw her, she wasn't mine. Would never be. Just like Jules would never belong to me.

They'd both always be Scratch's. He had them first.

He'd been the one to deserve them. I was just walking away before any more damage was done.

It was the smart thing.

Why I still felt like shit for it, I had no idea.

We rolled through town, the deafening rumble of ten bikes catching everyone's attention.

Everyone's attention except for the blonde on the sidewalk, who was running, arms flailing, as she waved us down in the middle of the damn street.

Daemon stopped, the rest of us taking our cue.

"It's Jules," the blonde panted. She didn't seem to notice that her waist-long hair was tangled around her neck and shoulders and down her arms. "She's freaking out. Said something about how he's got her."

"He?" Daemon asked.

Fuck!

"Where is she?" I growled.

The blonde pointed down the street. "At the salon, waiting for you guys. But my sister Callie just got to the daycare and…"

Her voice trailed off. Fuck. Sophie.

He has her. Rob. That douche of an ex-boyfriend? How in the fuck had he shown up in town without anyone noticing?

I didn't wait for instruction. I revved my engine and pulled out and around Daemon and the blonde, breathing a sigh of relief as I heard the bikes behind me doing the same thing.

"Where is she?" I demanded, pushing open the door to the salon. I hadn't taken off my sunglasses and everyone stared at me.

A blonde—a mirror image... fuck, two of them?—looked at me with wide eyes and I snapped. "Where the fuck is Jules?"

Her mouth dropped open but she slowly pointed. "In the back, my sister's getting her some water."

I nodded, kept moving as I heard the door behind me open and the stomp of familiar booted feet enter behind me.

"Holy crap," the girl muttered. Scared or in awe, I had no idea. We could be a lot to handle.

But I didn't stop moving until I pushed through the back door and saw Jules sitting at the table.

Her back straightened and she jumped to her feet as soon as she saw me.

She looked white, white as the walls behind her, and her eyes darted to someone on the other side of the room.

Her back was to me, but damn... I took in the long blond hair and then she turned. Fuck. Three of them? I'd just met three beautiful, identical-looking triplets in the span of minutes. Typically, my dick would be thinking for me at the endless possibilities in that type of scenario.

Instead, I focused back on Jules.

"Rob?" I growled.

She wiped the tears from her cheeks. "He's got her. I know it. He called and laughed, said something about it being easy and I just... I don't know what happened."

"My sister Callie went to the daycare to get Sophie and bring her to the salon. Jules said something about calling Liv, but when I did, Daemon answered."

Which explained his rage.

"We just saw Callie, Jules." I took a step toward her, stopped when I saw her shoulders tighten as I got close. God, I didn't want to be the one to tell her. I looked to the blonde, who gasped and instantly covered her mouth. "Sophie's gone."

The most pained sound I could ever experience filled the room as Jules's knees buckled. I rushed forward and grabbed her right before she hit the floor.

My knees sank to the floor beneath her weight as she collapsed into me, and I pulled her into my lap, shifting so my back was against the wall.

Her hands curled into fists and she beat me. She cried out in such a way that I felt the walls rattle from the sheer intensity of her anguished moans filling the air.

The blonde across me from sniffed. "Sophie?"

I met her questioning eyes as my hands went to the back of Jules's head. I couldn't help it. Her fists had given up using me as a punching bag and were now wrapped around my back. I pulled her head to my chest, feeling every sob, every pained groan escape her lips. My shirt was drenched with her tears, but I tightened my grip on her.

"We'll find her."

It was a fucking promise.

That asshole—whoever had taken Sophie—would bleed.

Chief Garrison sat across the table from Jules and me. She hadn't moved from my lap since I'd picked her up, and I had no idea how long ago that was. I wasn't in a hurry to get her off my lap, either.

She felt right.

Her eyes stared at the chief blankly as he wrote on a small notepad.

"Anything else you can tell us, Miss McAllister?"

"Jules," she said. Her voice was raw, barely audible.

My hand tightened its grip on her waist. I could feel her patience wearing thin with the overweight cop asking her questions over and over.

That, and she'd already told him four times to call her Jules.

"Shouldn't you boys be looking for my daughter?" she asked. Again. Chief didn't seem in any big hurry.

It'd taken everything I had to let him question Jules in the first place. But when the daycare had realized Sophie was gone, and the blondes out front had realized the same thing, everyone had called the cops.

They'd swarmed the salon in minutes, and the only thing Daemon and I could do was wait.

Wait until they were done with their questions and we could take care of this shit on our own.

When Daemon had heard as much as he needed to, he and the men had taken off at my nod of approval.

As soon as I heard their bikes rumble on the road, my chest had been able to inhale a breath.

Now, hours later, I was still stuck with the damn chief asking Jules questions with a doubtful expression on his face, and Jules's parents sitting next to him at the table.

As if it was her and me against them. Against the world.

With the way she leaned into me, and didn't throw herself into her mom or dad's arms when they entered the room, I decided I was perfectly okay with that.

As soon as we got Sophie back, it'd be Sophie, Jules, and me against the world. Fuck them belonging to Scratch. Maybe it made me a dick that I was consumed with thinking of Jules in my life as she went through the most horrific experience of her life, but I did.

I wasn't leaving her side until we got Sophie back, and after that, we had some serious shit to discuss.

It didn't sound as terrifying as it did weeks ago.

"We done?" I growled. My hand tightened at the back of Jules's neck.

The chief looked to Jules's dad and he nodded.

"We'll have more questions. We'll need to know where to get ahold of you best."

Her dad opened his mouth to speak but I cut him off.

"My house. My phone. She'll be with me."

"Son—"

I silenced the mayor with a glare. I saw his fear and his anguish at the thought of his granddaughter being missing. The decent part of me also knew he was just worried about his girls.

But they weren't fucking his anymore.

Mine.

I shook my head and sneered at him. "I'm not your son."

His nose twitched. Jules's mom laid her hand over her husband's clenched fists. They seemed out of place with his designer suit and slightly gelled comb-over.

"I think we're all just really worried. Jules should come home— she'll be able to rest in her own place, in her own bed."

"No," Jules croaked.

It was the first sound she'd made that wasn't a direct answer to the chief's questions for the last two hours.

All she'd done was sit on my lap, grab ahold of my leather cut, and stare—completely terrified—at a speck on the wall across from her. She hadn't yet looked at her parents, and they were in the same room as her.

Jules's mom sighed. I almost liked the woman. She seemed to know how to handle her pissed-off husband as well as calm the tension suffocating everyone in the room. Didn't mean I was unwrapping my arms from Jules's waist anytime soon.

"Jules, come home and get some rest and let the police find her."

Understanding dawned. Of course her dad would want all this done by the book.

I licked my lips to speak, but Jules beat me to it. I felt her rage boiling off her as she squirmed in my lap and finally faced her parents.

"If Daemon said he'll handle this, he'll handle this."

"Miss McAllister."

"Jules," she snapped, and pushed off me. "My name is Jules, chief, and you know this because you've known me since I was four." She inhaled a deep breath, possibly her first good suck of air in hours since we'd been crammed into the small room. "You do what you need to do to find my girl. And Daemon will do what he has to do to. But I have to tell you, chief..." She leaned forward, rested her palms flat on the table.

Something like pride suddenly swelled in my gut. She had finally found her fight. And it was fuckin' hot.

"Right now, I'm *really* liking the way that I know Daemon and his boys will take care of this sick fuck once they've got my girl safe."

Revenge. She wanted it. I could feel the thrill of someone's death—someone who deserved to die—clawing at Jules as the words were hissed across the table. She looked pissed—a mama lion protecting her cub—and who could fuckin' blame her?

Her dad looked appalled and I noticed a slight nod from her mom. I doubt she'd admit she wanted the same thing, but something told me *every* mom would want the same thing.

I stood from the chair, wrapped an arm around Jules's waist, and pulled her close. "You know where she'll be if you need her."

I didn't give Jules a second to change her mind. If she came back to reality and remembered how I'd pulled a disappearing act for the last two weeks, I didn't think she'd want anything to do with me.

Not that I wouldn't deserve it.

But we had Sophie to find. And once we did, I planned on changing a whole lot of shit.

18

Jules

I hadn't spoken since we left the salon. I didn't even remember leaving, or climbing on the back of Jaden's bike as he hauled ass to the clubhouse.

I didn't even know if it'd been days our hours since Rob's slick, ugly laughter rolled through the phone. Maybe it'd only been minutes.

Nothing registered in my head.

Sophie was gone. Taken in an attempt for me to go back to Rob. Once Jaden had wrapped his arms around me, allowed me to cry and scream and wail against him until I'd bled every terrified tear from my body, I'd finally been able to realize that was Rob's play. Knowing that, knowing what he really wanted—me—kept my terror in check. He wouldn't hurt her.

I knew it. Had to *believe* it, or else I'd die.

It fueled my anger toward Rob. How I'd been able to answer all of the chief's questions without losing my grip on reality and shoving his sharpened pencil through his chest as he continued droning on incessantly, asking me the same questions over and over, I had no clue.

I'd barely registered my parents' attendance at all. Knew my dad had found out, probably as soon as the cops got the call.

While I was grateful for their presence, they weren't what I needed.

I needed blood. I needed Rob's head sacrificed on a stake, not the calm and comforting yet empty assurances my parents would provide.

That was the only reason I left with Jaden, willing to spend time with him. Nordic Lords took care of their own, and Sophie was theirs. As we pulled into the parking lot at the clubhouse, I'd briefly scanned the lot.

A sick, satisfied grin twisted my lips with pleasure as I realized no one was there.

They'd all been dispatched. I knew it immediately.

And I freaking loved it—loved the thought of what Rob would do as soon as someone like Switch showed up in front of him. Switch might be old, but he was huge, strong, and intimidating as hell. Besides that, he'd grown a soft spot for Sophie, and I knew if anyone was itching to get her back safely, it'd be Switch most of all.

He and his old lady, Marie, had become completely taken with her, treating her like the granddaughter they'd never had. Which made sense in some way, since they'd practically raised Scratch and Jaden.

"Let's go inside," Jaden said, waiting for me to climb off the bike. "I'll get you something to drink, check in with Daemon, and see what he's got."

I nodded, partly because I was still pissed at Jaden—pissed at the way he'd turned his back on Sophie so easily, and even more upset that he thought he could swoop back in, acting like he suddenly gave a shit.

But the pain in his eyes told me he did. I saw a sparkle of fury in his dark brown eyes when he removed his sunglasses and grinned.

Yeah. Rob wouldn't know what was coming for him.

As soon as we the hit the main room in the clubhouse, strong, thin arms immediately assaulted me, pulling me tight and yanking me off my feet.

"Oh my gosh, Jules! I've been completely freaking out! Are you okay?" Liv let go of me, planted her hands on my shoulders, and pushed me back.

My head snapped from the whiplash of her sudden movement.

Tears began falling down my cheeks before I knew they were coming, and I collapsed into her chest. All the emotions I'd been able to hold in check during questioning spilled over into Liv's incredibly strong and warm embrace.

With her arms wrapped around me, she led me to a couch and pulled me down with her.

"We'll find her," she declared with utmost confidence.

"I know." I sniffed and wiped away my hair that had fallen in front of my face. It was wet, stained with my tears as I pushed it behind my ear.

When I opened them, Jaden stood in front of me, hands on his hips with a mixture of pain and lust written all over him.

Asshole. I tried to ignore the lust and focused on his pain and anger.

"What?" I asked.

"That asshole hit you?" He narrowed his eyes on me, dared me to argue with him.

I pressed my lips together. Talking about Rob had been hard enough in front of my parents. Answering the chief's questions had been harder, but he hadn't asked me that question.

But Jaden wasn't stupid.

I flinched from the intensity in his stare. It heated the room and I blew out a breath. "Not sure what that has to do with Sophie," I responded, trying to get him to focus on the issue.

I figured Rob was dead either way, once they found Soph. I didn't particularly care *how* he died. Just that he did.

He gritted his teeth. "Answer the question."

"No—and why do you care anyway?" I snarled back. I couldn't help it. Screw him. He'd avoided us for weeks, and just because he now swooped in to play the hero didn't mean I had to take it. There were dozens of other Nordic Lords men searching for Sophie. Any one of them could handle things.

Liv's hand rubbed my back, trying to soothe me. She failed.

"Maybe this isn't the right time for you guys to be hashing this out."

I glared at her, caught Jaden doing the same thing, and wondered how she didn't whither under our angry stares.

Jaden snapped his head to me. "I want to know how slow and painful to make his death once I find the fucker. That's why it matters."

Yes. A sick, oily feeling slithered down my spine at his words. It was evil… but thoroughly agreeing with Jaden.

I nodded. "Just find my daughter, Jaden. Please."

He swallowed, and a thick lump bobbed down his throat as he did. Grabbing his cell phone from his back pocket, he turned and disappeared into the bar area.

When he returned, he had a bottle of tequila, a bowl of cut-up limes, and two shot glasses in his hands, along with a fuming angry look on his face.

"Take this." He set out the tequila limes and poured me a shot. "Don't get fuckin' wasted, but it'll help you stay calm."

"What happened?" I choked, blood drained from my face. Oh my God. I could have been horribly wrong. Maybe Rob took Sophie because I didn't agree to go back to him. Maybe this was his way of getting revenge.

"Nothing new, yet," he said, and the way his eyes hit mine I felt instantly calmer. Relief fell from my shoulders. "But the men are on the highway heading south. I'm going to meet up with them."

"Call me when you know something."

"Of course."

I watched him walk away, Liv's arm tightening around me.

When he hit the door he turned around, and the force of his confidence smacked me in the chest, even from across the large space.

"I'll bring her back to you, Jules. I fuckin' swear it."

The door slammed behind him, and Liv handed me the shot I hadn't yet taken.

Night fell, and only a few of the men had returned. When they did, their eyes shot to mine in disbelief and frustration.

Liv, Faith, and Marie had tried to keep my mind moving. They chattered endlessly about upcoming weddings, constantly trying to pull me into the conversation. But all I wanted was to see lights shine through the windows of the clubhouse—Jaden pulling up in his truck, with Sophie safely tucked neatly in the cab next to him.

Completely safe.

I let out a shuddering breath, my arms crossed around my waist, as I stared out the window.

"She'll be fine," Faith said. It was almost all she'd said since she showed up with taco salads from her favorite Mexican restaurant.

I knew from experience that they were delicious. Tonight I felt like I could throw up after two bites. The tightly wound knot of fear in my gut took up all the space inside me.

"I know." I reached up and held onto her hand, which had fallen onto my shoulder. We stared out the side windows, me praying for Sophie to come home, praying they'd find Sophie safely, when my phone began vibrating on the table.

I looked at the dancing, black piece of plastic as if it was a cobra ready to strike, and my eyes flew open wide.

"Xbox!" Liv yelled from the couch. All of us stared at the phone until Xbox, a club member with apparently crazy-ass hacking skills, nodded the okay. He'd set up my phone at some point to track incoming calls. I didn't know how. I didn't *care* how.

I reached out with shaking hands and exhaled a breath of relief when I saw the caller.

"Jaden?" Blood buzzed through my entire body.

"We got her, babe."

My knees collapsed and tears of relief fell down my cheeks. I felt someone's arm wrap around my shoulders and pull me to them, but I couldn't tell if it was Liv or Faith. Or Marie. I didn't care, either.

"How?" I sobbed, my shoulders shaking. "Is she okay?"

"Tired. She's sleeping, but she's good. I swore to you I'd get her back to you and I meant it, Jules." His voice sounded so strong, so sincere.

I wiped away my tears as more fell. "Where is she?"

"In my arms. Just waiting for a truck so we can get her home."

"Where are you?"

He hesitated. I heard the hitch in his breath and fear tore down my spine. "Jaden?"

"We'll talk about it later, okay?"

His tightly clipped voice left no room for argument, so I nodded. Then I realized he couldn't see me nod.

"Okay, Jaden. When will you be back?"

"Not long. I'm having Finn come get you and take you to my place."

I thought about arguing, then realized that'd be stupid. I didn't care where I went, just that Sophie was safe and I got to see her. Hold her. Check over every inch of her skin to make sure she was injury-free.

"All right." I paused, emotion choking my throat, and I heard him heave a deep breath. "Jaden? Thank you."

My throat burned with new tears as he said, "Anything for you, Jules. And Sophie."

19

Jaden

"You owe me for this," the chief told Daemon right after I hung up the phone with Jules.

I didn't have time to erase the sound of her voice, the fear mixed with relief that had come through the phone, before I hung up and turned to face the man who had helped us.

Fucking helped us. It paid to have the chief of police in your back pocket, but never had he handed over a witness into our hands, knowing what we'd do to him.

The moron who had taken Sophie, though? He'd handed him right over as soon as two of his cops pulled the dumbass over on the highway just south of town.

With Arizona license plates.

It would have been comical if it wasn't Sophie in the backseat— no car seat, no seat belt, terrified alligator tears streaming down her pink-stained cheeks.

She had been hysterical by the time the chief had called us.

I had grabbed Sophie, throwing her out of the backseat of a run-down, gold Ford Taurus where the paint mixed perfectly with the rust, and hadn't let go until she calmed down.

Now, I was staring at Sophie, sleeping peacefully in my truck as if she hadn't just been scared out of her damned mind all day. I was thinking about how crazy Jules must have been goin' all day long, waiting for word from us on gettin' her back.

And as much as I wanted to thank the chief for letting us take that piece-of-shit, two-bit kidnapper off his hands, I wanted to punch him in the face.

"Pretty sure we've already paid you, so now we're even." Daemon crossed his arms over his chest and glared at the cop.

"Pretty sure giving up a kidnapping is worth more than that."

He was so slimy. I grinned, thinking of how we'd taken care of that kidnapper and wondering if it'd feel as good to do it to the chief.

Daemon must have known what I was thinking—or maybe it was the growl that I didn't hold back—because he speared me with a look, telling me to stand down.

"Miss your chance at nationwide fame?" Daemon asked and raised a brow.

I snorted.

The chief's sweaty, fat cheeks puffed up with rage and turned red. Ah, hell. That's what this was about?

I threw my head back and laughed. "All right then, chief. We owe you." I shook my head. Fucking greedy fat bastard. I threw a look to Daemon, tellin' him to go ahead and give up Sporelli to the police, and shook my head again. "I gotta kid to get back to her mom."

Before I climbed back into my truck, I watched the faint light of five of our men. I kept watching them as their flashlights began shining more bright when they exited the cover of the trees.

We were at a rest stop twenty minutes south of Jasper Bay, and completely out of Chief Garrison's territory. Why we let him follow us, I had no clue, but he wanted our reassurances that this wouldn't end up back in his jurisdiction, so what-the-fuck-ever.

I couldn't have cared less when Ryker, Tripp, Johnny, and two other men hauled Peter Taylor's scrawny, greasy-haired ass out to the woods. Two bullets and a deep hole dug four hours later, and they were done.

Sweet justice, I figured. Except Jules' ex, Rob, was still livin' safe in Phoenix, a country away from shit he'd just put into motion and hadn't been man enough to handle himself.

I pictured blond hair, girly hair shit in his hair, khaki pants. Or maybe pink and gray plaid golf shorts. A rich, entitled asshole, willing to pay to have shit done, but didn't have a big enough cock to do it himself.

Part of me was pissed that Jules had settled for some asshole who beat her and tried to kidnap her kid.

The other part knew that was what she deserved—country clubs, fancy lobster dinners, and designer clothes.

I couldn't give that to her. Didn't fucking want to give that to her.

But I was also past the point of caring. Or running. If anything, Sophie missing today had told me exactly what I wanted.

And I was done fucking it up intentionally.

With that, I slammed my hand on the hood of the truck and waved a goodbye to the assholes still standing around, cleaning shit up.

I caught Jules and Finn sitting on the wood steps leading up to my apartment as soon as I pulled my truck into the parking lot.

I could have had Finn take Jules back to her apartment, but I didn't trust the safety of it—not until we had a chance to make sure Rob wasn't sending more men after her. I wanted her far away from where he could find her easily.

Besides that, I just fuckin' wanted Jules and Sophie in my apartment.

She saw my truck as soon as I pulled in. Before I had slammed the gear shifter into park, Jules was at the passenger side of the door, ripping it open, frantically untangling and unhooking Sophie from her car seat.

"Oh my God." She chanted the words over and over as tears fell down her cheeks and her shaky fingers worked the locks and buckles.

As soon as Sophie was unhooked, she pulled Sophie's still sleeping frame in to her body and rocked her frantically.

Something expanded inside my chest when Jules's eyes locked with mine. Tears fell down her cheeks shamelessly. My hands froze on the steering wheel.

"Thank you."

The words fell from her raw throat, and for not the first time that day, anger clawed at me, wanting its release. Not having the satisfaction of killing the man who had caused Jules this amount of pain didn't help shit.

"Let's get you inside." I climbed out of the truck, knowing questions would come soon, and knowing even more that she wouldn't like the answers I had to give her.

Finn met us at the stairs, extended a hand to me, and clasped it tightly. "Did good today, mate."

Something haunted his eyes as he watched Jules still rocking Sophie, tears still rolling down her cheeks, which she didn't bother to wipe away.

"Daemon will fill you in when he gets back to the club, but this ain't over."

"What?" Jules gasped, her large eyes on me.

"Inside, Jules."

She took a step away from me, and I gritted my teeth at her small movement.

It wasn't about me, but ever since finding Sophie—fuck, ever since Daemon had made the smartass comment about me playing the daddy role—I'd fought that urge to wrap Sophie in my arms and protect her from harm.

I had failed her today. Jules's terrified eyes hit my gut as if I'd been punched.

"I want to know," she said, taking another step back.

Finn caught my eye, and even though he was closer, knew that small movement ate at me so he stepped back at the same time I stepped up.

"Jules," I said. My hand cupped her chin firmly. "Let's get you inside, and I'll fill you in, babe."

Something sparked in her eyes. Something I liked.

She nodded and turned toward the stairs that creaked under the weight of our footsteps.

"Jules?" Finn called as we reached the top. We both turned, watched him shove his hands into the pockets of jeans and he nodded toward Sophie. "Glad she's in your arms, Jules."

Her voice choked. "Thanks, Finn."

He nodded once, turned and headed toward his truck.

"C'mon," I told her, my hand at her back. "Up you go before Sophie wakes up. She's had a long day."

"Haven't we all."

I locked the door after she entered and headed straight toward the couch. In one fluid movement, she had her back propped up against the back of the couch, Sophie in her lap, and one hand running through Sophie's blond hair.

My stomach tightened.

"Need a drink?"

Jules kept her eyes on Sophie and shook her head. "I'm okay."

Okay. Jules wouldn't be okay for a long time, I figured. If I was as terrified and angry at the thought of Sophie being taken, ending up with God-knows-who in God-knows-where and having God-knows-what happen to her, Jules had to be a fucking wreck.

But besides her trembling fingers and the tears that still fell sporadically, she looked tough as nails.

I poured myself a drink and met her in the living room. I only had the one couch, so I sat at the opposite end of the small, tattered piece of furniture and stared at Sophie's bare feet. One over the other, toes curled in, I could see every wrinkle line along the soles.

I wanted to run a finger along every crease, but resisted.

"What happened?" Jules finally asked.

I hesitated, unsure of how much she really wanted to know. Debated how much she truly *needed* to know.

But then she pierced me with her bloodshot eyes, her blue eyes looking damaged yet fierce, but still showing more red than blue.

"Rob hired someone to take her back to Arizona. Figured by the time they took her at the daycare, he'd be hours on the road before cops would be behind them. Fuckin' dumbass he hired was dressed as an air and cooling maintenance man."

I shook my head. So fucking stupid. So damn cliché. I'd spent hours throughout the day rehearsing the hell I wanted to unleash on the daycare workers who let someone into their building.

"I don't know if Rob got cocky, figuring they were safe enough by the time the guy had Sophie, or if he thought you were too stupid to figure out what he meant when he called you, but either way, his fuck-up probably saved her."

Jules sucked in a shaky breath. I hadn't taken my eyes off her, even though it felt like she was looking through me and not at me. I had a feeling she hadn't been seeing shit all day long. Not since that phone call.

I couldn't keep the small distance between us anymore. I wanted to be there for her—*had* to be there for her. Whatever shit that had gone down with us before today had changed the second she crawled into my lap, sunk into my hold, and cried her damn eyes out.

I moved closer, shifting on the couch. My one leg bent, Sophie's feet rested on the inside of my knee. My other leg propped on my stained, chipped wood coffee table I'd picked up on the side of the road five years ago. My arm went to the back of the couch and my fingers ran over Jules's shoulder.

She stiffened, looked at my fingers and then up at me—then through me.

I let her, but I wouldn't let her continue not seeing me for long.

"Jules, Rob is still back in Arizona. Xbox is tracking him and we got men on it, but it's gonna take some to figure out his next move, or what he intended to have happen with this last play, but we'll take care of it."

Her eyes dropped to the top of Sophie's head. I watched her wrestle with her emotions; too many flickered through her eyes for me to be able to name.

My hand tightened on her shoulder. The firm movement caught her attention and she looked at me, inhaling a breath as she did.

"I swear to you. He'll pay for this."

She shook her head, her eyes dazed. "I don't even understand why he'd do this. Why…"

"Doesn't matter why. What matters is that she's safe and the fucker who took her is buried six feet under and unrecognizable."

Her lips parted on another quick gasp. "You guys?"

"You want specifics, I'll tell you. But I'm thinkin' it's better you don't know."

"No." Her eyes glossed over with more tears and she sniffed. "I don't want to know."

"Okay, then." I moved my hand from her shoulder to the back of her head, cupping it and digging my fingers into her scalp slightly. I couldn't help it; I had to be closer. Needed Jules to know she wasn't alone in this, that the club—that I—would fight for her. How that all changed, I didn't know. Didn't care anymore, either. "Why don't you two get to bed? We can talk about the rest in the morning after you've had some sleep."

Her eyes darted from mine to the small living space. "Where?"

I felt a small grin tug at my lips. "Come on."

Uncurling my legs from the couch, I stood in front of Jules and offered her a hand. I tugged her gently as she fought to keep her arms around Sophie and not lose her balance.

Then I moved her down the hallway. My heartbeat pounded inside my rib cage, because what in the hell would she think when she saw my second bedroom—the room I'd always kept for storing shit, but I'd recently cleaned out?

Opening the bedroom door, I bit down on my bottom lip and cast a quick glance at Jules.

She had Sophie propped on one hip, hands wrapped around the little girl's butt. She frowned at me as I pushed open the door so she could see inside.

Breath got stuck in my lungs.

"Here." I swallowed, stepped out of the way, and watched Jules duck her head in the doorway as if she was afraid I'd sent her into a room filled with snakes.

She gasped, her head whipped around to face me. Her pale blond hair snapped her in the cheek when her eyes flew wide open.

"You did this? Why?"

Frustration replaced nerves as she shot me a glare—of confusion or anger, I didn't know. Suddenly didn't want to take the risk of knowing either.

"Go to bed, Jules. We'll talk in the morning."

I left her there and marched back to the living room, back to my drink, and didn't look back.

There was only the quiet sound of the door clicking shut as Jules and Sophie entered the room I'd made for the little girl.

All that fucking pink. I'd felt like a fool at the store. Felt like a bigger fool now as I sat alone in my living room, drink in hand, while Jules was in the room with Sophie.

I huffed a breath, sank lower into the couch cushion, and took a large swallow from my glass half-filled with whiskey. Hell, she'd been through enough today. The last thing she probably expected to see was a room decked out for Sophie. 'Decked out' might be exaggerating: a bed with a pink comforter and a small buckets of toys and books was all I got. At the time it had felt like a ton. At the time, I didn't know why I did it except I'd been drawn to the toy side of the store instead of buying the food I'd gone there intending to get.

Now I just felt like an asshole, knowing I'd probably given Jules whiplash in the hallway with my constant mood swings.

"You're such a dick," I muttered to a dark, silent room.

20
Jules

I stared at the bed—the *pink* bed—and readjusted Sophie in my arms.

For the first time since Rob had called me at the salon, I finally felt as if my lungs could exhale full breath.

Sophie was *safe*, and in my arms. God, I never wanted to let her go again. Never wanted her out of my sight again.

How Rob could find us was no big secret. Where else would I have gone except head for home? That he could find out where Sophie's daycare was, only weeks after her starting, and find out where I worked, scared the hell out of me.

And why he was so obsessed with getting us back terrified me even more.

Every time I closed my eyes, I saw him. I saw his twisted lips as he backhanded me. His furrowed brow as he hit me in the ribs.

I had thought I was free of him, for good. Knowing he could get to us so easily left me feeling paralyzed.

Marginally, I felt better in Jaden's apartment for the first time in months. Something about knowing he probably not only kept a gun tucked beneath his vest, but that there undoubtedly had to be weapons stashed in this very apartment, had a slight calm permeating my terrified shell.

But I'd think about all of that tomorrow.

"Come on, pumpkin," I whispered, my lips pressed against the top of Sophie's head. "Let's get you to bed."

I moved hesitantly to the pink bed. There wasn't much in the room, and even with only the street lights shining through the open window blinds, the comforter seemed too bright. Pulling down the covers, I gently laid Sophie on the bed and began removing her shoes and her clothing.

My pulse increased as my eyes roamed her skin. It was the first time since I'd gotten her back that I was able to examine her.

Bile rose in my throat. Oh God, if that asshole hurt her... touched her—

Stop.

My fingers trailed her pale, soft skin, seeking any abrasion or scratch—any mark that would show me she was hurt—but after several minutes of my trembling fingers roaming her skin, I found nothing.

Safe. She was safe. I was safe for now, and all I wanted to do was hold her. I climbed into the small bed, trying to ignore what it meant that Jaden had done this for Sophie when he'd spent the last two weeks ignoring and avoiding us.

Sophie curled into a ball next to me. She seemed so unaffected by what had happened, sleeping so peacefully and calmly next to me just like she always did.

I didn't think I'd be able to sleep for weeks.

At least I wouldn't tonight. I had no idea how long I lay in bed next to her, my hands moving from her hair to her head to her heart just to feel it beneath my fingertips. But no matter how long I lay there, my mind wouldn't settle.

I couldn't close my eyes and stop the nightmares I'd thought about all day from invading the darkness behind my eyes.

Reluctantly, too afraid my continued touching or restless shifting in the bed would wake Sophie, I climbed out from behind her in the bed, careful not to disturb her.

The apartment was dark when I closed the bedroom behind me, all except for the muted sound and light coming from the television in the living room.

My feet moved slowly, as if I was invading someone's personal space—which in effect, I had—as I headed toward the living room.

When I reached the end of the small hallway, feeling as if the six-foot trip had taken me hours, my breath again caught in my throat.

Jaden sat on the couch, an empty drink on the table in front of him, his arms spread wide along the back of the couch and his now bare feet on the floor—knees spread wide and open.

He looked like a god commanding his throne. Even if his throne was a threadbare, ugly couch, he still consumed the space in a way that spoke of power and force.

"Hey," I said, swallowing the lump in my throat and the sudden warmth that rushed my body.

Jaden tilted his head, took his eyes off the TV, and slid them to me. He nodded once but didn't say anything.

Nerves flooded my blood at his silent but heated inspection.

"You okay?"

My hand went to my hair. My fingers ran through it, fidgeting as my feet felt glued to the worn carpet beneath them. "No," I admitted, shaking my head. "I'm really not."

Jaden said nothing, but kept watching me. Slowly, he pushed off the couch and headed to the kitchen.

My feet became unstuck and I followed him.

"Have this," he said, sliding me a glass of whiskey.

I scrunched my nose, already smelling the liquor that would burn my throat. "Got anything else?"

A silent laugh fell from his lips and he turned, opening the fridge. "Just beer."

"Beer's good." I hated beer, but one would hopefully make me drowsy enough to sleep and wouldn't burn my vocal chords in the process.

I heard the hiss of him popping the top before he slid a metal can in my direction.

"Sophie sleeping?"

"Yeah, she's totally out." My eyes squished close as the cold, bubbly, and nasty-tasting beer hit my throat. "Amazing... considering."

Jaden walked around the counter and stood in front of me. I only had a split second to take him in before his arm reached out, tugged my hand, and I tripped, smacking my head straight into his chest.

"Uh."

"Shut up, Jules."

His voice was tight, as if stretched like a rubber band and could snap at any moment. But I listened and kept my mouth shut—mostly because one of his arms wrapped around my waist, and the other arm wrapped around my shoulder. His hand made its home at the nape of my neck, his fingers entangled in my hair.

I forgot how to speak—how to ask him what he was doing—but he seemed to need it, and frankly, I needed it too. Needed to know there was something stronger and braver than the hell I'd faced today.

I relaxed into him almost instantly. My head turned so my ear felt his heart beating through his chest.

Seemingly on their own accord, my hands wrapped around his waist. I didn't know if I pulled him to me or he pulled me to him, but we pressed closer to one another and the only thing I heard in the room was the mixture of our hearts beating.

"Jaden?" I murmured.

His head dipped and his temple rubbed across the top of my head, brushing back and forth lightly. It sent the strangest tingling sensation across my skin.

"Shh." His arms squeezed tighter.

"But." I tried to push away, feeling something I probably shouldn't have been feeling when I had just gone through a wrecking ball of emotions over the course of the day. My body, strung tight with fear all day long, suddenly released a new course of adrenaline through my veins.

Jaden didn't allow it. His arm muscles coiled until he pulled me against him so tight I could barely breathe.

"You can let me go now."

He squeezed tight and then listened. As soon as I could, I took a step away and reached for my beer, hoping like hell he couldn't see or hear me gasping for breath.

"What was that?" I asked. "And the crap with the room?"

Jaden scowled at me, pressing his lips together. "Maybe I just wanted to do something nice for Sophie."

I swallowed. That sounded... nice. And strange. "I don't get it—not after you spent the last two weeks ignoring us." My hand went to my hair and I messed with it, wondering if shaking my hair would make my jumbled thoughts make sense.

It didn't help.

Jaden watched me, slight smirk on his lips, but his eyes never left mine. I couldn't read his look.

"I'm not trying to start a fight. It's the last thing I want tonight. I just want to understand why you'd do that when you ignored for us so long."

Especially since after the last time I saw him, he'd been staring at my newly pierced nipples as if they were that night's dinner. And dessert. And next morning's breakfast.

He seemed to catch the wicked thoughts in my head because he crossed his arms over his chest, tilted his head. His smirk grew. He shifted, resting his hip against the counter. The move looked relaxed, but the intensity in his eyes told me he felt differently.

"This really what you want to talk about tonight? You want to get into what happened at your place? Or why I decorated Sophie's room?

Why you curled into my lap earlier today and fell into my arms tonight and let go of all the shit you're holding in?"

He leaned forward, bracing himself on the counter with one hand as his arms fell from his chest. When he spoke again, his voice was rough, deeper. "Do you really want me to stand here and explain what being around you does to me?"

My eyes fell from his eyes—straight to his crotch. I caught the bulge behind his denim and jerked my eyes back up. Volcanic heat hit my cheeks as Jaden watched.

Oh God. He totally caught that.

"No." I snapped it quickly and turned away, gripping my beer. I had to get away from him. I'd had a feeling my presence around him did the same thing his presence around me did. The straining denim told me I was correct.

But no way was I getting into that now.

"Can't expect me to not get turned around you, Jules, when I know what you feel and taste like when you're coming against my tongue."

Holy shit! My eyes snapped to his and I quickly looked away when I saw his eyes trailing my body in another perusal. But his eyes stopped on my chest, and I knew exactly what he was wondering.

I collapsed into his couch, pressing the cold beer can against my flushed cheeks and forehead.

"Stop, please."

He pushed off the counter, making his way to me with the smoothness and stealth of a panther. I watched every long, muscled limb move with grace and ease until he took a spot on the opposite side of the couch.

"I think I made my point, anyway."

Oh hell, had he ever. My entire body thrummed with a need I desperately wanted to ignore.

He leaned forward and rested his elbows on his knees, and then dropped his head, running his hands through his hair.

"Besides, we have more important shit to talk about. Like Rob."

Rob. Disgust filled my stomach at the sound of his name. "Don't want to talk about that, either." I shook my head. No way.

Silence sounded good. A beer to make me drowsy, drunken in silence with UFC reruns on television in front of me. I didn't know the fighters, didn't want to know—didn't even want to sit and watch men beat the shit out of each other, but all of that was a better option than telling Jaden about Rob. Or what that pink room meant.

Jaden read my mind.

"Have to, Jules. We need to know what we're dealing with and last I heard, Xbox hadn't been able to find out much about him."

"He wouldn't, either." Because I knew. I knew Rob's dad covered up a multitude of his sins behind the veil that came from having a dad as one of the best defense attorneys in the country. Rob could do anything he wanted—and get away with it.

The thought chilled me to my bones, and I shivered.

"Jules."

I blinked, shaking my head. "Not tonight. I can't talk about him, Jaden."

He pulled a face, but nodded. "All right. Then we can talk about that room I made for Sophie. Why I avoided you for the last two weeks, and what I feel, knowing that you're in my apartment right now."

"Rob," I quipped. Lesser of two evils, absolutely. "I'll talk about Rob."

Jaden chuckled and I couldn't help but look at him. Big mistake.

His brown eyes narrowed on me instantly and he shifted so we were facing one another. I felt the heat between us prickle instantly, leaving needle pricks all down my arms.

"Is it that bad?" His voice dripped like warm honey from his tongue: thick and smooth, a bit of sweet. "To know the effect you have on me?"

He was playing a game. Had to be. No way did Jaden want me.

My brain lost the ability to think before speaking as one word fell from my lips.

"Terrifying."

I looked away, stared out the window and felt him move. I didn't see him, I just felt the tension shift in the room until Jaden was sitting on the coffee table in front of me. His knees spread wide so they surrounded me and his hands went to my knees.

I jumped from the contact.

"Jules, look at me."

I didn't. My teeth went to my bottom lip, and I bit down until I felt the slight sting of pain. I fought back tears that suddenly wanted to fall. My eyes already felt too raw, too dry from the crying I'd done all day.

This was too much.

His closeness, his honesty, and damn it, the way he felt when he touched me—like he *cared*.

I shook my head.

"Rob hit me." The words slipped from my lips, and I again cursed my ability to think before I spoke.

A deep, animalistic growl rumbled from Jaden. "Already figured that out."

"Yeah, well, he did it. A lot." I ran my hands through my hair, already feeling like I was going to throw up again. Which would be awesome to do it in front of Jaden—again. "But it didn't matter, because regardless of how many times I went to the hospital, or how many times I tried to file charges or restraining orders, they never went through."

Jaden tilted his head to the side, cracking his neck. "Not sure I follow."

"Rob's dad is a defense attorney, definitely the best in the state of Arizona, most likely the most sought-after criminal defense attorney in the Southwest. He gets called into cases all over the country to consult. And I don't want to talk about what he did to me, or why I let him do it for so long…" My voice trailed off and I paused. I couldn't think or talk about Rob without remembering the last time he'd hit me, or the way he'd promised I could never leave him. Had it not been for his incessant calling and stopping by at random times to see me at my apartment, I might not have ever came back to Jasper Bay.

"Jules," Jaden said quietly. Lethally quiet. When I looked at him, his lips were pulled into a twisted, wicked grin. And not the good kind of wicked. His eyes gleamed with something unidentifiable. I figured it was the excitement of death. "You don't have to be afraid of him anymore."

"I know." I choked over the words and tried again. "I know I don't, but that doesn't change the fact that Rob could get away murder. Literally. His dad has every statement I gave to the police, every medical file on my injuries buried so deeply that Rob thinks he can do whatever he wants and his dad will cover him."

Jaden leaned in closer. His hands slid from my knees to my thighs and he yanked me so I was sitting at the edge of the couch. I tried to ignore the way his secure handling of me made me feel all hot and bothered—just inches from where his fingers lay on my skin.

"I think you're forgetting who we are, and that we have charters all over the country. Men have been called, and trust me, he won't get away with this."

I wanted to believe him. Wanted to trust that whatever had happened with Jaden weeks ago, whatever he'd said to me tonight—all of it—was the God's honest truth, but I'd been tricked and deceived enough.

I was strung too tight and too exhausted to give him much credence.

But I also lacked the energy to argue or disagree.

"Okay."

His lips pursed as if he didn't believe my trust in him or his club, but he let it go. Then he leaned in closer; his hands started moving again until they were wrapped around my hip bones.

His thumbs moved slowly back and forth, over the black skirt I'd worn to work.

Heat pulsed through my body. Everywhere.

"Jaden." I shook my head, looked down at his hands.

His hands squeezed my hips and then his breath was at my ear, his slight stubble scratching my cheek. "I'm only going to say this once. Don't think I've said it in my entire life, but I'm sorry for being a dick to you. Sorry for taking my eyes off Sophie and not protecting you the way Scratch would want me to."

Scratch. Emotion clogged my throat.

My breath hitched as his lips moved from my ear to my jaw. He didn't kiss me, just lightly ran his lips down my skin until I shivered beneath him. His touch, the scent of him mixed with whiskey, clouded my judgment.

I opened my mouth to speak, when Jaden kept talking, pulling away from me slightly. "I also don't give a shit about Scratch right now, don't care that you and Sophie are his. All I care about right now is that you're in front of me. I've wanted you for years, watched while my brother got you instead, and I'm tired of waiting to have you."

21

Jules

My head spun.

It was too much to take in.

Although I liked the sound of all of it.

Wanted me. Jaden? God. How had this happened? Yet I couldn't deny it, either, because I'd wanted him ever since I got back to town... just kept brushing it off as some fucked up thing with him reminding me of Scratch.

But he didn't anymore. He was harder. Rougher. Tougher. Jaden was a force bigger than anything Scratch could have ever been.

Scratch was a biker, but kind and carefree. Jaden got all the rough parts of the Dillon family, and over the years had sharpened the roughness to jagged edges and sharp looks.

They were nothing alike.

The way Jaden touched my body, whispered dirty words against my skin, left my body craving something it'd never felt before.

I didn't have time to react before Jaden's hands gripped my hips and pulled me toward him. I gasped, straddling his waist on the coffee table, and my ankles instinctively wrapped around his hips.

"Wha—?"

My confusion and shock was cut off when one of Jaden's hands cupped the back of my neck, pulled me to him, and then his lips were on mine.

Hard. Fast. Demanding.

He parted my lips and thrust his tongue inside, not giving me time to consider stopping him. Not that I wanted to.

I instantly melted into him. My hips shifted against him on their own accord and my hands flew to his shoulders, gripping him, pulling him closer to me just as he was holding me against him.

A mewl of desperate need escaped my lips. Jaden swallowed it instantly as our tongues wrapped around one another. His fingers dug into my hair, gripping it and tugging, tipping my head back.

He growled into my lips. The deep rumble went to straight to my core, which now felt soaking wet against my swollen, tender skin.

It also shocked me back to reality.

Because what the hell was I doing?

I ripped my mouth off Jaden's, both of us panting, and his eyes opened—searing me.

"What the fuck?" he asked as I scrambled out of his hold and to my feet.

My hands flew to my hair and I shoved them back, clasping my fingers together at the back of my head.

"Jules." He stood. His breath heaved and his erection was evident.

I couldn't help but look—didn't bother trying to hide it, either, as I moved quickly to the other side of the couch.

"We can't do this." I pointed at him, trying to stop him. "Not tonight."

"You want to tell me why the hell not?"

"Because." I slapped my hands to my thighs, exasperated. "Sophie's in the next room, and the last time I let you do something to me, she woke up and you took off."

"Won't happen again."

I shook my head. "Maybe. Maybe not. But this is crazy, and my day—God, Jaden." I spun around, headed toward the whiskey. A shot would help calm me, even if it burned my vocal chords in the process. What kind of shitty mom was I? Making out with a jerk when my daughter had been kidnapped. The full stress of the day fell onto my shoulders. "It's not right."

I shook my head, terrified of what I'd see if I looked at Jaden.

I reached the counter and grabbed the bottle of whiskey when it was suddenly ripped out of my hands, slid down the counter, and Jaden's arms were at my sides, caging me in from behind.

And damn it all, his breath was at my ear. Again. His tongue licked my sensitive skin and I felt lust pouring off him in palpable waves. Thick, needy waves. I felt every inch of him when he pressed up against me from behind.

"What happened last time won't happen again."

I swallowed, losing the ability to think. My eyes stared at the whiskey bottle, wishing I had superhero powers that could vault it through the air into my hand, or drain the entire bottle without having to touch it at all.

We said nothing else. All I could hear was our mingled, harsh breathing as I fought to calm down. Fought to forget what his lips felt like, how the bulge in his jeans felt against my core, and what it felt like to be taken by someone who was so strong and powerful, my body simply moved and shifted however he wanted.

It was so damn hot.

"I need to check on Sophie."

His hand clamped down on my hip, pinning me against the counter. "I'm only saying this one more time, but what happened last time won't happen again."

He sounded so serious, so sure of himself, I lost all doubt that he actually meant it.

I relaxed into his hold, chewing on my bottom lip until his grip loosened enough for me to turn around.

When I did, he smirked.

"Let's say it doesn't," I said. "But I'm a mom, Jaden. A single mom, and the last time we were alone you had me pinned against a wall where Sophie could have easily seen me. And that shit's not cool—at all. I can't keep making out in living rooms where my daughter can see me."

He opened his mouth to say something, but I cut him off. Based on the glint in his eye, it would be totally indecent. Probably something I desperately wanted, too, but I couldn't afford to be stupid when it came to Sophie anymore.

"I need to check on her and go to bed. Can we just... talk about this some other time?"

He smiled wide. It stretched from cheek to cheek but didn't reach his eyes. Then he nodded. "Sure Jules, we can talk about this another time."

I started to smile but was immediately caught off guard when he pressed his lips to mine again. He was like a ninja, moving faster than I could have anticipated. He kissed me forcefully again, his hands cupping my chin and my cheeks.

I didn't bother resisting. I rolled onto the tips of my toes, my hands flew to the back of his neck.

And I let him devour me.

When he pulled away, my entire body trembled beneath him.

One side of his lips lifted into a grin. "Goodnight, babe."

I stood on shaky, wobbly knees and watched Jaden head to his bedroom. My hands held me up by the countertop behind me as I watched him disappear, and it took minutes—maybe hours—for me to find my secure footing again.

I went to the bedroom where Sophie slept, climbed in behind her, and tugged her close.

She rolled into my arms, making quiet sucking sounds with her lips like she still used her pacifier, even though she hadn't used it in months, and sighed.

The sun was just beginning to rise when I finally closed my eyes, hoping like hell I hadn't just made another huge mistake by falling for the wrong type of man.

But it couldn't be helped. By the time I'd replayed every single one of my interactions with Jaden over the last few months—the change in how he was today and tonight, a vast difference from the past—I knew it was too late.

I was already gone.

When I woke up, the bed next to me was cold, although my body was hot and sweaty from the nightmare that had awoken me: Sophie screaming in my ear as a gloved hand ripped her out of my hold, yanking her into darkness.

I shuddered at the memory of screams, the reality that it was a dream calming me only slightly. I jolted up, throwing back the covers and checking over the edge of the bed to see if Sophie had fallen off the floor.

It took me another minute to realize the sun was shining brightly into the bedroom, and I was in a bed with a hot pink comforter. A small bag of neon colored blocks sat in the corner next to a bucket filled with... princess books?

My instant panic at not finding Sophie next to me began to subside as I remembered where I had fallen asleep.

Jaden's house. Where Sophie and I were safe.

I inhaled a deep, trembling breath and pulled my hair off my neck. Using a band I kept on my wrist at all times, I quickly threw it up into a messy bun and climbed out of the bed.

When I did, I saw a T-shirt and pair of athletic shorts folded neatly on the floor. Based on the Viking helmet, skull, and crossbones, I instantly recognized the Nordic Lords logo.

Glancing down at my own wrinkled button-up shirt and black skirt I'd worn to work yesterday, I gingerly reached down to pick up the clothes.

They smelled like Jaden. A familiar warmth began trickling its way through my body.

He'd left clean clothes for me.

The very idea of him doing something so nice, so caring, had a quiet giggle escaping my lips before I could stop it.

Quickly I threw on the clothes, cringing at the thought of having to keep dirty underwear on, but didn't stop to think about it too much before I quickly remade the bed.

I smiled even wider as I realized Jaden had bought this stuff. He'd made a room for Sophie—as small and sparsely decorated as it was, he'd made the effort. Even in the weeks he'd avoided us, he'd bought her stuff, wanting her in his place.

The thought was too large to continue considering without coffee.

Lucky for me, as I walked out of the room and into the hall, my nose was instantly hit with the precious smell of caffeine and... bacon?

I was still fighting a smile when I hit the living room and saw Sophie on the couch, her head propped against the armrest and her eyes focused on the television.

Animated cartoons filled the room, and she didn't realize I was in the room until I was right in front of her, scooping her into my arms.

"Mommy!" She threw her arms around my neck, her legs around my waist, and held on tight as I tickled her side. "Put me down."

"Never," I mock-growled into her ear. "I will never let you go."

My sinuses instantly began to burn as she fought out of my hold. Setting her down, I pressed a firm, quick kiss to her cheek and ruffled her hair. "God, I'm glad you're here."

"No cry, mommy. Be happy."

I sniffed, wiped away the tear Sophie focused on with a slight frown. "Mommy is happy, pumpkin. So happy."

My hands pressed her cheeks together, smushing her face, and I kissed her again.

She instantly wiped my kiss off her lips and turned to watch TV.

It was how we started almost every day, and something about the normalcy of it had me pushing down the rest of my tears.

She was okay. Uninjured. Safe.

I ruffled her hair one more time and moved away. Far be it from me to mess with a girl's *Dora* time.

When I stood up, intent on getting that coffee, I caught Jaden staring at me from the kitchen. His hands were braced on the counter, spatula in one hand, and his intense gaze on me.

But this time there was no scowl. Just a look of heated desire that I could feel increasing with every step I took closer to him.

22

Jaden

Damn, she looked good. My shirt fell to Jules's mid-thigh and my shorts went well past her knees. She looked like a little girl playing dress-up in her father's grown-up clothes as she shuffled her feet toward me in the kitchen.

My thoughts were anything but familial as she pushed away a stray strand of her blond hair, her cheeks turning a deeper shade of pink as she reached me in the kitchen.

Mine. All fucking mine.

My hands tightened at the edge of the countertop so I didn't reach out, pull her into my arms, and give her the kind of kiss that was completely inappropriate in front of a two-year-old.

"Mornin'," she mumbled on her way past me. Her eyes were trained on the coffee pot in my kitchen, and working hard at avoiding me.

That wouldn't do.

I reached out, snagged an arm around her waist, and pulled her to me.

She let out a small, quick gasp of surprise before I silenced her with a kiss. My lips pressed against hers firmly and my arm pulled her tight against me.

Then I let her go, smiled as she rocked back on her heels and her eyes snapped to mine.

I grinned wider. "Good morning."

Her eyes widened, the pink on her cheeks blaring hot red. "Um."

I pointed over my shoulder as if we hadn't just made out like raunchy teenagers in my kitchen with her kid ten feet away. "Coffee's ready and the bacon's done. How do you like your eggs?"

She frowned but headed toward the coffee pot. "Scrambled," she finally said after she'd poured her coffee, added two drops of milk, and took her first sip.

Her eyes seemed like they awakened as soon as the coffee hit her throat.

"Comin' right up."

I worked in silence, scrambling her eggs as Jules snagged two pieces of bacon. She stood at the counter, drinking her coffee and munching on the bacon, keeping her eyes on Sophie the entire time.

When I slid the plate of eggs in front of her, she looked down, smiled her thanks, and took a bite. "When did she wake up?"

"Right after I did a couple hours ago."

Her eyebrows pulled in. "What time is it?"

I shrugged and looked at the clock on the microwave. "Eleven."

Jules gasped. "Holy crap! Why'd you let me sleep so late?"

She turned to me, looking aghast at the fact she'd actually slept in. I had almost wanted to wake her as soon as I'd heard Sophie leaving their bedroom this morning. Not knowing what kind of condition the girl would be in after yesterday, I figured she'd want her mom.

But then she'd walked right up me, crawled into my lap, and murmured, "Miss you, Uncah Jaden."

I had figured Jules could use the sleep after the day she'd had yesterday, so I let her sleep, figuring if Sophie needed anything, she was right there to help anyway.

"Jules." My head dipped down to the crook of her neck. "You

had a shit day yesterday, probably have a couple shitty weeks until we can take care of this Rob shit, and Sophie was fine. I figured you could use your sleep."

My lips pulled into a small grin as her pulse along her collarbone sped up.

I wanted her. Wanted to see her naked, in my bed, writhing beneath me and calling my name as I rode her hard. And deep.

I cleared my throat, took a step away before I attempted to take her in the kitchen, and watched a soft smile spread across her lip.

"What?"

"Nothing." She shook her head, shoved another bite of eggs and bacon into her mouth. "You're just being nice. I'm not used to it."

I deserved that, so I took it. I'd been a complete asshole, but I planned on changing that, too. Not sure how, seeing as how I'd never had to be nice to someone before, but I figured it couldn't be too hard to not be a dick all the time.

Instead of letting her see how much it concerned me that I could possibly fail at that, I wrapped my arms around her waist and pulled her against my chest. I kept my eyes on Sophie, knowing she was totally hypnotized by some bandit fox on the television, and rocked my hips into Jules.

She groaned. She might have collapsed into the counter if I wasn't holding her, but damn it, just being near her made me hard. Her in my clothes, in my apartment, sent another thrill straight to my dick, making it try to jump out of my jeans.

Straight into her.

"I can show you nice," I rumbled in her ear. "The question is, how nice do you want me to be? Soft and slow as I make your entire body shake with pleasure? Or do you want it hard and fast so you're screaming my name until all the neighbors hear you shouting in pure bliss?"

"Jaden –"

Her soft moan vibrated down to my dick.

"Later." I released her from my arms and smiled with sick satisfaction when she braced herself against the counter. She went back to her coffee and breakfast while I thought of all the things I wanted to do her tight little body.

When she was done, I cleared her plate. She arched an eyebrow at my gesture.

"I can be nice, babe." I tossed her a scowl for good measure, but it was fake—and based on her instantly playful look, she knew it.

"Ah, there's the Jaden I know."

"Right." She wanted that Jaden? She'd get it. Because we still had shit to discuss and she wasn't gonna like it. "How about we go to my room and talk?"

"Talk?" Her voice was husky and doubtful.

I bit back a groan. "Fuck, that's tempting," I growled, and then schooled my features into seriousness.

She noticed instantly and her back straightened.

"Talk. I got shit to tell you."

Her eyes darted to Sophie for a second before they came back to mine. She chewed on her bottom lip before nodding.

"Sophie, keep watching *Dora* while Uncle Jaden and I talk in another room."

The kid didn't move a muscle until Jules snapped her name again. "Sophie."

She looked at her mom, keeping one eye trained on the television. Damn. It was like I could see the show rotting her brain right in front of my face. "Stay here, okay?"

"Otay," she mumbled and went back to a slightly zombified state on the couch.

"Do all shows knock kids out like that?" I asked as I followed her into my room.

"Just *Dora*. Which means we have about ten minutes until the show is over and she starts climbing through your cupboards and knocking your bags of sugar and flour all over the place."

I didn't have shit like flour or sugar in my house, but I let the slightly joking comment slide. In about two minutes, Jules wouldn't be finding anything funny.

"Here's the deal," I started, my hands on my hips, and then thought better. "You might want to sit."

Jules frowned at me, but did what I said. I fought back a grin at the thought of her obeying my every command—especially when she was in my bed.

"That fucker hired a PI to follow you. He knows where you live, where your parents live, and obviously where you work and where Sophie goes to daycare. He even knows about the club and that you hang out there."

Jules gasped, but I kept on talking, figuring this shit should be like ripping off a Band-Aid.

"Why he thought he could take Sophie and not have fallback from us is anyone's first fuckin' clue. But you're not leaving my side until I hear word from our Colorado charter that he's been dealt with."

"Dealt with?" She raised her eyebrows.

I ignored her and kept talking. "Finn and Tripp headed to your place early this morning, searched the whole place to see if we could find anything, and they found two cameras—one in your kitchen, facing your front door, and one in your bedroom."

Jules eyes flew open and she leaped off the bed onto her feet.

"He had my house bugged."

"Yup." I nodded. "Also had that shit done somehow before you ever moved in, so he's been watching you for weeks." I couldn't help the grin of cocky satisfaction that spread across my lips. "Also means he saw me and you that night."

Her cheeks turned dark red and she sucked in a breath. "Oh my God. That's… that's sick!"

"Actually, it's fuckin' awesome."

Her mouth dropped. "Awesome? You think it's awesome that my asshole ex, who's clearly unstable and stalking me, saw me… and…

you?" She swallowed. Took her awhile to do it as I watched her remember everything I'd done to her that night.

God, I'd been out of control. Would have taken her against the floor if Sophie wouldn't have screamed out. Now, I fuckin' regretted it.

"The good thing about it is that I'm guessing he watched you light up in a way you'd never done with him. I figure it pissed him off, and whatever plan he had in place, whatever time he was thinking of taking to get you back, went out the fuckin' window. He got frantic and sloppy, and because of that—Sophie is sitting in that living room out there, watching fucking cartoons, instead of who knows where and having who in the hell knows what happen to her."

I gave her a minute to process all that, and when she did, she huffed, crossed her arms over her chest, and glared at me. "Well, you don't have to sound so pleased with yourself."

"Trust me. I won't be pleased with myself until I'm buried balls deep inside you, watching you fall apart."

"Jesus." She swiped a hand across her forehead and patted her red cheeks. "Do you have to be so blunt about that?"

"Only way I can be, babe."

When in the hell had I started calling her *babe?* I shrugged. Who gave a shit? The nickname rolled off my lips and I liked it, so I was going to keep doin' it.

A small smile stretched her lips. "Okay, so what does that mean for us?"

"Us?" I almost choked over the word.

"Me and Sophie."

Right. Not Jules and me. What in the hell was I thinking?

"Means I'm moving into your place so I can keep an eye on you. I'd make you move in here, but all your shit is there, you got a new lease, and it's Sophie's home so I'm figuring she'll do better if she's around her own shit."

"You're... what?" She shook her head. "You're not."

163

I crossed my arms and gave her a look that would usually have her turning away from me, but this time, she straightened her shoulders and propped her hands on her hips, ready to fight me back.

My dick twitched.

"Then you're movin' here."

"I can't do that! I have a job! And a life."

I shrugged, not giving a shit. "Then I'm there, Jules. I'm not fuckin' kidding. That asshole bugged your apartment and tried to take your kid. How pissed do you think he's gonna be now that he learned he lost that move?"

"Probably even more pissed if he sees another man living with me."

"Not living," I sneered. "Staying to keep you and Sophie safe."

She scowled, her lips twisted into a furious expression before she finally exhaled. "Fine, but only for Sophie."

I took a step forward, watched her breath hitch immediately as my chest brushed against hers. Then I kept walking, forcing her to step back to the bed.

Her knees hit the mattress and she collapsed.

I followed her, until my body was completely aligned with hers.

I bent down, dragged my nose along her throat and back to her ear. She smelled fucking fantastic, and every time I touched her, her pulsed jumped. I fucking loved it.

"Keep tellin' yourself it's just for Sophie. I'll let you lie to yourself for a little bit longer."

Her hands went to my chest and she tried to push. She had the force of a mosquito behind her, and I bent down and nipped her earlobe.

Her hips arched into mine and I had to bite back a groan.

"How long do you think it's going to be until I can finally have you naked beneath me?"

"Never."

How cute. She thought I couldn't tell she wanted me. This would be fun.

"Right," I whispered against her skin, licking the column of her neck down to her collarbone. "I give it a day, with how much you're showing me right now you want me."

Her hand reached out and gripped the front of my shirt. Her scowl matched mine, but then she grinned.

It lit up her entire damn face, and I loved it.

"Sophie's show is going to be done in about two minutes. Why don't you shut up and kiss me?"

My pleasure.

My lips hit hers and my tongue thrust in, not waiting for her to open up. But she did, quickly and willingly, and by the time Jules caught the end of *Dora's* theme song playing in the living room with some sort of super-sonic mom hearing, I was well on my way to having blue balls from my dick pressed so hard up against my zipper.

23

Jules

I relished the feel of my satin cami top sliding over my breasts, down my ribs until it hit my hips. It was a cute pajama set, with white, eyelet trim and a bright teal color that seemed to brighten my skin.

Today had been long and my shoulders sagged with relief that it was almost finally over.

I shimmied into my matching teal satin bottoms, loving the cool feel of the fabric on my freshly bathed and shaved skin, before heading into the bathroom.

Once Jaden had brought me and Sophie home, he hadn't left. We'd spent the entire day hanging out at my place, being bombarded by Olivia and Faith, and even the girls from the salon had stopped by. They brought us dinner.

They made us laugh.

They cried happy tears as all of the women took turns wrapping their arms around Sophie. She'd handled the day remarkably well until it all ended in a temper tantrum to beat all tantrums when I'd told her no chocolate milk after she'd already brushed her teeth.

Seeing that Jaden was at his maximum capacity of loud and chatty female company, and that my daughter was on the verge of completely losing it, I'd packed everyone up and sent them on their way an hour ago.

And as soon as the door shut behind them, the thick tension between Jaden and I had shot up to epic proportions. I could feel his eyes everywhere I turned, even when I couldn't see them.

So I did the only sane thing I could: ran to my room, locked myself in my bathroom, and took a bath. A bubble bath. I stayed in there until I began shivering from the cool water and my skin resembled prunes.

Sophie had acted fine all day, and was now peacefully sleeping back in her bed. I figured she truly didn't understand the magnitude of yesterday's reality. Seeing her calm and sweet, loving all the company we'd received that day, had helped me calm down as well. That didn't mean I was rushing to jump into Jaden's arms, though.

Not that I didn't want it.

I just didn't trust it wouldn't end abruptly again, and after he'd spent the last two days being so oddly nice—but nice in a way that felt comforting and incredible—I was completely lost for him.

He'd shown me a different side of him, but it didn't mean I wasn't waiting for asshole Jaden to return and for the kind, updated version—that made my insides flutter every time he looked at me—to vanish.

I figured avoiding him when we were left alone was the smartest and most logical choice I could make.

With the water running as I brushed the teeth, I didn't hear anyone enter the room until a shadow fell across the doorway to the bathroom.

I choked on my toothpaste when Jaden's incredible frame filled the doorway.

"You scared the hell out of me," I said, spitting out my toothpaste. Grabbing a rag, I washed off the excess toothpaste and tried not to drool as I looked at Jaden through the mirror's reflection.

"Sorry." He winked and his eyes slowly raked down my back. I felt his eyes touch me *everywhere* as they slowly descended down my sexy but modest pajama set, fell to my butt, and kept going. "Never mind. Totally not sorry at all."

When his eyes met mine in the mirror, I tried to look away.

Unfortunately, my brain stopped working and my eyes wouldn't move. No amount of silent cursing as Jaden pushed off the doorframe and entered the small bathroom made them work, either.

It was as if he silently froze my eyes to his by some imaginary string.

When he stood behind me, his hand came to my shoulder. With his thumb and forefinger, he gently tugged on the thin, satin strap, slowly running it through his fingertips. He hadn't touched me at all, except for the brief contact he made when he touched the strap, but the barely-there contact sent a surge of electricity straight to my core.

My thighs tightened to relieve the pressure as his hand gently slid down my back, down the satin fabric that seemed torturously arousing against my skin, across my ribs, and settled on my hip.

I swallowed a thick ball of drool in my throat.

Without saying anything, he let me go, plopped a black bag onto the counter, and looked away from me.

The move unfroze my own eyes as he took out his toothbrush and toothpaste and turned the water tap on.

I frowned. "What are you doing?"

He held the toothbrush, now filled with paste, in the air. "What's it look like?"

I pointed out the door. "There's a bath in the hallway you can use. This one's mine."

He paused, toothbrush frozen right before it hit his teeth, and grinned.

Stupid, sexy, nice-guy grin.

"Not using a bathroom that's filled with Barbies and princesses and pink shit."

"You put pink shit in your apartment."

A muscle jumped in his jaw and I wondered if it bothered him that he did it. But I didn't care to ask. He shrugged his shoulder and began scrubbing his teeth.

How he could look hot and sexy, and like someone I was fighting the urge to run my hands all over, even while toothpaste foamed in his mouth and he spit into the sink, I had no idea.

But he did.

My hands curled into tiny fists at my side.

When he was done wiping his mouth off with the same towel I'd just used—*ew*... and maybe I was jealous of the towel—he looked at me, his face filled with amusement.

"I'm staying in your place, sleeping in your bed, and I'm not going to use a bathroom that makes my dick want to shrivel up and fall off."

Sleeping in my... Huh?

"You're not sleeping in my bed."

"No?" He crossed his arms, shifted so his hip rested on the counter and he was facing me. "Not sleeping on the couch, and I'm pretty sure I'm not sleeping in Sophie's bed."

My lips twisted in anger that he'd so quickly situated himself into my life, given the circumstance. Also, I wanted to kick my own ass for being angry.

I had the chance to sleep next to Jaden and that body, and I was complaining?

"No," I stated, standing as tall as I could.

When his grin grew, I knew my voice lacked the conviction necessary to tell him I was serious. He leaned forward and put his nose right at the crook of my neck, right where he always seemed to place it.

He smelled so damn good, and when his breath washed over me in one of the most sensual ways I'd ever felt, I pushed down a moan of pleasure that threatened to escape. It was like every warm exhale from him against my skin somehow awakened something inside me.

Something I'd locked down long ago.

Something I was certain I didn't want unlocked—not by a man whose mood swings and tantrums could rival Sophie's.

"Think you can kick me out?"

He winked, pushed off the counter, and by the time my feet were moving, Jaden had already disrobed, leaving a pile of dirty clothes all over my clean floor, and climbed into bed.

"This isn't going to work," I muttered, fluffing my pillow for the umpteenth time since I'd given up the fight of kicking Jaden out of my bed.

I could have shoved him, maybe, but I was small and he was huge and I figured any attempt on my part would be completely futile. Better to save my strength for a fight I could win.

Jaden laughed a low, quiet but thick rumble that made my stomach flip-flop.

He hadn't touched me since I'd climbed into bed. He hadn't moved a muscle. No, Jaden just laid on his back, facing the ceiling with one thick, muscle-corded arm draped over his eyes.

The only sign I had that he wasn't sleeping yet was the way he kept laughing every time I flipped around, fluffed my pillow, and muttered immature curse words in his direction.

"Can't you go to the couch?"

"Nope."

Argh!

His presence was driving me to distraction. Every time I moved or shifted, I questioned how close I could get to him without actually touching him.

Except that I wanted to touch him. I wanted to haul my little frame on top of his lap and screw his brains out.

Which had my panties damp and uncomfortable and there was no way in hell I was getting out of bed to change them. No way was I going to let him know the illicit thoughts filling my head just because he had to be a bossy jerk and sleep on *my* side of the bed, for crying out loud.

My side!

"You're infuriating," I mumbled into my pillow. "And I hate you."

Another rumble from him. Another belly flop from me.

"If you're stressed, I can help you relax."

"I don't want your help." Liar, liar.

"That's okay." I could practically feel the heat of his grin, and his stare boring into the back of my head. "I don't mind watching you relax yourself, either."

"Argh!" I flew up, gripping my pillow with two hands, and swung.

Hard.

It smacked Jaden right in the face, and a victorious surge rushed through my veins.

"There," I huffed, throwing myself back down on my bed. "Now I'm relaxed."

I rolled to my side, shoved one hand under my cheek, the other under the pillow, and blew out a breath through puffed cheeks.

I stayed like that for maybe two seconds before an arm reached out, hooked around my side, and pulled.

I was flipped and on my back before I could blink, one of his arms wrapped around me, and the weight of his body on top of me.

Gulp.

Gone was his grin and his laughter. He'd replaced it with something else entirely. His intense gaze roamed my cheeks, nose, and stopped directly on my lips.

His hand under me squeezed tighter. That one tug radiated through every pore of my body and my jaw went slack as I stared at him—mesmerized by his hard lines, narrowed eyes, and crooked, scarred nose.

My voice went breathy and needy. Damn it. "What are you doing?"

His hips rolled, pressed into me, and it was then I realized he was completely naked, as his thick erection pressed against me. And I felt something… rub against my inner thigh.

Double gulp.

Holy shit. He wasn't kidding about being pierced. The chilled metal tickled my skin and sent a blast straight through my clothing.

My hands flew to his chest to push him off. Instead, he leaned against my hands. Against my own volition, my fingers dug into his hard chest, feeling his coarse chest chair.

I cleared my throat.

"What do you think I'm doing?"

I shivered from the heaviness in his words. He rocked his hips, languidly rubbing his hard dick along my thigh, teasing me. My core pulsed with the need to have him.

"Jaden." It was a warning—a weak one. Or a plea for him to do it already. To screw me until I saw stars and couldn't breathe, or walk straight for a week.

He bent low, ran his tongue along the sensitive skin on my neck, tasting me.

With his arm wrapped around my back, he pulled. He shifted onto his knees, bringing me with him until I was kneeling in front of him.

His eyes settled on my breasts and he grinned. I knew what he saw; I saw it earlier.

"I want to see you."

He spoke, his eyes on my breasts. I could have been annoyed that he was staring at them like they were his next meal.

But screw it: I wanted him. I wanted him for more than sex, but sex with Jaden wouldn't be the worst decision I'd ever made.

Crossing my arms against my front, I grabbed the hem of my cami top and lifted my arms above my head, pulling it off.

24

Jaden

I couldn't decide where to look first. Jules kneeling in front of me, knees parted and dressed in only tiny, silky shorts that didn't cover shit, almost made my head explode.

And my dick.

"Hell." I raised my eyes to hers, saw her eyes flicker with nerves, and I unfroze.

My eyes dropped to her breasts, and I licked my lips and gripped her hips, pulling her to me.

She came willingly and easily until I had her nestled against me, pressing my hard-on into my stomach.

My hands moved up her ribs until I cupped her tits, small but full, and fuck if that jewelry hanging on her right nipple wasn't the sexiest thing ever.

"Why'd you do this?" I asked, my thumb running slowly over it.

Her breath hitched, and I knew it was because metal through the sensitive skin made the sensation five times more of a rush.

I pulled my eyes off her tit and onto her lust-filled blue eyes. "Jules?" I asked again, still rubbing her pierced nipple. I wanted to tug on it, suck it in between my teeth, but held back. "Why'd you do this?"

She cleared her throat, rolled her shoulders as if she was trying to gather her confidence, and then pinned her half-lidded eyes on me. "Because I wanted to know what you'd do if you saw it."

Fucking shit. I clenched my jaw together to prevent it falling open in shock. Not what I expected her to say at all, but she was serious, too.

I gave the ring a slight tug, licking my lips.

Jules's hips shifted right into my dick. My balls pulled tight, and the anticipation of my orgasm releasing deep inside her while I sucked on her tits made me move.

I threw her back down on the bed, instantly moving in between her parted legs.

"You're about to find out, then." I leaned down, kissed her. She instantly opened her lips and my tongue met hers in a firestorm of epic proportions.

God, she could kiss. As small as Jules was, as timid and proper as she could be, when her tongue hit mine and her hands began roaming my body—my shoulders, my back, and then settled on gripping my ass—she was a fucking a fireball in bed.

I pulled my lips off hers and shifted, moving further down. Her hands moved to my hair, gripping and tugging as I set about licking all the way down to her tits. I licked her piercing, and she ground her hips up into mine. I could feel her wetness spread across my lower stomach as she rolled and shifted.

I teased her nipple, sucking it into my mouth and tugging slightly. Her nipple hardened, and the feel of the cold metal on my tongue and teeth encouraged me.

That and the way she pulled on my hair, holding me against her and moaning my name.

My name. No one else's.

"Fuck, you're amazing," I growled, lifting off her nipple and moving to the other one. I lavished them both equally. Her clean, sweet taste and the moans escaping her mouth had me needing her. *Now.*

I arched back, rolled off her until I could grab my jeans. Finding a condom, I rolled it on, not wasting any more time.

"You want me?" I asked, holding the condom and the base of my dick in my hands. Jules looked down, legs spread wide, and I grinned, realizing she'd taken off her shorts.

She was naked beneath me. Exactly where I wanted her.

"Yes," she panted.

"How bad?" I asked, running two fingers along her swollen clit. So damn hot. I teased her again, flicking her clit, running my fingers slowly around it and only coming close to her opening.

"Jaden," she moaned. I felt the word in my balls as it rolled off her swollen lips and tongue. "I need more."

She'd get it. Climbing closer to her, I pushed her thighs back until her knees were pressed against her chest. She was fucking wide open for me, dripping her moisture onto her sheets.

Jesus. She was sexy as hell, spread open for me. I wanted to bend down and taste her, knowing how good and sweet she was.

But she moaned again, clawed at my hands behind her knees.

I raised up on my knees, moving closer until the head of my dick was at her opening.

"You ever fuck a man with a piercing?" I asked, pushing inside her.

"No." She shook her head.

I stopped moving right as her body swallowed the tip of my dick. Hell, I could have exploded right then. A deep groan rumbled from my throat.

"Fuck, you're tight."

I felt her smile, but I couldn't take my eyes off her glistening pussy.

"You're just really big."

I pulled back, biting back a laugh. She mewled and her fingers clawed the sheets at her sides. When she lifted her hips against me, I knew I'd found that perfect spot, where even through a condom, the ball of my apa would scrape against her.

"Oh shit," she moaned, pushing her head back into the bed and arching her back.

God, she was beautiful.

I wanted to go slow, tease her, and fuck her into next week all at the same time.

Instead she leaned up, grabbed the back of my neck, and pulled me toward her.

"I need more," she moaned, as my dick began sinking further inside her. "Now, Jaden."

Fuck slow. I'd do slow next time.

My hips rolled, pushing my dick inside her until I was buried balls deep. Her pussy pulsed around me, creating a friction and squeezing my dick so hard it was amazing I didn't end things right then.

I closed my eyes, gathering my self-control before pulling out. And then we moved.

It was fast as I crashed my hips into hers, pushing and pulling. My thumb tugged her nipple and she cried out.

She grabbed my hair, taking all of me, and pushing back when I tried to pull out.

Our bodies became layered with sweat and the stench of sex filled my flared nostrils.

"Jaden!" she cried out, turning her head into her pillow before biting down.

"Close, Jules," I grunted, my hips rocking back and forth with force I didn't know I had, but I couldn't get enough of her, couldn't get deep enough inside her. "Get there."

"Fuck," she chanted, over and over again. I fucking loved it.

Loved watching her fall apart as her hands gripped my shoulders, her nails clawing into my inked back.

"Fuck," I groaned, right as the walls of her pussy began pulsing and clamping down on me like a fucking vise grip.

"Jules," I groaned, feeling my balls tighten. She exploded beneath me; her entire body bucked and arched into me. Her pussy tightened and pulsed so hard until I couldn't take any more.

I slammed into her, felt my balls smack against her ass, and then I came.

Hard. Stars exploded behind my closed eyes as I pumped into her, wringing every last drop out of her orgasm and mine at the same time.

Fucking hell. Amazing. Best orgasm ever.

I couldn't move when I was done. I collapsed onto her, my arms giving out, and I found my favorite spot as I fell down, wrapped an arm around her waist, and pressed a kiss to her neck.

"Holy crap," she panted. I felt her heart racing against my chest as if she'd run a marathon.

Or had the best sex of her life.

Knowing I just gave that to her made my barely softened dick begin to harden again.

"You're heavy." She pushed against my chest with weak arms, but I got her point.

I raised off her, loving the way her heat clamped around my dick as I pulled out of her to get rid of the condom, as if her body rejected the idea of my dick leaving.

"Be back." I took care of business in the bathroom and when I was done, I climbed back into bed, immediately climbing under the covers, and then tugged Jules into my side.

"Jaden?" she asked, her voice thick with sleep. "Why are you holding me?"

Why? No fucking clue. I'd never, ever, wanted to hold a woman after I'd screwed her.

I brushed my nose against her hairline. "Shut up and go to sleep."

She snorted, but didn't argue.

Then she relaxed into my chest, one of her hands landed on top of mine at her waist, and her breathing evened out just minutes before sleep pulled me under.

"You headed to the garage today?"

The question sounded so domestic, Jules watching me at the kitchen counter, coffee mug in one hand, hip propped against the counter.

It should have made me queasy. It didn't. I'd been staying at her apartment for almost a week. Five days of waking up with Jules's legs wrapped around mine. Somehow she became an octopus while she slept, all clingy limbs suctioning themselves to every part of body.

That should have made me nauseous too. But it didn't.

Even better than the mornings was the way we ended the nights… me with my dick buried deep inside her.

This morning she arched a brow, waiting for my answer.

"Sorry." I quirked a matching arched brow. "Your tits distracted me."

"Shut up." But she grinned, and pushed out her chest.

Well, fuck. Now her tits *were* distracting me. I checked the clock on the microwave, rapidly trying to figure if we could get a quickie in before she had to be at work.

Five minutes would be enough for me, maybe for Jules if I—

"Jaden!" She snapped my name, scowling.

"What?"

She leaned forward, glanced at Sophie on the couch behind me, and whisper-hissed, "We're not doing that this morning."

I coughed. Loudly.

"Again." Her cheeks flushed. I didn't know if the blush was her remembering the way I snuck into the shower and took her from behind hard and fast just thirty minutes before, or if she was embarrassed that I'd brought it up.

Who gave a fuck, really? Jules was fucking hot. All the time.

"You haven't told me if you're going to the garage."

"I'll be at the clubhouse. Fuckin' call me if you need me."

It was her first day back at the salon, but we were done with daycare. Sophie was coming with me again, which again, should have my stomach rolling, but didn't.

It'd been a lot of adjustment during the week, and I knew Jules hated that someone in the club was on her at all times, but what hadn't felt strange was the way Sophie had begun clinging her pudgy little—usually sticky—hands to me whenever I was within eyesight.

Instead of it making me want to throw up, it sent some strange, warm sensation buzzing through my chest whenever her fingers wrapped around one of mine—or my leg, as she normally did when I got back from the clubhouse.

Jules's eyes darted to Sophie and worry made wrinkles line her forehead.

"She'll be fine."

"I know that," she whispered, "but he's still out there."

I stiffened, unable to look at her, certain she'd see the deception in my eyes. "We'll find him. Soon."

Except we already had. Our Denver charter had deposited one Rob Walters to Jasper Bay during the middle of the night. When I'd gotten the text in the morning, it'd taken every ounce of self-control to not bust the hell out of the apartment before Jules and Sophie woke up.

So I was lying to her about where I was going. But it was for a good cause. And Sophie would still be safe with Liv at the club.

Everybody wins.

Except for Rob.

"All right, all right," she muttered, finished off her coffee, set it on the counter, and picked up her keys. She walked to me, kissed me with abandon in the kitchen, right in front of Sophie, and didn't care when I grabbed her ass, hauling her up my body so she was flush against mine.

I ended the kiss, set her back on shaking knees, and grinned.

"Be good," I told her.

She scowled teasingly. "You too."

I'd be good. It'd be the best kill I'd made yet and I had to fight a smile, knowing I was looking forward to it.

25

Jaden

Shit, the guy could scream like a little girl.

The jagged cuts pouring thick red blood down his thighs and his arms probably didn't help.

I grinned, re-entering a storage room at the club's salvage yard—one of the legit businesses we ran in addition to the auto garage at the clubhouse.

Rob looked exactly how I figured he'd look: brown hair, which had probably been gelled back in a nice and preppy look days ago. His black dress pants, light gray dress shirt, and his dark red tie had been discarded hours ago, leaving him only in a pair of black boxers. His hair was a matted with sweat, hair shit, and blood.

But I still hadn't been able to vanquish the evil glint in his light blue eyes, no matter how many times we'd sliced the guy. The deal had been simple once we'd confirmed how powerful his dad was. The last thing we'd wanted was to have blowback coming back to the club just because we fucked with the wrong kid.

Yet this asshole knew it—knew he was untouchable—and after Daemon nodded for me to go ahead and end this shit, I was ready.

Rob's eyes met mine and he smiled. A full set of perfectly straight white teeth gleamed bright in the poorly lit, hot and airless room. At least they had been. Now they dripped blood from the cuts inside his mouth from repeated punches to his jaw. One of his eyes had swelled and he could barely see out of it, but that hadn't stopped him.

His skin was lighter, most likely due to the blood loss, but the dipshit was so crazy he was still smiling like he knew at any second we'd be untying him, sending him home to dear old daddy.

He hadn't said much to me, except telling me to fuck off when I pressed him about his plans for Sophie and leaving Jules the hell alone.

But somehow, in my brief disappearance from the room, something had changed in him. Something registered in his expression when he looked at me.

"You're the brat's dad."

A muscle in my jaw tightened—partly because he kept calling Sophie a brat, and partly because he was starting to click puzzle pieces together.

"Nope." I raised my .38 and aimed it at his head. "And I'm pretty sure I've told you not to call her that."

Next to me, Tripp and Finn snickered. They'd been doing that all morning long, acting like they were sitting ringside in Vegas at UFC Championships. At one point, one of the bastards had actually left to make popcorn.

"But you like her," he taunted.

I moved closer and the idiot wasn't scared enough to flinch. I almost admired his ability to look death in the face and stay the course of crazy-fucked-up-ness.

My hand tightened on my gun, and my thumb flicked the safety. "You gonna leave her alone?"

His head dropped, falling forward slightly, and I glanced at Daemon. Silently he shook his head, telling me not yet. We still wanted to know what he'd planned, who else he'd hired, who else was following her, and until we got that information, it was best to keep him alive.

"She tastes good, doesn't she? So warm and sweet when her thighs are spread wide for you—"

"Enough." I took a step forward, my gun inches from his damn brain.

"Jaden." I ignored Daemon's warning that came in a low, husky growl and kept my eyes focused on the dick in front of me.

Red fury boiled my veins as his smile increased. My hand tightened on the trigger.

"You know that bitch screams her lover's name while she sleeps? For months, all night long, I fucking had to listen to her scream for Scratch."

I heard the screech of a metal chair scraping on concrete, felt the heat of a body behind me, one as tightly coiled as I was. I didn't move when I vaguely registered Finn's voice.

"Jaden, mate."

Rob leaned forward, pressed his forehead against the barrel of my gun. "And she screams his name when she comes, too. Might not at first, she might be able to fake it with you, too, but eventually, she'll start wanting him more…"

My hand was shaking. This fucking dipshit was telling me everything I'd already worried about.

That no matter how much Jules thought she'd get over Scratch, she never would, and I was just an easy substitute.

My arm shook slightly, my muscles trembling from tension at hearing this slick bastard describe the way Jules was in bed.

"And eventually, it'll drive you mad," he continued. "She'll have your dick so pussy-whipped, you'll do whatever it is you can do to beat that asshole's name and memory out of her head."

The blast from the gunshot reverberated loudly in the small room. Daemon jumped, moved behind me, and swore.

"Fucking hell," Finn muttered when I lowered my gun. "That looks like shit."

I looked at the guy, now practically missing a head, his brain matter splattered all over the wall behind him, and on my chest and cut.

Shit.

"Jaden."

I turned to my Prez, my best friend, and pressed my teeth together. Daemon clasped his hand on my shoulder and shook it back and forth.

"We'll clean him up, get the hell out of here."

I couldn't speak. My hand still held the gun as if I'd need to use it again immediately, as if the threat hadn't just exploded all over the walls behind me.

And maybe it hadn't. Because in two short sentences, the dead prick had voiced every concern I'd had about finally getting Jules under me.

She'd always compare to me to my brother.

"I got it."

Daemon pulled me closer, whispered in my ear so the others, who were already beginning to bag his body, couldn't hear. "Get the fuck out of here and go get your shit together."

My teeth ground together, my nostrils flared as I panted, the adrenaline from killing a man still loading my veins with an inexplicable high.

Nodding, I slid the gun to the back of my jeans and took one last glance at the dead asshole on the floor at my feet.

An almost empty bottle of Jack Daniels dropped loosely from my fingertips. I'd popped the top on it hours ago, after I hauled my ass back to the clubhouse to my small room and showered Rob's blood and brains off my body.

Too fuckin' bad I hadn't been able to erase his words.

Sophie had somehow sensed my mood when I'd shown up, and chose to stay close to Liv instead of following me and clinging to me like she'd done for the last week. Could have been due to the blood I had drying all over me, but I tried not to think about it.

Tried not to think about the fact that maybe she only stayed so close to me for the last week because I reminded her of 'picture daddy.'

And certainly tried not to think that maybe that psychotic prick had been right: that Jules looked at me and saw Scratch, my brother, and not me.

For a moment, common sense had shouted that I was being a stupid asshole to think about it… to think about Scratch.

But then the haze and burn of cheap whiskey flooded my veins and irrationality consumed me as I sat in my room, only dressed in the towel I'd wrapped around my waist after leaving the shower hours ago.

I only knew time had passed because the sun was no longer glaring into my western-facing windows. Daemon had stopped by to tell me Rob had been taken care of.

And Faith, once she showed up after her shift at the tattoo shop, had talked Ryker into bringing me dinner.

It still sat on a tray next to me, completely untouched.

A shame, really, because the steak Ryker had grilled probably would have soaked up some of the liquor and made me clear-headed.

But that wasn't what I wanted. I craved the darkness the whiskey provided, an escape from the weight of knowing I'd taken a man's life. Regardless of how much he deserved it, that shit weighed on your shoulders.

So when Shania-Shayla opened the door to my room, her bleached blond hair covering whatever small scrap of clothing she wore, barely covering her tits, I felt my lips spread wide into a grin.

I leaned back against my pillows as she shifted her stance against the doorframe to my room.

She propped a hand on her hip, pressed her surgically enhanced boobs out, and flipped her hair. "Wanna invite me in?"

I brought the whiskey bottle to my lips, wishing I could give her a different answer than the one I already knew was going to fall from my lips. When I opened my mouth to answer, a woman's voice floated from the hallway, straight to my dick.

"He's busy and taken."

My dick seemed to like the possessively clipped tone. It pressed up against the towel, instantly pushing for freedom.

I didn't bother hiding my reaction as Shania-Shayla's eyes dropped to the bulge. I grinned at her and shrugged, more of a 'sorry-not-sorry' response, but she didn't seem too disappointed as Jules appeared in the doorway.

Both of the women sized the other one up, in that bitchy way all women have in them, before the club bunny pushed off the doorway and threw her hands in the air.

"Just checkin' on the man," she grinned, backing away while Jules walked inside my room, ignoring her.

"Go check on someone else," she said, still not looking at the club bunny. "I think Pappy's free."

From behind Jules, Shania scowled.

A twisted laugh escaped my throat as she walked away.

"That wasn't very nice."

Jules shrugged, closing the door behind her. "What? Getting rid of your toy?"

"Sending her to Pappy. The man reeks."

Her lips twitched as if she was fighting a smile. Then it broke through, for just a second, before her lips pulled into a tight, thin line. My expression matched hers as soon as I remembered why I'd gotten so drunk in the first place.

26

Jules

I'd been at the club for two hours, showing up after work to pick up Sophie, and wondered why Jaden was hiding. Daemon and Ryker had filled me in as soon as I showed up, telling me about Rob. At least, telling me parts about Rob.

My heart almost stalled in my chest when they told me Jaden took care of him. I didn't need to know what they meant specifically.

Jaden had killed a man. For me. For Sophie. And while Rob was a jerk of the worst type, a man who thought he could beat women and stalk them and kidnap their kids with no thoughts of consequences to their actions, tears fell from my eyes when they told me he was dead.

Tears of relief because he was gone, and tears of gratitude because I was thankful for it.

What kind of sick person did that make me?

But when I'd looked at Sophie, warm and safe in my arms, her little brows furrowed as she wiped away my tears, I realized it didn't make me a horrible person at all.

It made me a mom. It made me someone who would fight, willing to do anything, for the safety of her children.

And I didn't care who was hurt, as long as my flesh and blood would be safe.

That didn't fully explain, though, why Jaden had been holed up in his room for hours, according to Daemon. Although he'd warned me that Rob said some things—things about Scratch—that had fucked with his head.

I could only imagine what those would have been.

Nerves running rampant, I made my way to his room, leaving Sophie with Faith and Ryker as they plopped her bottom onto one of the pool tables and watched as she smashed the pool balls into one another and flung them across the felt top.

My steps faltered when I saw one of the club bunnies, scantily dressed and leaning against the doorway to Jaden's room, breasts pushed out in offering. I almost stopped and turned away.

Then I remembered the way he'd looked at me all week long in my apartment, a powerful, possessive, searing gaze in his eyes whenever he caught me worried.

Now I stood in his room, sweaty palms pressed against the outsides of my thighs as I tried to hide my body's trembling response.

He looked at me with clouded, whiskey-filled eyes, laying back on his bed, two pillows resting behind him and only a towel wrapped around his waist. The bottle pressed to his lips, he looked at is if he'd forgotten he was holding the thing. Probably because it was half empty and he'd spent the last few hours guzzling it in an attempt to forget something.

I inhaled a deep breath, ignoring the way—from even feet away—I could smell his masculine body wash that had somehow, in the last week, permeated the space in my bedroom and bathroom.

I'd probably never be able to get the smell out of my apartment or my pillows—not that I wanted to.

"Daemon told me what happened today," I began, and quickly forgot the rest of what I was going to say when Jaden pushed himself unsteadily off the side of his bed.

"Yeah?" His eyes flashed and darkened. "He tell you I had to scrub the asshole's brain matter off my face, too?"

Jesus. I flinched. But I only saw the visual image behind closed eyelids when I squeezed them shut and quickly opened them.

Clearing my throat, I choked out an answer. "No. Not that part."

"He tell you what the asshole said to me? Taunted with me with?"

Fury rolled off his shoulders and his thick biceps with such palpability, I could almost see his blood boiling beneath his inked and tanned skin.

"No, but –"

"But nothing." His hand gripping the bottle of Jack Daniels lifted and pointed at the door. "Get the fuck out of here."

My knees shook. I looked at the door behind me before facing Jaden with my own confused expression. "I came to tell you thank you." My voice was meek, quiet. But it broke through the intensity of Jaden's drunken, angry scowl.

It almost made me laugh. Only a week and I'd forgotten how much I'd hated and lusted after his hardened features.

God, I was whipped. Totally done for.

I took a step toward Jaden, and then another. Watched as his expression darkened further and a storm raged behind his dark brown eyes. He was fighting for something, I could feel it.

Perhaps it was absolution over taking a life. I'd give him that.

My eyes caught the bulge underneath the white towel as Jaden stood frozen still in front of me, his chest heaving with slow, angry breaths. If he was horny, I'd take care of that, too. Something about seeing Jaden all pissed off again made me want it.

Want him.

He caught the way my cheeks flushed, the way I licked my lips with heightened anticipation, and reached out, gripping my shoulder.

His hand wrapped around my shoulder, elbow locking so I couldn't move closer.

"You going to fuck me while thinking of Scratch? Going to scream out his name when it's my dick inside you?"

Or… perhaps that could be his problem.

I jerked back, but his grip on my shoulder was strong—tight and digging into my skin.

"What?"

He leaned forward, hissing, and I tried not to wrench away from the massive whiff of whiskey that filled my nose.

"You think of him when I fuck you? Just like you did with that asshole? Scream Scratch's name when he's making you come?"

I leaned back, smacked his hand off my shoulder. "That's what's got you so pissed right now?" I huffed a breath, took a step back to put space between us. Tears stung my eyes at the memory, the night I'd done that with Rob.

The first morning after he'd used me as a punching bag. All night long I'd been tormented of nightmares of Scratch's death, the meaninglessness behind all of it, and how he would have been so damn disappointed in the decisions I'd made since he was buried.

And yeah, I'd woken up screaming his name. With Rob on top of me.

The memory of that morning, the tears that had fallen like a forceful waterfall, with Rob taking what he wanted from me—what he thought I owed him—without any regard to how I felt or what I wanted, slammed into me, knocking me back a step.

I wiped tears from my cheeks, eyes stinging with salty memories that fell before I knew I was crying.

"You're an asshole," I whispered, spinning on my heels.

Jaden called my name, his throat scratchy, sounding unsure of himself.

I shook my head and cleared my eyes, wiping the stain of tears from my cheeks before I looked back.

"You think I don't remember Scratch? Jesus, I do. Every damn day I think of him, wondering what he'd think or how he'd smile when he saw Sophie take her first step, say her first word. God—how would his face have lit up when she had her first smile? I know the pain of living without him, Jaden. I feel that ache burn deep every single damn time Sophie's eyes light up."

I swallowed, not taking the time to see the look of regret flash across Jaden's eyes as I continued. "You think I don't feel the burden of his death? That had I not been scared to tell him I was pregnant that everything would have ended differently? That's all it would have taken to keep him alive—one fucking phone call from me—and he'd be here, raising his daughter. I live with that guilt, that regret, every single day, knowing my immaturity killed him."

I stopped, wiping my cheeks again, and inhaled a shaky breath.

"But I've also mourned him. I've buried him and I've let him go as much as I can. That doesn't mean he doesn't—and won't always— be someone I love, but it means I know I'll be able to love again. Not the same way, but it'll be different, and it will be just as important to me as my love for Scratch."

When I pulled my eyes to Jaden, his sorrow matched mine—that love for his brother that I knew he still felt deep in bones—and I finally realized his struggle.

Screwing his dead brother's girlfriend carried the same weight— the same questions—as it did for me to be sleeping with Jaden… to be falling for him.

He blinked, shook his head, and swayed on his feet.

I stepped toward him, put my hands on his shoulders, and pushed him to the bed. His knees hit the mattress and he sat down, whiskey bottle still enclosed in his tightened fist.

"I used to see him," I admitted slowly, "when I showed up here and first saw you. Hell, for the last few months I saw him when I saw you. And it killed me, catching glances of you hating me while you looked so much like him."

A muscle in his jaw jumped and he opened his mouth—probably to say something that would make him an absolute asshole. I covered his mouth with my hand.

"Shut up and let me finish."

He murmured something indecipherable beneath my hand but nodded.

"You're different than him. You're angrier and you're stronger and you carry a darkness inside you that Scratch didn't have. But when I'm with you, all I see is you."

Slowly, I let go of his mouth and dropped to my knees in front of him.

His eyes widened and his jaw went slack when my fingers dug into his towel.

"You don't—" he started to protest, but I reached into the towel and wrapped my hand around his thick erection. "Fuck."

"Not yet," I whispered, smiling up at him. A growl escaped the back of his throat as my hand firmly ran from base to tip, my thumb slowly wiping across his piercing. His thigh tensed beneath my other hand, the coarse hair on his legs tickling my palm. "I don't know what's started between us. I don't even know if I'm something besides someone to fuck to you, but don't let Rob's lies and bullshit ruin it."

I pleaded with him with eyes wide open as I bent down and ran my tongue along his cock, so thick, and warm, salty mixed with the smell of his soap. The metal piercing hitting the top of my mouth and the back of my throat sent a shiver of excitement through me.

"Fuck, Jules," he growled. He dropped the whiskey on the floor, and his hands went to my hair. The bottle clunked and rolled until the top of the bottle hit my knee. The warm liquid spread on the floor and around my knees, making me wet and sticky as I took his dick into my mouth as far as I could. Slowly. I pulled back, my hand continuing to glide up and down his cock.

He was beautiful. His jaw clenched and his eyes narrowed on me as if he didn't know what in the hell I was doing—or why I was doing it.

"I only see you," I repeated.

His tortured expression told me he needed to hear it. I didn't give him time to reply before I leaned down and ran my tongue down his cock, and then gently sucked one of his balls into my mouth.

"Oh, fuck," he groaned. His hands tangled in my hair and held me in place. I shook my head, signaling for him to ease up. Surprisingly, he did, letting me have control. My tongue licked all over his balls, gently sucking and licking the sensitive skin before I trailed along a vein on the bottom of his cock. I ran my tongue up to the tip, sucking it into my mouth, my tongue playing with his piercing.

His hips rocked toward my mouth and his pleasured curses and groans filled my ears before I took him deep, as far as I could without gagging.

"Jesus you're good at this," he moaned, his hands pulled my hair.

I wrapped one hand around the base of his dick, pumping in time with my mouth as I continued playing with the tip of his dick, gently pulling on his apa and loving the way he moaned my name—or a stuttered variation of it. *ShitJules, FuckJules, ShitfuckhellJules,* all rolled off his tongue repeatedly.

Every desperate moan increased the moisture and the need between my legs until his cock swelled inside my mouth. My other hand moved to his balls, and I squeezed gently.

His hips bucked off the bed as he screamed, "Fuck!"

And I smiled, loving that I was driving him crazy, and at the same time driving myself to the edge.

My hand fell from his balls. I pumped his dick with my hand and my mouth, and my other hand went down my shorts.

I flicked my own clit in time to the way I fucked his dick with my mouth.

"Shit, Jules, I gotta see this,"

I shook my head. Not moving, too close to my own orgasm.

My hips rocked frantically as Jaden brushed hair out of my face. I stared up at him, his drunken, half-lidded eyes watched my hand and my mouth.

"Gonna come," he growled. His thighs tightened at the same time he gripped my hair. My own thighs began to shake.

It was so hot, getting myself off with Jaden watching, his dick in my mouth.

His hips rocked. I groaned right as my own body began releasing an orgasm that left my thighs trembling.

I moaned around his dick and he was gone.

He cursed and pulled me closer, until my nose was at the base of his cock as hot streams spurted into my mouth. I swallowed his thick, salty cum until he stopped pulsing in my mouth and my own orgasm had subsided.

He reached down, grabbed my wrist, and brought my wet fingers to his mouth, sucking my own taste off my fingers.

"That was incredible, and you taste even better."

He sounded sleepy and I grinned, bracing myself on his knees to stand up.

"Trust me," I smiled. "It was my pleasure." With my thumb and index finger, I wiped off the remaining taste of him from around my lips.

He tilted his head back and I inhaled sharply, getting lost in dark brown eyes that seemed to say so much more than I thought Jaden might ever be able to say out loud.

He exhaled and his forehead dropped to my stomach. His arms wrapped around my waist.

I waited. Gave him time to slow his breathing. Then he mumbled, slightly slurred, "That asshole fucked with my head. Made me think of Scratch, and all of this shit is such a mess in my head… wanting my brother's girl… his fuckin' kid. Fuckin' hell, I'm a mess."

I tried for playfulness, pushing him off my stomach, and he fell back to the bed. But in truth, his admission of wanting not only me— but Sophie, too—meant he wanted me for more than just sex. He wanted *me and Sophie*.

"You're drunk and won't remember this shit in the morning," I grinned, shoving his knee with mine as I fixed my shorts and ran my fingers through my hair. "And I need to get Sophie home to bed."

"Stay here."

A lascivious need pulsed from my heart and spread throughout my veins. His eyes were closed, his head tilted to the side, and he looked like he was seconds from passing out. But still, I relished his request, even if I couldn't say yes.

"Sophie needs her bed, and you're going to pass out."

I moved, but his warm hand clasped onto my wrist and held me in place. His other hand went to his face, his fingers rubbing his eyes, but they never opened.

"You're more than a fuck, Jules. Fuck… so much more than that to me. Always have been."

I inhaled a sharp breath but he didn't move after that. It was possibly the most romantic thing he could say to me. Jaden wasn't hearts and flowers, he was straight up—always telling you exactly what was on his mind. His words wrapped around my heart, and I knew in that moment, I was irrevocably chained to him—in lust or in love, I was yet to figure that out.

I couldn't resist him. Leaning down, I brushed my lips against his and then unpeeled his fingers from my skin.

"Good to know," I replied, but I said it too softly and he was already snoring.

For a moment, I thought about trying to shift him onto his bed, but I chose not to. A part of me wanted him to wake up, feet resting on the floor, completely naked, and have his first memory be of the way I had sucked him off.

I closed his door behind me, grabbed Sophie from the pool table, and left the clubhouse with a smile on face that didn't disappear until sleep finally took me an hour later.

27

Jules

Light movement brushed my arms, tickling the sensitive skin at the crook of my elbow, and I shivered. With my eyes closed, I brushed my arm and tried to burrow deeper into my comforter.

"Go back to sleep, Sophie," I muttered, my voice thick from sleep.

It was too early.

I groaned when hot breath hit my ear.

"Not Sophie, babe."

My eyes jerked open and I gasped. Jaden knelt on the bed, mostly covering me. His morning scruff scraped across my cheek. I quickly registered that he was completely naked. And hard.

"Oh my God," I rasped, my heart pounding in my ears. "Quit scaring me."

"I woke up naked on top of my bed at the club house with only a vague memory of you sucking me off so hard last night, my brain almost exploded."

Fire flashed on my cheeks. I tried to turn away, but Jaden's warm hand cupped my cheek and held me inches from him.

"You were pretty drunk." My throat bobbed with a thick swallow when I couldn't place his burning look. "Perhaps your memory is skewed."

He shook his head, then dropped it to the crook of my neck and sucked.

My eyes rolled back into my head. "Oh shit, that always feels so good."

"I know." He raised his head, a slight smirk on his lips. "And you taste fucking phenomenal."

"Why are you here?"

Jaden looked down at his erection, bobbing between us, and back at me with one eyebrow raised.

"Sex." I swallowed a lump of disappointment. It didn't surprise me: we'd been having it a lot. Yet somehow, I had come home from the club the night before imagining something had changed between us. That we'd gotten past the hurdle of Scratch between us and become more.

Or I was just really good at blowjobs and Jaden wanted one he could remember without half of a bottle of whiskey sloshing in his stomach.

I blinked, trying to keep the disappointment at bay, when Jaden began removing my shirt and my shorts. I let him, although my heart started beating faster—faster for something more than a quick morning lay before the sun rose and life began.

Jaden surprised me when he rolled off me. One leg thrown over me, and an arm over my waist, he tugged me to him so I was almost laying on my side, but pinned under the weight of his leg and arm.

"I wasn't so drunk last night that I don't remember everything," he started, an odd, serious expression on his face that made me take notice. "And I'm pretty sure the last thing I said to you was that you were never just a fuck to me."

"You did." I nodded, chewed on my bottom lip.

He reached out and pulled my bottom lip out with his thumb.

Slowly, his callused thumb swiped across my lips. I opened them, nipping the pad of his thumb.

His hips shifted into me, pressing his erection against my thigh.

Jaden grinned and then it disappeared. "Need to talk to you."

"Okay." My pulse increased. Nothing good ever came from a sentence that started with that need.

Jaden's eyes danced between my own and I watched his Adam's apple bob as he took a minute. A minute for what, I didn't know, but he seemed to need the time to compose himself so I gave it to him, all while my pulse began thundering like I was at the horse track.

"I'm a dick," he started, hesitation clear in his voice.

I licked my lips but stayed silent.

"Always have been, always will be. I'm not going to apologize for the shit in the past, because I figure we both made choices with Scratch we wish we could do different, but I figure nothin' can be done about that and it's time to put that shit to rest."

His eyes raked down my body. His fingers tightened on my waist before he raised his eyes, staring at my mouth.

"Woke up this morning, thinking of yesterday and last night, pissed about that asshole and bunch of other shit. But mostly I was pissed you weren't next to me."

My eyes widened in shock. I cleared my throat. "Why?"

He shook his head. "Can't explain it fully, just that shit's better when I wake up next to you. I'm not as pissed when I wake up curled next to your body."

It wasn't much. But for Jaden, it was everything. My heart began thundering against my rib cage. "What are you saying, Jaden?"

He rolled his lips, as if searching for the right words. His hand on my waist came up and smoothed back the hair from my face. The move was so gentle… so calming and yet strong… so *not* like Jaden. I couldn't help but smile when he leaned forward and pressed his lips against mine before leaning back.

"Saying I like this shit that we've got going on right now. I like being in your bed, waking up and having coffee with Sophie. I like knowing you two are safe. Mostly I like the way you scream my name when I'm deep inside you and your pussy is clamping around my dick so hard I think you're going snap it off."

I coughed over the harshness of his words, all while moisture flooded my panties. "That doesn't sound good."

"It's fucking magnificent." His hand on my hair moved back around to my neck, tugging me backward so my neck was completely exposed to him. "You're always so tight wrapped around me. I can't stop thinking about you. Wanting you. Needing…"

His voice trailed off as he began sucking and licking my skin, peppering the column of my throat down to my collarbone with sweet brushes of his lips. My hips shifted, the center of my thighs needing release from the pressure building.

"Jaden," I rasped out, my throat not working while he continued slowly driving me crazy. "I don't know what this means."

Although I did. I just needed him to say. I needed to hear it.

"It means…" He pulled back, intensity in his darkened brown eyes that left me struggling to breathe and see straight. "That you're mine."

I lost the ability to think after that. Or answer him.

Because Jaden quickly went to work proving exactly what that meant to him.

And two painfully silent orgasms later, he left me to clean up and shower for work while he made coffee.

I entered the kitchen dressed for another day at the salon, and the day looked exactly like it had the day before: Sophie watching her cartoons, Jaden fixing breakfast at the kitchen counter, full mug of coffee on the counter waiting for me.

It was so domestic.

So similar to twenty-four hours ago, but based on the way Jaden's eyes stayed glued to mine, a brightness in them that I'd never seen in him, I knew everything had changed.

I was completely, irrevocably, his.

"Faith and Liv and I are going out for dinner and drinks tonight. My mom has Sophie for a few hours. Liv said she'd drop Sophie off sometime this afternoon if you're still taking her to the clubhouse," I told him, taking my first sip of coffee.

I stood behind him, watched as the muscles in his back tensed and rippled with a small hitch before he glanced at me over his shoulder.

"Men are still on you."

My nose twitched with annoyance, but I stayed silent.

"And yeah, I'm taking Sophie to the club."

"All right then." I turned, poured the rest of the coffee into a to-go mug, and pressed my lips to his rough cheek. "Have a good day."

I'd leaned back to grab my keys when his arm came out, snagged my waist, and pulled me back to him.

His lips covered mine, quickly and fiercely, and I gasped, opening my mouth to him instantly. He devoured me with his tongue and the taste of him. And when he pulled away, I was grasping for breath. "Mine," he growled. "On my bike. You might have men on you, watching you, but don't forget that."

On his bike. Hell, I knew what that meant. Yet still, hearing the words made my pulse begin to race.

"I don't particularly like bikes anymore," I whispered. He wasn't talking about his bike, literally. I knew what that mean to bikers, to have their women on their bikes. But besides the couple of times I'd needed to take a ride from him, the very idea still terrified me.

His hand on my waist moved until it was at the back of my neck. He dropped his forehead to mine and let out a harsh breath.

"You'll get over it." He pulled me back, our eyes inches from each other. In the silence, I knew exactly what he was saying. "I had to, too."

Vulnerability flashed in his eyes and they darkened to black before he blinked it away.

But it was that one glimpse, seeing it, that almost had my heart dropping to the floor and tears stinging his eyes. He'd never shown me his pain about Scratch, always been so quick to toss it all into my lap.

This was different: this was Jaden lowering his guard, and I wanted to wrap myself around him with my legs and my arms and comfort him, knowing no one had been there to do it for him.

Instead I nodded, and forced my lips into a small smile. "I'll try."

Then I gave him another quick kiss, pressed my lips to Sophie's, and headed to work.

Placing my cell phone on the receptionist's desk at the salon, I felt a wistful smile tug at my lips. It wasn't easy to turn down a full-time substitute position, thanks to a teacher going on early maternity leave due to pregnancy complications, at the school I'd been dying just weeks ago to get into.

But things had changed. And quickly.

"You okay?" Cammie asked me as she walked up to the counter. "You got the job."

"Yeah." I ran my hand through my freshly highlighted hair—thanks to Cassie—and shrugged. "I can't believe I turned it down, though."

Her eyebrows shot up. "You did? But you've wanted this."

My hand dropped to my neck, rubbing the back. "I know, but I guess things have changed a bit."

And there was no way I'd be able to keep the job once the school figured out I was involved with Jaden, and close with the Nordic Lords. My initial relationship with them had prevented me from getting the job in the first place.

But besides Jaden, other things had changed, too. I *liked* the salon—although what girl wouldn't love free haircuts, highlights, manicures and pedicures? I also really liked working with the sisters, not to mention the flexibility they gave me with Sophie and needing time off. They'd been there for me when she was taken. No way would that have flown had it happened if I'd been in the middle of a school day. I'd be handed my pink slip faster than I could blink.

My stomach felt unsettled from knowing I just turned down a job based on a guy who'd only that morning told me he wanted me, wanted us to try whatever it was we were doing—but hell, I couldn't stop my reaction or my craving to be with Jaden at this point even if I tried.

I also didn't want to try to stay away from him.

"Anyway," I said, pushing away thoughts of Jaden and the club and the job opportunity I'd wanted and just turned away. "Liv and Faith are taking me out tonight. When you close up shop tonight you can join us if you want."

Cammie blinked and looked around the salon nervously. I frowned, watching her odd reaction. "Oh, thanks. Maybe we will later."

She turned on her hot pink high heels and walked away.

I brushed it off as a client came up. After ringing her out, I smiled when Faith sauntered into the salon, black purse slung over her shoulder, black hair falling straight down her back, and a giant smile stretched wide across her face.

"Let's get your party started!"

I shook my head, laughing. "Tell me you're not planning something."

Faith reached the counter and leaned in, carefree mischief written all over her face. I grinned, because God—she'd been through hell, and by the look on her face, you'd never guess it.

"You didn't honestly think we'd forget your birthday, did you?"

More like hoping. It'd been the last thing on my mind for weeks, and with all the drama happening in my life, I'd completely pushed it aside.

"Forget? No… just figured it wasn't important, given everything else going on."

"Ah." She pushed off the counter, slapping her hands down on it. "But see—that's where you're wrong. Because what I've learned—and what Liv was so quick to teach me herself—is that when the shit hits the fan, the best thing you can do is party it off and remind yourself to enjoy life as long as you can—and as much as you can."

Who could argue with that?

"All right, where is Liv anyway?" I grabbed my purse and met Faith on the other side of the counter.

"She, um, had something come up at the garage, so we're picking her up there."

"See you girls later?" I called out to the triplets, all busy with clients in their chairs. Bella Salon was packed all day long, which only had me smiling as they turned to me in unison.

Callie pulled a comb out of her lips. "We'll do our best!"

"Come on," Faith said, tugging my hand until we were outside. "We've got partying to do."

28

Jules

Blaring rock music rattled my eardrums as we climbed out of Ryker's truck at the clubhouse. I turned my head toward the outside grass area, mostly hidden behind the garage.

"What's going on over there?" I asked Faith as she met me at the front of the truck.

All the lights in the garage were off, the doors pulled closed as if everyone had closed up shop early for the day and started their partying earlier than normal.

Faith threw an arm over my shoulder. "With these men? Who knows? Let's go find Liv."

I was dragged along by Faith's quick-moving legs until we hit the back corner of the garage and my eyes flew wide open.

"Oh my gosh," I muttered, my fingers covering my dropped jaw. My gaze snapped to Faith's. "You did this?"

She grinned and pulled me further into the yard, which was all decked out in birthday decorations. A huge banner hung across a tent that had been set up and an outside bar, completely packed with Nordic Lords standing around and helping themselves to what looked like enough alcohol to keep a small country drunk for a decades.

Bottles and tapped kegs were everywhere.

Plastic cups already littered the ground like one of the few college frat parties I'd attended years ago. But these weren't preppy frat boys in designer shirts, partying on their parents' dime.

From the corner of my eye, I caught Liv standing off to the side, smiling and animatedly talking to a very unhappy Daemon.

I snorted, a grin beginning to stretch wide on my lips, knowing girly decorations splattering his yard were probably not making him happy.

"Jules!" she shrieked when she saw us, turned her back on Daemon, and came running across the yard, throwing her arms around me. "Happy Birthday!"

I untangled myself from Faith and wrapped my arms around Liv. "You're crazy."

"I know!" she shouted in my ear and pulled back. "Hey!" She turned around, one arm still wrapped around my shoulder, and pulled me toward the center of the yard. "I didn't spend all freaking day decorating this damn place and filling it with liquor for you jerks to ignore the birthday girl."

Her loud shouts echoed through the yard, and on cue, every man and woman in attendance turned to me, their glasses raised high.

My eyes scanned the yard, feeling heat blossom on my cheeks when I didn't see Jaden at first.

All the men cheered, did their best to try to at least act like they gave a shit for a reason to party, but when their half-hearted attempt made Liv frown, I didn't mind.

"Where's Sophie?" I asked, still scanning the crowd, not seeing her anywhere. Or Jaden. A small ball of disappointment began growing in my gut, but then disappeared as quickly as it showed up when a few men parted the circle they were standing in and I saw Sophie, propped on Jaden's hip, both of them smiling at me…

With my parents?

My eyeballs almost popped out of my head as they began heading my way.

"How in the heck did you manage this?" I asked Liv, shock making my words disjointed.

She nudged my hip and let me go. "Just asked them to stay until you got here, that's all."

"Wow."

My pulse increased and my hands became sweaty as I met my parents—Jaden with Sophie still propped on his hip, looking oddly pleased with himself and sexy as hell holding my daughter—in the middle the yard.

I hesitated to look around, but I felt dozens of eyes on all of us. My two worlds colliding left me breathless as my mom reached out and hugged me.

"Happy birthday," she whispered in my ear, and then because she couldn't resist and knew Jaden couldn't hear her—or perhaps because she knew he could, she continued with her motherly warning: "Be careful."

"Thanks," I mumbled before she handed me off to my dad.

His eyes darted uncomfortably around, seeing the men, before he tugged me into his side and pressed a kiss to my temple. "Not sure how I feel about my girl being involved in all this again." In contrast to my mom, who tried to hide her disapproval, my dad spoke plain and firm. Across from me, Jaden's back stiffened and his eyes narrowed on my dad.

"It's just a party, Dad," I said, my hands falling to his stomach as I pushed off him.

"It's not a party, it's a life." He looked down at me and all his fears for me, swimming in his eyes plain as day, made my breath get caught in my throat. His nose twitched and I felt Jaden behind me before his hand clamped down on my hip. My dad saw Jaden's hand on me, glared at it as if he was trying to set it on fire, and then raised his eyes to mine.

"The men in this life got Sophie back to me, and got me free of Rob for good."

"Don't defend us, Jules."

I snapped my eyes to Jaden, only to see his hardened stare matching my dad's intensity. But where my dad's radiated concern for me and his granddaughter, Jaden's were alight with something so much more visceral.

"He knows what kind of men we are."

"Already saw you shattered by losing one of them, Jules," my dad warned, resetting his eyes on me.

Jaden's fingers twitched on my hip, but his eyes lost their anger. "Doing my best to make sure that doesn't happen again," he drawled. I closed my eyes, exhaling and wishing Liv would have kept my parents out of this.

A quick glance around the yard told me the rest of the men and their women were watching the mounting tension in the middle of their party—my party—with eagle eyes, ready to step in if needed, but trying to act as if nothing was amiss right in front of them.

"Yeah? Pretty sure your shitty treatment of her after your brother died was part of what shattered her in the first place."

Jaden stepped forward, pulling me with him, and rolled his shoulders. I felt the coiled tension of his back muscles radiating down his spine.

"Pretty sure that shit's between Jules and me" he clipped, lips pulled into a thin line.

"All right," I said, stepping forward between the two of them. With quick hands, I grabbed Sophie off Jaden's hip. "Hey, pumpkin."

I kissed her cheek, hoping to diffuse the tension bouncing off Jaden and my dad. "Happy Birfday. We got cake!"

"Yay!" I kissed her again, set her on feet, and patted her butt before my mom scooped her up. "We'll get some in a minute, okay?"

She grinned, that perfect smile filled with gaps between her teeth. "Otay!"

"This isn't the place," I whispered to both the men before I turned to my dad. "Thank you for being here. I can come tomorrow for dinner so we can celebrate at home, if you want."

My dad shot a glare to Jaden before he sighed, and then his hands cupped my cheeks. His voice was thick and raspy. "Worried about you, baby girl."

"I know." I covered his warm hands with mine. "But I'm good, I swear it."

Whatever fight he still had in him, he breathed out on a frustrated exhale and pressed a kiss to my forehead. "Be safe."

"Will do," I whispered, fighting tears that stung the backs of my eyes. He was concerned and I appreciated it, but I wouldn't let him talk about Jaden that way on Jaden's property. "Have fun with Sophie."

He harrumphed, took Sophie from my mom, and headed toward the parking lot.

I watched him go, watched him carrying Sophie in his arms in a protective way, probably like how he'd always done to me, when I felt my mom's small, warm hands cup my chin the way my dad had just done.

"He's just worried about you," she whispered to me, smiling sadly. "You know we love you."

"I know." I sniffed, and then felt instantly strengthened when Jaden's palm pressed against my lower back.

With a nod of her own, she looked up into what I knew was Jaden's gaze and let go of me. "Thank you for getting Sophie back, and while I don't want to know—*at all*—at how you managed that and taking care of Rob, thank you."

She reached out her hand to Jaden, who let go of my back to shake hers. When she had him in her grip, she leaned up on her high-heeled tiptoes and pressed a kiss to his cheek.

"Welcome." Jaden's gruff voice caught my attention and I looked to him, smiling down at Mom in some oddly soft way. Such a contradiction to the hardness in which he usually carried himself.

She pulled back and swiped under her eye, muttering something about allergies before she lifted her hand and waved goodbye. "See you tomorrow for dinner?"

I smiled and waved back. "You bet."

She turned, carrying herself in the confident way she always seemed to, and met my dad and Sophie in the parking lot. I stayed rooted to the spot while I watched them strap Sophie into her car seat, climb into her car, and pull out of the parking lot.

Once they were gone, I felt oxygen leave my lungs. "Well that was fun."

Jaden's arm hooked around my neck and he pulled me to him. "They just care. Ain't nothing wrong with that." He looked down at me and scowled. "Mind telling me why you didn't fuckin' tell me it was your birthday?"

I pressed my lips together. "Forgot?"

He made a harrumph sound similar to one my dad had made and I grinned.

"Come on," he said, tugging me toward the makeshift backyard bar. "We're going to get you wasted, then I've got birthday orgasms to deliver on."

"Orgasms?" As in plural? I immediately felt my panties grow wet.

"One for every year," he said with a smirk.

My lower stomach instantly exploded into flames.

Well… hell. Let the partying begin.

I was swaying somewhere along the line between more-than-tipsy and completely-trashed-off-my-butt, standing in a small circle with Faith, Liv, Marie, and a few other old ladies who had apparently decided to welcome me into the fold.

The chilled wind whipped through my short-sleeved baby blue top, but I barely felt it due to the beer I'd consumed, which was filling my stomach and warming my blood.

The night, so far, had been incredible.

I'd accepted more than my fair share of shots from some of the men, but after I downed the first couple, I started handing them off to Jaden, who rarely left my side unless he was huddled in some corner of the yard, seeming to argue quietly with Daemon.

I didn't know what it was about, didn't want to know what it was about.

I simply wanted to pretend that my parents' presence hadn't rattled me. That their warnings were simply made to their only daughter that they loved like crazy, yet were completely unjustified.

Standing outside with men and women surrounding a raging bonfire, partying like it was some sort of celebration instead of just my twenty-sixth birthday, it was easy to fool myself into thinking this was just a large, really loud, family party.

I pushed down the feeling of unease, tried to stay in the midst of the conversations with Faith and Liv as they prattled on about their wedding plans, but knew I was failing miserably when I caught Finn walking toward us.

I hadn't had much interaction with him since he'd basically called me a shitty mom for not being with Sophie twenty-four seven. Liv had assured me he had his own issues he was dealing with that made him grouchy and quiet, but I still resented his implication from a few weeks ago.

So it shocked me when he easily strolled into our circle of women, wrapped an arm around my shoulder, and tugged me to his side.

"Glad you got your girl back," he said quietly, squeezing my shoulder. That accent of his made my knees wobble. "And free from that dick."

I couldn't hide my shock. "Even considering you think I'm a shitty mom?"

The wide, easy smile he seemed to carry with him to hide the weight behind his dark eyes disappeared. "That's my shit."

His hand dropped and I watched the alligator ink on his arm twist and turn with the flex of his tightened muscles.

I let it go, because I didn't have a choice when he turned and I watched Gunner approach our small circle. When he reached us, he easily draped his arms around Liv's and Faith's shoulders and smiled directly at my chest.

"How's the birthday girl?" He arched an eyebrow, which was barely visible due to the guy being completely covered in ink. His short, buzzed, full head of black hair hid the ink I knew covered his scalp, but the only un-inked parts of skin I knew about were around his eyes and the palms of his hands.

My heart stuttered in my chest, leaving me momentarily speechless. Even in the dark, his impish grin shot a blast of embarrassment to my hardening nipples. I hadn't seen him since he'd pierced me, and for a moment I lost the shock that Gunner, owner of a tattoo shop, was partying with Nordic Lords.

I crossed my arms over my chest and Gunner let out a low laugh before raising his eyes to meet mine.

"Just checking on my work."

"Might wanna do it when her man isn't around, mate." Finn nodded his head toward Jaden, glaring daggers at our small group from across the yard.

Catching my eye, I swore I saw the faint hint of a grin on his eyes before he smacked Daemon on the back and headed our way.

"Nah," Gunner said easily, "your men need me too much to hate me."

His flippant attitude and quick perusal of my chest sent a cold, slithering feeling down my spine.

"Why are you here?"

Gunner's grin widened. "Faith and Liv told me it was your birthday. Didn't think I'd want to miss this party."

"Well, thanks." I shuffled on my feet, not understanding why I'd always felt okay around Gunner before, but didn't get the same easy feeling radiating off him that he was trying to project.

I jumped slightly when I felt a warm arm slide around my shoulder and instantly relaxed into Jaden's unmistakable strong embrace. "Gunner."

Glancing at Jaden, I saw his glare directed at the tattoo master and then dart to his arms, which were still wrapped around Liv and Faith. They didn't seem to care that he was touching them, but the heat from Jaden's eyes had Gunner dropping his arms and shoving his hands into his pockets.

"Not sure whether to kick your ass since you've seen my girl's tits or thank you."

Gunner nodded, a slight hint of that naughty smile quirking the edges of his lips. "Thanks'll do."

Jaden's slight smile matched his and he jerked his head up once.

I took that for a silent 'thanks' in man-speak.

"What's going on?" I asked, turning to Jaden and pushing down the awkwardness of Gunner. Maybe it was because I hadn't seen him anywhere else besides the GetInked2 that his presence rattled me.

No one else seemed to mind.

Jaden's arm dropped to my wrist and he turned so he was facing me, unease suddenly appearing on his wrinkled brow.

"Need you go to your parents' tonight."

My head jerked back. "What?"

A blast of cold shot up my arms and I scrubbed them, knowing it wasn't from the chill in the air.

Jaden's nose twitched. His eyes flickered to the group next to us before coming back to mine and he bit his bottom lip. His voice dropped, speaking low enough so no one else could hear, but the deep, gravelly rumble caused a tight, itchy sensation at the back of my neck.

"Got work to do tonight and I want you at their house."

His tone left no room for argument, but it didn't stop me from trying. "Why can't I stay here?"

I glanced next to me and saw Marie, Switch's old lady—and a woman who had practically raised Scratch and Jaden—eyeing me with a raised, curious brow of her own. Beneath the concern was a softness I hadn't seen from her since before Scratch died.

She smiled sadly and looked away from me.

"Just do it, okay, Jules?"

"What aren't you telling me?" I asked, suddenly thinking of Rob and Sophie. I knew there was stuff he had held back from me about finding him—about the whole day, really. None of it had made sense; how he'd found her so quick, yet it had taken him so long to get her back to me.

Jaden leaned down, cupped the back of my neck with his hand and pressed his lips against my ear.

"Club has shit goin' down tonight. You'll be fine, and Sophie's fine, but shit could get messy with this and I need you away from the club."

I swallowed, a lump in my throat quickly forming. Finally, I nodded and whispered, "Okay."

Jaden pulled me back and then dropped his lips to mine before I could blink. His lips pressed against mine with a ferocity. I sucked in a quick breath, instantly parting my lips, and didn't care that Jaden took my breath away with one touch and one brush of his lips.

"Break it up, fucker."

Jaden jumped back and spun around.

Daemon walked by him, smacked his shoulder, and nodded to Finn. "Time to roll."

"What?" Liv asked, her eyes widening.

"Got shit to do, baby. Party's over. Clean it up—club's going on lockdown."

"But—"

Daemon pinned his eyes on her, rolling his shoulders and rolling off the vibe that had made him the President he'd become. Power pulsed off his leather cut as if he could summon the force at will. Even Liv looked as if she was attempting not to shrink under the heady weight thundering off him.

"Liv."

He narrowed his eyes and all the fight drained from Liv instantly. "All right, Daemon," she said softly and closed the small space between him to press a kiss to his lips. "Be safe."

"Always."

She snorted.

I felt Jaden's fingers dig into the back of my neck. He nodded his head toward Marie and back to me. "Marie will get you home."

Unease rolled through me. I had never been around the men when they got a call like this, had never witness how they so quickly flashed from men drinking and having a good time to the predatory looks and stances they all seemed to switch on in the blink of an eye.

All around me, men were grabbing their women, tossing their drinks, and heading toward the lot.

"You all have been drinking."

Jaden's grin was quick and then gone. "We're good."

He blinked and something unspoken flashed in his eyes before he dropped his head to my neck, and bit.

I jerked from the sudden sensation, the playfulness amidst the tension, and smacked his chest. "Hey."

"Just wanted one last taste." Then he stole my breath again with another deep kiss that left me shaking on my slightly drunken feet as he sat me down. "Be good." He pointed a finger at me and winked.

"Be safe," I whispered, but he had already turned his back, slapping an arm around Finn's shoulders as the two headed toward the parking lot and their bikes.

29

Jules

"Well, crap," Liv said.

I looked at her and her pouty frown.

"That's not how I wanted your birthday to end up."

I shrugged, feigning nonchalance. Reality of what it meant to be in the club began settling like a dead weight on my shoulders.

Was I really cut out for this kind of life?

Marie sidled up to my side. "Let's get you home."

Her warm command left no room for arguing and when I opened my mouth to say something, Liv and Faith smiled at me.

"Go, we're good here."

"I can help clean up," I offered half-heartedly.

They disagreed when they leaned in, both of them kissing my cheek.

"Jaden wants you gone, go. It'll give him a clear head to know you're doing what he wants."

The quiet warning came from Marie, and I turned to her, frowning.

I nodded, speechless, and not sure why. The air had shifted, as if the men had sucked the oxygen straight from the air when they turned their backs on the yard, leaving only tension and fear in the women as we watched them climb aboard their bikes.

"Okay," I muttered, but it was useless. Marie was already tugging me toward her car, speaking quietly to me, although I didn't register any of it over the thunderous rumble of the bikes as all the men started their engines simultaneously.

Near the front of the row of bikes, I caught Jaden glance back at me over his shoulder before shouting something to whoever was next to him—Ryker, I thought, but couldn't be certain.

I walked silently with Marie as the men peeled out of the lot, two men standing guard by the gated entrance as the bikes whipped out onto the street.

The vibrations of their engines rattled the concrete beneath my feet.

"Come on," Marie said, and opened the door to the car for me to get in.

I sat, folded my hands in my lap like a good little girl, like I knew what was going on, but so… lost.

God. The entire night had been strange—something I couldn't put a pulse on, but it was off. They all had been, all night.

Or maybe that was alcohol clouding my brain and leaving me unable to think straight.

I didn't notice Marie starting the car, or pulling onto the street.

My head spun. Jaden leaving. The look he'd given me. The way he'd kissed me. As if he didn't know if he'd see me again.

A boulder settled in my stomach as I stared out the window, seeing the trees and the road along the winding road to my parents' house, but none of it registered.

Marie's soft but wise voice brought me back to the present. "I told Liv months ago not to worry when this happens. Our men are strong, and they're fast, and they're smart. Somehow, they always come back to us."

Not all of them, I thought.

Fat raindrops plopped down on Marie's windshield.

"I knew it smelled like rain earlier." She frowned, flipped on her wipers as the rain began to pick up.

"How do you do this?" I asked, watching the rain splash against my side window, drops splattering the glass with increasing size and speed.

"It's the life we signed up for, Jules."

My eyelids closed, and I thought of Scratch—the last time I saw him smile, when I told him about Sophie.

God, had I known it was the last time I would have ever seen him… so many things I would have told him.

So many things I would have done differently, if only I had known.

"Jaden's different with you."

I swallowed the tears already forming in my eyes and turned to face Marie. With my head on the headrest, I pressed my lips together. "I'm not sure I can do this." My shaky voice was barely holding on. Had I gotten so swept up into lust with Jaden, the way he'd originally reminded me so much of Scratch, that I'd lost perspective? I'd already buried his brother.

I didn't have the strength to bury another.

My chin wobbled as she reached over and squeezed my hand. Air Supply filtered through the speakers, barely audible over the rain now barreling down on us.

"You get used to it," she said, her voice full of confidence and experience.

"Not when you've already lost one."

With only the entryway lights on inside, my parents' monstrosity loomed in front of me as Marie drove slowly up their curved driveway. The rest of the house was dark.

Like the night. Everything felt creepy, like an evil filth was languidly thickening the air. I couldn't describe it, I could only feel it.

"Jaden's always wanted you, you know."

I snapped my head toward Marie. "What?"

She smiled, like an omniscient mother, and I suppose she was, considering she'd practically been the only mother Jaden and Scratch ever knew. "I heard the boys arguing back before you and Scratch got together. Almost tossed the boxing gloves at them and told them to fight it out for you." She smiled wistfully, replaying a memory I had no knowledge of, in her head.

"I didn't know."

"Probably why he's always been a jerk to you... trying to keep his distance. But I've always seen it—how he looks at you."

"With hatred and loathing."

"With guilt over wanting his brother's girl," she quickly snapped back. "And now he's got you—something he's wanted for a long time—and I can't for one second think that doesn't weigh on him, whether or not he's gonna admit it to you. He knows—you both know—what it's like to lose someone. Hell, even I still miss Scratch most days. And Jaden has a heavier side to him that he doesn't let anyone see, but don't let that anger in him make you think he doesn't care."

I blinked quickly, fighting off the burn at the back of my eyes. "I don't know what I was thinking, getting involved with him, but the unknown... I don't know if I can handle it."

"You can," she said, reaching over and squeezing my hand firmly, "and you will, because you love him. Besides that, I know he loves you and he's too much of a stubborn asshole to die. Trust me, Jules... you'll get time with him if you give yourself the chance to take it, but he won't leave you like Scratch."

I inhaled slowly, breath leaving my flared nostrils.

God. How had I been so stupid to fall in love with brothers?

"Get inside," she said, squeezing my hand before letting it drop to my knee. "They'll be done and back tomorrow and everything will seem better in the daylight. Not as scary."

I nodded, too afraid to speak, terrified of what would come

out of my mouth if I did.

I unlocked the door to my parent's home and quietly let myself inside the house, only seeing a faint light on in the living room and knew it was my dad—who had some uncanny ability to always be awake when shit hit the fan around him.

It only made me certain that Marie had been wrong.

Nothing would be cleared in the daylight.

Everything would change.

30
Jaden

I slid my leather gloves on my hands and cursed the rain that had decided to fall. That was all we needed with shit already starting to fall apart.

A fucking rainstorm, making hands and weapons slippery.

Not to mention the unease and dread that was coiled tight at the base of my spine.

I narrowed my eyes, trying to see through the rain and turned to Daemon.

"This isn't right," I told him, scanning the lot at the docks.

He'd gotten a call just two hours ago that Sporelli had a shipment being dropped off.

Wasn't nearly the timeframe we usually had, and gave us shit time to plan.

The rain wasn't helping, but neither was the uncertainty that kept flashing across Daemon's eyes.

"None of this shit is right," he muttered before reaching for the gun inside his cut. It wasn't his only one. Out of the twenty men who had left the clubhouse thirty minutes earlier, we were all packing.

Shit would end tonight. Daemon had decided. I wanted to be out from Sporelli too, and drug-running was a bitch with pain-in-the-ass consequences, but I didn't agree with handling it this way.

I didn't get a say either, so I sucked it up and did what I was told, regardless of the tightness in my gut. Mostly it stemmed from leaving Jules at her birthday party. I saw it—the fear and uncertainty in her eyes as I walked away from her.

And I knew what she was thinking about. Scratch. The way he'd left her and never come back. Fuck if I was going to let that be me, but I couldn't blame her for wondering if a life with an asshole like me, a life like mine, was good enough for her. If it was what was best for her.

I was smart enough to know I wasn't.

I was selfish enough to not give a shit because I wasn't letting her go, either—even if she tried to run.

"Men are in place," Finn said on my other side.

I nodded, watched as the shadows that had descended onto the docks disappeared and melded into their surroundings.

We had enough men.

Enough firepower to end this, or create a war bigger than anything we'd dreamed of.

"Chief ready?" I asked Daemon.

"Should be."

Wasn't the best response, but nothing we could do about it.

"Go, then. We got your back," I told him. Then I watched from a distance, on a slight ridge overlooking the docks, as Daemon and Switch headed down to the docks.

It only took them minutes, but my fingers already tightened around my gun, ready to go if needed.

I hoped to fuck it wasn't.

"Shit, this doesn't feel right," Finn said, uttering the words that continued replaying in my head. I knew what he meant, though. My shoulders tried to roll off the nerves but nothing worked.

"Finn?" I waited for him to look at me out of the corner of my eye. "Shut the fuck up."

He snorted quietly before turning back to watch.

The rain rushing down on my face and body didn't help me see shit clearly either.

Fuck. This was a disaster.

Three figures stepped out of the shadows. The scenario felt so similar to our last run to the Cities that my back instantly went straight. My eyes scanned the horizons for movement, but all I saw was a black sky through the rain.

I tried to push it down. Two hours hadn't given us enough time to plan, but no way could Sporelli have that many men called and ready—sneaking into our town without any word they were coming either.

"Fuck," I muttered, rubbing my hands down my face. "When we're done with this shit, I'm getting fucking wasted and laid."

"With Jules's pussy?"

"Fuck off, Finn." But I grinned. I didn't want another guy thinking of Jules's pussy, but hell if it wasn't always the first thing on my mind, anyway.

"Here they come."

We watched as Daemon and Switch met the men. Words we couldn't hear were spoken.

Then I grinned, seeing the shadows of the chief and his men stepping out from behind a barge, guns pulled.

We couldn't hear the screaming over the distance and the rain as all five men, Daemon and Switch included, pulled their guns.

No shots were fired, though.

Sporelli's men raised their hands and then dropped their guns on the pavement. More men, local police, surrounded the five. In total, fifteen men from the local force and surrounding areas had been called in, in order to bust Sporelli during a drop-off.

Daemon said the club had been granted immunity. I doubted

the honesty of Chief Garrisson's promise, and was still expecting everything to go ass-up, when something shifted in the area.

I breathed a sigh of relief as I watched Daemon and Switch lower their weapons, setting them on the ground and sliding them toward the cops.

Everything looked as if it was going according to plan.

Cops stepped up, handcuffed the Sporellis. I only hoped it was Erik Sporelli—the son of the Sporelli patriarch, Angelo.

Daemon and Switch stood with their hands behind their backs, uncuffed, as the men were led away.

I turned to Finn, doing another scan of the dark lot, unable to see shit with the rain and thunder booming around us—when I saw something.

A quick glint of movement catching my attention under a streetlight.

"Finn!" I shouted, instantly drawing my gun toward the movement. "Your six!"

He spun on his heels, gun pulled, but it was too late.

Shots immediately began filling the air, smoke billowing from behind darkened hiding spots right as hidden men came out of the dark and into the light.

"Fuck," I screamed. A burst of searing pain hit my gut. My hand flew to the spot, only to come away wet and sticky.

"Shit!" I heard Finn scream, but couldn't find him.

My knees hit the ground, but still I raised my gun, firing off the last rounds as my body weakened.

I saw someone in the distance go down.

Or maybe it was my fucking imagination.

I couldn't see shit.

I couldn't feel shit besides a burning sensation that had started in my abdomen but now spread throughout my body.

The gun fell from my hand.

Both of my hands slipped to my stomach as I collapsed onto my side.

Wet rain pounded against my skin like a thousand knife slashes.

Pain radiated from my gut outward to every nerve in my body.

I was hurting—everywhere.

Finn's narrowed, concerned eyes appeared in my vision. He shouted something I couldn't hear.

Then everything went black.

31

Finn

"Damn it you fucker!" I gripped Jaden's cut.

If I could beat the shit out of the bleeding asshole, I would. As the paramedics jumped out of the ambulance, I still shouted at him to stay the fuck awake.

His skin turned white, blood mixed with water creating a river that pooled and washed away as soon as they left his body.

Behind me, the gunshots had stopped. So many damn men were gone, and it was such a waste.

A fucking waste.

Death was brutal. The pain of those left behind to deal with the death never fully healed.

I knew. I knew it in my bones, and there was no way my fuckin' brother was dying under my watch.

Paramedics loaded him up, quickly wrapped his bleeding gut, and began shouting orders as soon as they'd checked his pulse.

"Paddles!" they shouted.

Quick movement came from the back of the ambulance as Daemon reached me, shouting, "Jaden! NO!"

My arm reached out and stopped him. Daemon was smaller than

me, but a tough fucker. Fear flashed in his eyes before quickly being replaced by revenge.

"Clear!"

Jaden's entire body jerked on the small bed before two fingers were pressed against his throat.

"Fuck!" Daemon's hand flew to his hair, swiping the rain from his face before he locked his fingers at the back of his neck.

"Go!" a paramedic shouted.

The doors slammed shut and the ambulance took off.

Daemon fell to his knees, taking me with him, as other men reached us.

"What the fuck happened?" I asked, still stunned we'd been ambushed.

"Fuckin' Sporelli," Daemon growled from his knees on the pavement. His hand smacked the cement before he released a cry of pain mixed with grief and fear into the air.

"Twelve down." I snapped my eyes to Ryker as he reached us, slightly out of breath from running up the hill from the docks where Jaden and I had been. "Not all ours, though, but Jaden's the worst. Cops cleaning it up, we gotta go."

Daemon stood up and shook my hand off his shoulder. With a blink of his eyes and a roll of his shoulder, our President returned, the fear for his long-time friend pushed to the back.

"Get to the clubhouse. Get the word out make the calls. Get every fucking charter we can find. Angelo Sporelli will burn."

He leaned in, intimidating as all fuck even to me, and I'd lived my whole life with shit darker than anything this club could have thrown at me. Fuck, considering how I'd been raised, the shit I'd seen, this club was still like a damn vacation most of the time—even with the drugs and violence.

I nodded, hopped on my bike.

Jaden.

I closed my eyes, sent up a silent prayer to a God I already knew fucking despised me because he'd never answered me, but still—I hoped this one damn time—He would let Jaden pull through.

32

Jules

A phone call at four in the morning was never a good thing.

It buzzed in my hand, my fingers tingling from the vibration of the phone and the terror that immediately assaulted my senses.

Across from me, my dad's exhausted eyes settled on me, a frown twisting his thin, worried lips.

"Hello?" I croaked.

"It's Jaden, Jules," Liv said. My eyes snapped to my dad immediately. As if knowing already, he uncurled from the couch and moved to sit beside me. "You need to get to Northern Hospital immediately."

My body shivered, immediately going ice cold. I replayed the words in my head even as I asked the question, "What happened?"

"I'm not sure." Her voice came through, quicker—more panicked. "Daemon just called me and I'm on my way now, but something went wrong tonight and a lot of men are hurt."

A lot of men are hurt.

I blinked, immediately seeing funerals. Burial plots and headstones of granite flashed in front of my eyes.

I saw Scratch. His casket. His hands crossed over his chest, buried with his cut that I only got a glimpse of before the men in the club had created a barrier, not allowing me to get close to him.

All thanks to Jaden.

Pain gripped my heart, squeezing it as I tried to blink the vision, the memories, out of my mind.

"Jules…"

"I can't," I croaked, my throat dry.

Next to me, my dad squeezed my hand in my lap, but I barely felt it.

"You have to," she whispered. "You love him."

As if I needed the painful reminder. But I couldn't do this again. Not now, not when I'd stayed up all night long with my dad—waiting for news like this.

We hadn't spoken at all. He'd sat, reading a James Patterson book, his reading glasses perched on the tip of his nose. But I could tell by how quickly he turned the pages, how often his eyes flickered to mine, that he was only pretending.

We had both stayed up waiting for news like this. Me with my eyes staring out into the stormy darkness, letting the storm roll by, thunder shaking the foundation of our house, and I had only remembered.

I couldn't go through this again.

I couldn't bury another Dillon.

"I…" I swallowed, a sob breaking from my throat before I could stop it. My fingers ached from their grip on the phone. "I can't… Liv…" I bit my lip, willed her to silently understand. "You… Faith… Jaden… Scratch—I can't do this again. I can't stand in another hospital waiting for someone to die."

"Jules -"

"Tell him I'm sorry."

Before I could change my mind, jump off the couch, and rush to the hospital, I hung up, barely hearing Liv's protesting voice coming through the line.

My dad's arm went around my shoulder, and he pulled me to him as I sobbed into his chest.

"I'm sorry, sweetie."

My hands tightened on his shirt, gripping it until my knuckles hurt, as tears spilled from my eyes. I pulled my feet under me, curled into a ball inside my dad's protective embrace, and released all my fears, all my pain in his arms.

Wiping the tears that wouldn't stop falling, I eventually tried to pull away, to regain control of myself and my emotions, but my dad's hand on the back of me made me pause.

"This is what you wanted," I sobbed through a choked cry.

His warm lips pressed against the top of my head, his hand threaded through my hair, comforting me like he did when I was a child. "Not like this, Jules. Not like this."

I barely heard him over my own wrecked grief.

But I didn't move away again. I let him hold me, finding a painful solace in the arms of my father, knowing… I could never go back.

Not again.

I wasn't strong like Faith. Wasn't born into the life like Liv. And didn't have the confidence and assurance Marie possessed.

All I wanted was a quiet life filled with love and laughter, and a stable home for Sophie.

Jaden couldn't—the club couldn't—ever give me that.

33

Jaden

I reached for consciousness and failed.

Again.

My arms pushed, swimming through a foggy sea with no end except for the faint glow I could barely make out in the far distance.

Every limb felt liquid, dissolving into the thick air in front of me. Every gray, foggy matter my fingers reached for, clung to in hopes of sifting my way through the clouds that surrounded me, disintegrated in front of me, but they kept coming.

Fuck, I hurt.

Everything did. Pain wrapped around my arms and my legs with wicked tendrils, sending shocks of searing torment through my nerves. My head pounded with the force of a jackhammer pounding my skull.

Occasionally I could focus on murmured voices, unable to make out their owners—just whether they were male and female.

Pissed off.

Sad.

Indifferent.

The tones I could decipher, the words jumbled together until the fog became too thick, too dark, and I was pulled back under.

The pain ebbed and flowed like I imagined the ocean's tide—pulling back, easing off, lifting the fog before the force slammed and pressed against my chest.

My heart.

The pain.

Voices came clearer. Liv and Daemon. I heard them. Shouted at them in my silence to tell me what the fuck was going on, but I was caught.

Captured.

Weak and helpless.

I hated every moment.

She isn't coming.

It came from Liv. It was the only full sentence I'd been able to make out and it was on constant repeat inside my head:

Sheisn'tcoming.sheisn'tcoming.sheisn'tcoming.

Until I finally understood the words.

And a harsher pain gripped my chest, squeezing and tightening until it made sense.

Jules.

I swore, my silent screams cut off from the fog until the pain blasted against my skull, to my limbs.

My body jolted. The pain lacerated my body from the inside out, until shouts filled my ears.

"Code Blue!" "Get out!" "Make room!"

"Clear!"

My body jolted.

The fog won.

The pain disappeared.

34

Jules

"It's been a week."

I tried to fortify myself from the bluntness of Liv's words and the coldness in her eyes.

I licked my lips, and my eyes darted to every corner in my apartment. Feigned indifference wouldn't work with Liv and Faith as they sat on the couches in my living room.

An intervention.

A get-the-fuck-over-yourself meeting with a side of coffee and donuts.

I knew I couldn't hide from my friends forever. Knew they'd be pissed when I finally let them into my apartment.

Knew I was being a coward because I couldn't even say goodbye. Not to Jaden.

Not to the man who consumed me, filled me with hope, with passion I never knew existed and would forever crave but could never have again.

"I can't go," I said, my face and my voice blank from emotions. It was the only way I could make it through—by pushing every feeling, every short memory, to a far corner in the recesses of my mind.

"It's been a week, Jules."

I shook my head. I couldn't. Couldn't see him in a bed filled with wires and tubes, knowing he'd already died.

Twice they'd revived his heart.

I couldn't be there if it happened a third time—and perhaps the next time, they wouldn't be able to revive him.

My lips cracked and pulled from dryness as I stared out my window. All I saw was the courtyard, wind whipping the falling leaves into a tumultuous storm.

Outside, it looked cold.

Winter was coming.

Death was coming… it was only a matter of time. And if I didn't harden myself for it now, the pain would become unbearable when the final storm came.

"I can't." I swallowed, the truth thick in my throat and in the hollowness of my eyes. "I've already said my goodbyes."

And I had—in the silence of my room every night while I wiped tears from eyes before they could stain my pillow.

A pillow that still smelled like Jaden, that laced pain to my heart when the scent hit me as I rolled, unable to sleep at night. It clung to me.

Yet I couldn't bring myself to get rid of it, either.

Liv's eyes softened with awareness and understanding. "I know this is hard for you, Jules. But you have to be there for him. You have to go see him—do what you need to do when he's okay—but don't leave him like this." She leaned over, squeezed my hand. "He's not Scratch. He's stubborn, and I have to believe he's going to be okay. All the men do, Jules. But he needs a reason."

"And I can't be the one to give him a false one."

I shook my head, a burn growing in the depth of my throat and the back of my nose. I drank my coffee, pushing it back.

"I need to find a way to move on." Again. How many times would I have to do that—pick up the pieces of my heart and glue them back together—before it would no longer work?

I pushed off the couch, headed toward the kitchen. I couldn't take their pitiful stares, their anger and disappointment with me that I knew was being held back behind a thin veil.

"You need to be there for Jaden and show him how much you love him."

I whipped my head up, staring at Liv. "Don't," I warned.

"But you do. And we all know it, and staying away because you're scared is not only stupid, it's beneath you. You're stronger than that." She stood on the other side of the kitchen counter, eyebrow arched, daring me to argue.

I inhaled and exhaled slowly, reminding myself Sophie was napping so I didn't unleash all my rage and frustration directly at Liv. She wasn't who I was mad at.

I was mad at fate. For giving me an incredible man, only to rip him away.

"Maybe I'm not," I said slowly, poorly masking my patience. "Maybe I've already buried someone I loved, and even if Jaden makes it, you can't guarantee that someday I won't bury him too. And you don't know what that's like, Liv." My eyes darted to Faith—who'd been relatively silent. I didn't know if she was here because she wanted to be or because Liv had figured there would be strength in numbers. "And you don't, either. Both of you are marrying your first loves, and mine is buried six feet under. Forever."

I exhaled, feeling like shit. And just… so over it all. The pain, the waiting, the worrying, the anger. My muscles ached, crying out for relief from sleepless nights.

I wanted warm hands and dark brown eyes to promise me everything would be okay. I wanted a scowl and a smirk. I wanted hot, spicy breath on the crook of my neck.

And Jaden couldn't give me that. He couldn't make those promises, and the last thing I wanted was more lies.

"Maybe we are," Liv said, unable to argue as the light caught the glint of her diamond. She glanced at it, almost looking embarrassed, but found resolve from somewhere. God, she was strong. She'd been through more than any of us, I imagined, so how she didn't understand what I was going through, I had no clue. "Maybe Jaden isn't your first, and he's not even your second."

She stopped, walked around the counter, and wrapped her hands around my shoulders. I stiffened when she smiled.

"But he could be your forever, and that's far more lasting than a memory of a man you haven't truly put behind you."

She dropped her hands, pressed a kiss to my cheek, and turned on her heels. Resentment flooded my blood—at her accusations and the loving way she dished them out. She may not have been completely wrong.

In all the years I'd thought I'd moved passed Scratch's death, this last week was a stark reminder of him.

Halfway to meet Liv at the door, Faith smiled sadly when she looked at me.

"I don't want you more upset, Jules. I know what it's like to lose hope in anything ever getting better. I also know what it's like to have to fight for what you want, despite how terrifying it is. You have the strength to do that, you just have to want it bad enough."

She blew me a kiss and followed Liv out the door.

It clicked shut behind them. But the quiet words of their warnings mixed with their hope and truth echoed in my ears, bouncing off the walls, long after they were gone.

Tormenting me on the dark nights and the dreary days that followed.

35

Jaden

Numbness. My mind swam in it. It filled my veins and my muscles until I didn't bother trying to fight.

Yet the fog lifted. The darkness turned to gray and then white before I felt a small tug of pain behind my eyes and then blinding, scorching white light.

I clamped my eyes closed. Orange light radiating behind my closed lids.

I groaned. Or tried to. I felt it deep in my throat, but couldn't open my mouth. I tried again, willed my lips to part, my muscles to work, and slowly felt the tear of dry flesh on flesh cracking apart.

"Fuck." I coughed. Cleared my throat. Through the dim of the leftover fog, I wondered if that was my voice.

Dry like sand. But harsher, like jagged rocks.

Damn, I felt funny. My brain sloshed in my head, woozy and disoriented. A ball of orange shone behind my closed eyes.

I tried again.

Slowly, I pushed my eyelids to open into small slits.

Instantly, the glaring lights overhead sent a fiery sensation to my pupils. I blinked, turned my head to the side, and opened them wider.

Olivia lay on a couch across from me, hands balled under her cheeks again the armrest, and her eyes were closed.

I frowned and continued moving my head, searching the room. Television mounted in corner, doors with windows and no blinds for privacy, rails next to the side of my bed. A dull throb began pounding at the base of my neck.

Tubes.

They were everywhere. My nose itched, and I felt the plastic shoved inside. It scraped across my cheek as I looked down. Plastic covered a fingertip, needles were inserted into the back of my hand and the inside of my elbow.

My head fell back onto pillow, making a scratchy sound.

"Fuck," I groaned again. In my other hand was a remote.

I pressed the red button. Red meant fire. Emergency. I took a shot.

Within minutes, the door to my room opened and a nurse poked her head in.

"Mr. Dillon." She smiled, her eyes wide with surprise. "You're awake."

I frowned. Cleared my throat, and winced from the jagged shards shredding my insides. "Yeah. Fuck it hurts."

She nodded, moved into the room and handed me a glass of water. "Two small sips. You're stomach's empty and too much will make you vomit, but it should help."

I wrapped my lips around the plastic straw, fought against the sudden urge to guzzle the whole cup. Vomiting wouldn't be good, but I figured it wouldn't be the worst thing in the world if I had ended up in the fucking hospital.

She tugged on my cup and the straw popped out of my mouth against protest. My throat screamed for it.

"Jaden?" Olivia asked, her voice thick from sleep. Her eyes flew open and her feet hit the floor. "You're up!"

She immediately rushed to my side; her hand fell on my shoulder and her lips hit my cheek. "God, I'm so glad you're awake." Her hand went to my hair, scrubbing it. The pain moved from the back of my head to the front.

"Enough." I flinched from the pain and the fuss.

"I'll go let the doctor know you're awake, but for now, small sips of water and try to rest." Her lips twisted into something bitchy before she shut the door.

"What the fuck happened?" I growled.

Liv grabbed a chair, pulled it to the side of the bed. My mind began to clear even as I voiced the question. My hand went to the sheets and I lifted them. Liv's hand covered mine.

I shot her a look.

Hers matched mine in concern and anger. "Leave it."

"Where…" I blinked, and the final haze lifted. *She's not coming. She's not coming. Jules.* "Where's Daemon?" I finally asked.

Liv's eyes went wide with shock and her lips parted. Surprised I didn't ask about Jules?

Maybe. My head hurt too much to think about anything.

Not until I knew what happened.

"I was shot."

Liv nodded. Her brown hair was pulled back into a messy bun, she had indentations on her cheek from sleeping, and she looked like shit. But her eyes went sad. "Badly, Jaden. Jesus—we almost lost you." Her chin quivered.

I closed my eyes so I didn't have to watch.

Lost me. I figured that meant I'd almost died.

Which explained why Jules wasn't coming. Didn't take a genius to figure out she didn't want shit to do with a biker who'd die on her, leaving her alone just like Scratch.

I wasn't fucking stupid.

I was too selfish to be stupid.

With fire in my eyes, I stared at Olivia. "Get her ass here, and Sophie's. Or tell her I'm showing up at her place, needles and pain and whatever the fuck else be damned."

Her lips twitched, fighting a smile. "Want me to use those exact words?"

Pain spread to my eyes, forcing me to close them. My head fell back and exhaustion and pain pulled at me. "Do whatever you fuckin' have to do."

Silence covered me like a thick blanket before Liv's hand went to my shoulder. She shoved something small and plastic into my hand. "Will do, J. And use this if you need more meds."

I mumbled something incoherent and went back to the fog.

The haze cleared more quickly the second time. Beeps and voices in the background became instantly sharp.

The bright light when my eyes were forced open was still blinding, but precise as it wiggled back and forth between my eyelids.

Which felt like they were being yanked and tugged open.

I smacked the offending light away.

"Settle, Jaden."

Daemon. His voice registered and I followed the sound until I opened my eyes on my own and stared at him. He was next to the bed, cocky grin on his lips, arms crossed over his chest, staring at a man in a white coat.

"Thanks, doc."

A man with a comb-over too obvious to ignore moved his glasses further up on his nose. He slid a thin flashlight into a pocket at his chest and rested his hands at his sides.

"How are you feeling?"

"Drugged."

He nodded, a hint of a smile in his eyes though his lips pulled into a thin line. "You're lucky to be alive." He glanced at Daemon but

I was too sluggish to follow the movement. "You were shot, Mr. Dillon—"

"Jaden."

He nodded once and continued. "Bullet entered your upper right quadrant, pierced your intestines, bile duct, and lodged into your right lung."

I squeezed my eyes closed, tried to make sense of what he said, but only focused on the important shit. Bullet… guts… lung… pain.

My thumb tapped on the button still in my hand. "How long have I been out?"

Daemon cleared his throat. "Nine days."

The fuck? My shoulders jerked, but shooting, stabbing pain in my gut quickly forced me back to the pillow. "Fuckin' hell," I muttered, one hand scrubbing down my face. My fingers got stuck on my cheeks and my chin, feeling the full, scratchy hair that had grown.

"Shit."

"We lost you twice," the doctor said.

I squinted to read his name but it blurred in my vision.

"It will take you weeks to recover, maybe months before you're back to full strength. You've received two blood transfusions, your oxygen is still low, and you have twenty-eight stitches on your right side."

Which explained the horrendous stretching, pulling sensation clawing at the skin above my right hip.

"I get it," I told him, not wanting to hear any more.

No wonder Jules was fuckin' gone. The fact she was the first thing on my mind, my first concern—even as pissed as I was that she thought she could slink away without having to answer me—scared me.

When did I become such a pussy? *Perhaps death could do that you.*

I scowled at the thought, ignored the doctor as he droned on about rest and care and visitors and what-the-fuck-ever, before he left the room on a heavy sigh, pulling the door closed behind him.

"What happened?" I asked Daemon as soon as we were alone.

His hands ran through his hair and clasped together at the back of his neck. "Nothing you need to worry about. We've already finished it."

"Finished what?" I growled, straining to move but unable to.

He sighed, dropped to the chair next to my bed, and rested his elbows on his knees. "Sporelli ambushed us, knew that we were planning something and were there. But it doesn't matter now: Erik Sporelli was taken into custody, and Ryker, Finn, and Switch took off immediately. They've taken them all out except for Angelo, who fled back to Chicago."

A slow breath filled my nose and I let it out, processing everything. "Shit. What does this mean for the club?"

"That Sporelli will come back and try to kick our ass, most likely. But we've got four charters headed our way for backup. They won't get near us."

Almost satisfied with knowing we were done with their bullshit, I almost smiled. Not running drugs would hit our cash flow, but Daemon had never wanted into that shit in the first place.

Although I would have liked to be the one to help take them out instead of laid up in a fucking hospital bed.

"Who set us up?"

Daemon's eyes flashed with feral anger. A muscle flexed in his jaw.

"Who was it?" I gritted out. I knew that look. I'd seen it in him once—when he'd learned Olivia's father, former Nordic Lords President Bull Masters was responsible for putting a hit on his own wife and Olivia had gotten caught in the crossfire. Literally.

"Gunner."

"The fuck?" I gasped. Shock pulsed through my veins. Every nerve in me had me suddenly scratching to get the fuck out of the hospital, regardless of the blistering pain shooting through my side.

"Don't fuckin' make me repeat it. Once Angelo took off, Xbox went searching, and what he found was a trail of income landing in Gunner's account—whose real name is Maurice Sporelli. Found out he made a call as soon as he heard about us movin' out the night of the party."

My head spun from the information. Shit. And we'd let Faith and Liv both work for the betraying dickhead. Not to mention the number of men who got inked by him.

And Jules with her piercing.

My fingernails dug into my palms, my breath came faster than I could take it in.

"Hey," Daemon warned, watching a monitor pulse and beep, sending piercing sounds through the room. "Calm the fuck down. The important thing is that we took care of most of it, all while you were bein' a lazy fuck and sleeping on us. Plus, we saved something fun for you." He wiggled his eyebrows playfully, but there was nothing playful about the glint in his eye or the crooked smile on his lips.

My look matched his. "Gunner?"

His hand gripped my shoulder. "He's all yours once you're out of here."

He said it to break my fury, and it helped. Barely.

I felt my lips crack into a small smile—just a hint, but my racing heart slowed enough to calm the monitors.

"Can't wait," I groaned, my hand clutching my side.

"We'll fill you in on the rest later."

I let the weight of all I'd missed out on wash over me, and eventually we fell back into an easy banter, with football highlights we didn't actually give a shit about on the television set.

But it didn't matter. It eased the pain from my side and my head until night fell, and Daemon promised he'd be back the next day.

36

Jules

Olivia had been right. The last thing I'd wanted to do was admit it when she showed up at my apartment three days ago, telling me Jaden had finally woken up and was going to be okay.

But she got what she came for.

He deserved for me to say goodbye to him in person.

Except how did you say goodbye to someone you'd only just realized you loved, knowing you couldn't be with him?

The life was too much: too harsh, too difficult, and not something I wanted Sophie raised in. My heart alone couldn't handle it—no way would I expect her to be able to.

Regardless of knowing I was doing the right thing—the best thing for everyone—my palms felt slick and clammy with Sophie's index finger tucked inside my grip on one hand, my other hand clutching the strap of my purse.

The stark white hallway seemed to stretch and grow with every step we took closer to Jaden's room.

He was being released tomorrow. If I didn't see him in the hospital, I ran the risk of him showing up at my parents' home or my apartment, demanding to see me.

I figured with Sophie in the hospital room with us, the confrontation would be less dramatic.

"Mommy," Sophie said as we reached his room. Her large, scared blue eyes peered up at me and almost took my breath away. "I miss him."

"I know," I told her, running a hand through her hair. "You'll still see him. But remember what I said about today?"

She nodded, pushed her lips into a pout before she frowned. "He sick."

"And he might not look okay, but he's going to be just fine."

Despite not understanding, she nodded again. I didn't know how Jaden would look either, but I figured it was better to prepare her for the worst than have her scared when she saw him.

Forcing a bravery I didn't feel, I twisted the doorknob to Jaden's room and opened it.

My nerves and my fear instantly jumped to my throat as I took him in, helplessly laid out on a hospital bed that seemed too small for his intimidating frame.

Even with him sleeping, his eyes closed, with his arm draped over his eyes to block out the light, I felt my body warm.

God, he did things to me. My arousal began to pulse, just staring at him, as I uselessly tried to push it down.

It didn't work, but still I felt my feet to move toward the bed, hesitating only slightly when I wondered if we should come back later.

But I knew if I did, I might not ever make it.

"You're here."

My feet faltered at his gravelly voice. I saw his mouth move, but every other muscle in his body was still. I almost imagined I dreamed it or made it up until his full lips pulled and twisted.

"I am," I finally said, suddenly certain this was the worst idea I ever had.

Enclosed in a room with Jaden, even in a hospital, didn't provide safety from the anger rolling off him, or the desperation to flee coming from me.

Slowly, he removed his arm from his eyes and rested it over his stomach. He flinched when his hand made contact with his side.

Cracking open one eye, he caught my terrified gaze before quickly dropping to look at Sophie.

"And you brought your safety net."

I resisted the pull to cower under his sarcasm and his harsh glare. Even if he was right.

"Hi, Uncah Jaden." Sophie squeezed my hand, as if she needed to remind me that I was there and that she'd been anxiously asking to see Jaden for the last week. She wanted her piggyback rides and her trips to the garage.

"Hey, half-pint," Jaden said, and patted the bed next to him. Without hesitating, I lifted her and set her down on the left side of his bed so she could talk to him.

Jaden's hand gripped mine as soon as I let her go, unable to do it quickly enough so he couldn't touch me.

He tightened his grip when I tried to pull away.

I moved my gaze from his hand to Sophie. "She wanted to see you."

"That the only reason you came?"

I steeled myself for the lie I needed to give. "Yes."

He whispered "Bullshit" but dropped my hand. Sophie began showing Jaden her hot pink fingernails we'd painted that morning and her fancy Easter dress that she had already grown out of but insisted she wore to see him at the hospital.

I let them have their time, and like the coward I knew I was being, I slunk to the couch on the far side of the room, as far away from Jaden as I could get, yet not far enough. His pale skin didn't detract from the physical pull he always had on me.

Drawn to him, I watched him smile and laugh with Sophie. My heartbeat increased every time his eyes snapped in my direction, as if he couldn't take his eyes off me either.

Finally, I couldn't take it anymore.

"Sophie," I said, walking to the bed. Jaden's hand tightened on her thigh. "We need to get going."

"Not until we talk."

"Jaden," I started, then snapped my mouth shut when his eyes narrowed into slits.

"You running?" His anger rolled off his broad shoulders in palpable waves.

I hitched my purse over my shoulder, trying to buy time. "No."

"Bullshit."

My eyes snapped to Sophie. "Watch your language."

With a quick pat, he tapped Sophie's back. "Go play, half-pint."

Sophie looked at me, raising her arms. I picked her up, handed her my phone, pulling up a cartoon app, and slid it into her hand. "Go watch."

She toddled over to the couch, climbed up, and settled herself easily into the uncomfortable furniture.

Jaden's hand snapped out and gripped my wrist, regaining my attention, although he'd never lost it. I was just... avoiding.

"You can't run from me."

My eyes stayed focus on his hand, too afraid of what he'd see if he looked into my blue eyes: fear. It clung to me like cheap perfume, and I couldn't erase its scent no matter how hard I tried.

"Jaden," I said softly. "Maybe it's not about running," I raised my eyes to his. "Maybe it's simply about knowing what I can handle and what I can't."

"Bullshit," he growled.

"This isn't a fucking card game, Jaden," I snapped, watching his scowl slightly disappear. "I've seen Scratch die, I was in town when your parents were buried. I saw Liv in the hospital after being shot, Faith being kidnapped." Emotions raged inside, spilling into tears and down my cheeks. I leaned over Jaden so Sophie couldn't hear. "My daughter was taken." I pointed a finger at my chest. "My daughter. The only good damn thing I've got in my life, and she was taken from me."

"And we took care of the fuckin' problem," he growled, his fingers tightening along the pulse in my wrist.

And hell, it felt good. His strength and his confidence covered me like a thick blanket I couldn't shake.

"You're part of the problem," I hissed. "How many more people in my life have to die or be taken before I just fucking lose it?" I waved a hand in the air, making my point.

"For one," he sneered, pulling me forward slightly. The move pulled me off balance and my hand came down on the far side of his hips so I was bent completely over him.

Jaden looked down the gap in the front of my shirt and smirked.

"For one," he restated, "Scratch died because he was a jackass on a bike and he wasn't safe. Sophie was taken because you fucked around with a psychopath." Anger and humiliation boiled inside in me in equal measure.

I wanted to argue. But he wasn't wrong, either. Not really.

"And this club life is dangerous. You knew that before you let me take you against your wall, shoving your pussy in my face like you wanted me to devour you."

"Shut up," I huffed. But my body liked what he was saying. My panties grew damp, and my pulse pounded against my skin, beating in my ears like a rolling thunderstorm.

Jaden's hand dropped my wrist, and he pressed two fingers to the base of my throat. "Why would I shut up when the reminder of what I've done to you turns you on?" One side of his lips quirked.

The move distracted me. His tongue came out and he licked his lips before his hand moved to the back of my neck and he pulled me to him.

His lips were on me instantly. His hand dug into my skin, holding me in place against him, and damn it—I surrendered. My tongue met his and I soaked in the taste of him. My arms shook from the weight of trying to hold myself off his body, off his stitches and his injury, when the only thing my body screamed at me was "Yes! More!"

I fought against it—fought against the pull to throw myself into his arms, crawl into his bed next to him, and never let go.

I tasted every ounce of him that I could while he held my mouth to his, adjusting his grip on the back of my head to a better angle. I mewled into his mouth when he released a groan.

God, he was so sexy and tasted so damn good.

"Jules," he rasped, breaking our kiss and the trance his touch put me under. He pulled me down until my forehead pressed to his. He shifted, pressed his mouth against my ear. My hips ground against the edge of his bed when his teeth came down and bit my ear lobe. "You can try to fuckin' hide, but this is a small town. I'm in Sophie's life and I'll stay there. Go deal with the shit you need to deal with until you're not afraid of what's happening between us, but don't think for one second that you'll get rid of me."

I tried to pull away from him, but his hand tightened and he pulled me back until our eyes were inches from each other. Our shallow breaths mixed between us.

"You're mine, Jules. And I'll prove it to you."

"How?" I asked, unable to stop myself from being sucked into his spell. His eyes, his jaw, his slightly crooked nose… all of it was irresistible, regardless of how hard I tried. Not to mention his confidence and his ability to kill anything that risked harming me.

"Because," he grinned. "You won't be able to forget me, no matter how hard you try."

I pushed off the bed and his hand fell from my skin to his lap, leaving my neck prickled with chill bumps. I rolled my shoulders, fighting the feeling. "Don't be so arrogant. You don't know everything."

I turned to leave when his quiet, threatening voice stilled me.

"I know you love me."

Looking back over my shoulder, I opened my mouth to deny it, but I shut my mouth when I took in his chilling glare.

"Don't lie, Jules. Not about that."

I swallowed. A thick lump impeded the movement, but I turned away before he could see the truth, even though he knew it. But admitting it and him assuming it were two completely different things.

"Goodbye, Jaden."

His nose twitched and then his lips pulled into a wide grin. It stretched from ear to ear and light sparkled in his eyes as if I'd given him the greatest present in the world instead of the biggest brush-off.

"Temporary, Jules. Get your shit together, avoid me all you want, but I get my ass out of here and the first thing I'm fuckin' doin' is coming for you, and I won't leave until you admit it."

Squeezing my eyes closed, I reached for Sophie until she was safely in my arms. It gave me the semblance of protection from Jaden and his words, which I knew were completely truthful.

Jaden didn't bullshit.

Which meant I had only a few days to prepare myself for the fight of my life.

But as I walked out of the hospital, Sophie strolling slowly next to me with my finger gripped in hers, I no longer knew if the fight was going to be running…

Or staying.

Either one risked my heart—just in completely different ways.

37

Jules

Weeks passed. Every day that I went to work at the salon, came home, and sat in my quiet apartment after Sophie went to sleep, I grew more on edge.

Jaden had been released from the hospital three weeks ago.

I had yet to hear from him.

Liv and Faith came to my place every week for a girls' night that generally consisted of alcohol, but not nearly the amounts it would have taken to erase my constant thoughts of Jaden from my memory. They didn't say much about the club, but they dropped enough guilt-inducing comments in my lap for me to know that Jaden was being an angry asshole—worse than before—but that his wounds were healing well.

Everything they said filled me with relief that he was going to be fine, and regret for not being strong enough to stand by his side and help him. A small biting voice made me question who was taking care of him instead of me. Another voice yelled at me for being stupid. A third voice—one that continued to grow quieter and quieter as the days wore on—reminded me it was no longer my business who helped Jaden… I'd given up the right to know anything about him.

All of them left me feeling crabby and cranky and tired and just… sad.

But regardless of how I felt, the stabbing pain that hit my chest at the end of every day, reminding me that another day had passed and he hadn't even bothered trying to get me back was the most hurtful.

Not that it should have mattered. I had turned my back on him— not the other way around.

Yet, a part of me longed to hear his rough, gravel voice when he woke up in the morning. I wanted to feel his touch and be the one to make those rare half-smiles appear. But the parts I wanted weren't enough to make me admit my mistakes and my fears directly to him, to risk the possibility that Jaden had decided I wasn't worth the chase or the effort anymore.

So how I ended up here, sitting cross-legged on an old tattered blanket, I had no idea. When I had woken up I'd grabbed Sophie and a bag of her toys, knowing that at some point I truly did need to say goodbye to my past once and for all.

Maybe then I'd be able to see everything else more clearly.

I smiled, watching while Sophie played absent-mindedly as she ran around the trunk of a nearby tree. Her soft voice fluttered through the air, her feet crunched on the freshly fallen leaves tinged with red and yellow.

And I knew without a doubt that I had to be here, even if uncertainty still clung to me like wet dewdrops to the tips of the grass.

"I don't know what to say to you," I finally croaked. Closing my eyes, I slowly opened them and lifted my chin to the stone slab in front of me.

The etched name brought sadness to my eyes, but tears stayed at bay.

Scott "Scratch" Dillon
Brother, in life and in death
1989-2010

"You can't even hear me," I muttered, ashamed of myself that it'd taken so long to come and see him. The man I'd once I loved. The man who'd died just after finding out he was going to have a child, and I had yet to introduce them. And now that I was here, my selfish heart beat wildly against my chest.

The words I'd been holding close to me, too afraid to speak out loud, for fear that Fate would strike me again, fell from my lips, and tears began falling down my cheeks.

"I loved you, you know." I paused, shook my head, and continued. "I loved you as much as any twenty-two-year-old could have loved another, and I don't know if that would have been a forever kind of love or not anymore. Sometimes I wonder…" I wiped my eyes, tried to keep them trained on the headstone in front of me. My eyes kept flitting to Sophie, watching her play, completely oblivious to the current that was swirling inside of me like the eye of a hurricane. "I wonder if we would have made it. Once you got more into the club, would I have been the kind of woman who stood by and watched you do the things I know those men do?

"But I know you would have loved Sophie with everything you had," I sobbed, my shoulders began to shake. I stopped myself. The guilt over everything I'd questioned for the last several years fell on my shoulders, and yet I was freeing myself of it at the same time. "I don't know if we would have made it. It doesn't mean I love you less, or that I ever loved you less, but I mourned your death. I mourned the loss of your love and the fact that Sophie would grow up without a father.

"And… I fell in love again. He's scary and he's mean and he's angry almost all the time unless Sophie is on his hip—and even then his ability to be happy is questionable." I laughed to myself, thinking of Jaden and his angry brown eyes and his scowl that he wore as if the world would end if anyone spied his teeth. "It terrifies me, how I feel about him—knowing who he is and how much you loved him. I'm terrified that he'll end up buried next to you and I'll have to say goodbye to another Dillon brother who has my entire heart. I feel like life is waiting to crush me again, and I don't know if I can handle it. Or that I want to.

"I don't know how to handle this life that I've always enjoyed but never fully understood the true depth of. Where men kill and are killed, women aren't safe, and God—Scratch, what if something else happened to Sophie?"

I stopped bothering to wipe my eyes and let the tears fall freely. They wet my scarf and landed like raindrops on my denim-clad lap.

"And yet, I know that if there was anyone else out there in the entire world, that this is who you'd want for me."

I turned my head, searching for Sophie when I didn't hear her whispered songs filter to my ears. I squinted, tried to peer behind the large maple tree where she'd been playing. Leaning forward on the blanket, I still couldn't see her so I stood up, momentarily forgetting where I was.

Whipping my head around, spinning on my heels, my hand flew to my mouth and I gasped.

Behind me Jaden stood, one arm in a sling, with Sophie propped on his hip and her head resting on his shoulders.

He jiggled her, his hand on her bottom bouncing her to a more comfortable position. His eyes were on me as if he wanted to set fire to my soul.

"You're wrong." His eyes flashed to the headstone behind me and his lips twisted. "He wouldn't have wanted me for you. Scratch was smart enough to know I would never be good enough for you."

"I… uh…" Jesus. I needed to get a grip. "How long have you been here?" My eyes whipped around to the parking lot. I frowned when I didn't see his truck or his bike. Not that he looked in any condition to be able to ride his bike yet.

"That's what you want to know?" Jaden took a step forward, and then another one. With every slow movement of his, my heartbeat increased until it pounded so loudly inside my chest I was certain he could hear it from five feet away.

Four feet.

Three feet.

He stepped so close I could smell his cologne, and see his breath in the chilly morning air. It wafted from his lips and his nose into a faint plume of smoke before evaporating into the space between us.

I closed my eyes, breaking the intense heat his presence sent through me.

"Uncah Jaden hurt," Sophie said. She pointed at his arm and frowned.

"I know." My lips pursed. "How are you healing?"

"That's still not the right question."

What? My head spun. I blinked as I watched Jaden set Sophie on her feet, pat her butt, and watch her run to Scratch's headstone, where we'd set flowers earlier.

"Who dat?"

God, I'd failed at everything this morning. I hadn't even told Sophie who we were here to see. With an apologetic look to Jaden, I knelt next to Sophie on the grass and ran my hand over Scratch's name.

"This is your daddy, sweetie."

Her eyebrows pulled in. "Dat my dad?"

I nodded. "Yes, the one in the pictures from your book. Remember I said he died, but he loved you and watched over you all the time?" I pulled in a breath when she looked at the headstone, frowned, and back to Jaden. I didn't know if she understood, but I could see the wheels in her mind working furiously.

Slowly, she frowned at the slab of stone and shook her head. "Dat not my dad."

"Sophie," I gasped. "Of course he is."

She stood up, looking much older than any almost three-year-old should look. Her blond hair, piled into two pigtails behind her ears, swung in the cold breeze and she pouted.

"You tell me daddy yuv me, and play wif me, and help us."

I did tell her that. Every night when I showed her the book, I went through all the things Scratch would have done, would have wanted to do with Sophie and I, had he been here. But I frowned, uncertain where she was going.

When her head whipped around and she stared at Jaden, I inhaled a breath.

"Sophie," I started. But she was on the move.

She walked the short distance to Jaden and reached for his hand. With imploring, large blue eyes, she asked, "You yuv me?"

"Yeah, half-pint, I love you." His eyes softened and his entire face went slack when she wrapped her arms around her leg.

"You help me. You my dad."

I gasped again; the force of her confidence rocked me on my heels.

I went to move, to correct her, but before I could, her speech and her declaration stunned me into a block of ice, and Jaden squatted down in front of her.

He winced from the movement, his good hand gripping the arm in his sling until he knelt at her level and placed his good on hand on her shoulder.

She grinned a smile full of spaces between her tiny teeth. "You can be my dad."

"You had one, half-pint, and he was the best man I ever knew. But I love you just as much as he did. And if you want, I'll tell you all about him."

"Otay," she grinned, shrugged like something monumental hadn't just happened. Like Sophie hadn't just thrown my world and my fears into a tailspin with her simple, clearly spoken words. "Mommy, I go play now?"

I shook my head, and as I did, seeing the love Jaden clearly had for Sophie written so plainly across his face—a look that only intensified as his eyes reached mine—my fears fell to the ground and evaporated like the dew.

"Yeah, pumpkin. Go play."

I waited until she went back to dancing around the tree, singing her quiet songs, before I went to Jaden and offered him a hand. "Need help getting up?"

He scoffed. "No, getting up has never been my problem." He flashed me a look and looked at his crotch before raising an eyebrow at me. A strangled laugh choked my throat. Typical.

He grabbed my hand and pulled me down to him until I was on my knees in front of him.

"But my side feels like it's on fire, so sit with me before I have to get up again."

I did. I sat next to Jaden on the grass in front of his dead brother's gravesite, and wished I were anywhere else when I had to say what I had to say.

Yet somehow, it all seemed so fitting to be declaring my love for Jaden with Scratch so close, giving me the go-ahead to move on—the permission to be strong even when it scared the crap out of me.

As if he read my mind, Jaden reached out, cupped my cheek with his hand. "Scratch would know I wouldn't be good enough for you. I meant that earlier. He also knows I wanted you back before you went to him and that I'm a selfish prick—so now that I have my shot, finally have a good shot at you, I won't ever let you walk away from me."

"What makes you so sure that's what I want?"

He shot me an "oh fuckin' please" look. It was one I'd seen often. "I heard you, babe."

Babe. The word sent shivers to my spine. "Maybe I wasn't talking about you."

"I already knew you loved me, just been waiting for the words."

I swallowed, knowing he was right but unable to admit to him. Not face to face. Not when I'd just so quickly realized the depth of my love for him myself—a love so deep that I knew I'd stand by him regardless of what he did.

"And you?"

Jaden laughed softly, as if it was the dumbest question in the world. He leaned in, pressed his forehead to mine, and his hand moved to the back of my neck—right where I loved it when he held me. "Wouldn't be here if I didn't, Jules."

I blew out a breath I didn't know I was holding.

"I want that. Want to be the man Sophie thinks I am. I want that for you and I want it for her, but mostly, I want to be the kind of man she sees when she looks at me."

"You already are." My body burned for him. I couldn't sit here so close to him and not feel the connection we'd always seemed to have—one that had quickly changed from hatred and mistrust to something so beautiful and so much deeper. "Doesn't mean I'm not still scared, Jaden."

"I know." He pulled back until our eyes were inches from one another. "Club took care of Sporelli when I was out, you know."

I nodded, because I did. Liv and Faith had filled me in—even letting me know that somehow Gunner had been a plant from the Sporelli family for years. I also knew Jaden beat the shit out of him, then they returned him to Chicago, barely alive, but alive enough that Sporelli had guaranteed there'd be no blowback on the club if they let him go. I swallowed, that thick lump in my throat appearing whenever I thought about the reality of their life—potentially *my* life.

"I wanted to wait to come to you until all that shit was done. But we've taken care of Gunner, the club's done running drugs, and we've done a damn good job of cleaning up Jasper Bay. The only shit we'll get into now is in keeping it clean, and we'll do whatever we need to keep it a safe, clean place. Doesn't mean shit won't happen, but you need to trust that if a bullet in my gut and me dying two times already wasn't enough to take me from you, that nothing will."

I lost the fight I had in staying away from him. Everything he said was exactly what I needed to hear.

I couldn't help it. The pull between us was real. It was intense and it was built on a lifetime of knowing one another. Maybe not always liking one another, but I knew Jaden enough to know he didn't say shit he didn't mean. His word was his bond. Permanently.

"I trust you," I finally admitted, feeling emotions bubble to the surface. Before I could let them break, let him see more tears in my eyes, I leaned in and pressed my lips to his.

With a grunt of surprise, Jaden quickly pressed against the back of my head and took control. From my lips to my toes, everything exploded with desire and love for the man on his knees in front of me. Promising me the world.

Promising me the family I'd always wanted for Sophie.

It was so overwhelming, tears began to fall anyway. I sniffed, still reeling from the kiss when Jaden pulled back.

He wiped the tears off my cheeks and pulled me to him so my ear rested against his lips. "Love you, Jules. And Sophie. I'll be the man you need me to be, I fuckin' promise."

"I know," I choked out, my voice thick with emotion. "I know you will."

"I'd also love nothing better than to lay down and let you ride my cock until you're screaming my name, but the doc says I can't do shit like that for another six weeks so we're gonna have to find another way to make up."

And just like that, he broke the heaviness of the moment and filled it with something else completely more powerful… something I desperately wanted. Forever.

EPILOGUE
Jules

Eight months later ~ early June

"Finish it, babe."

Jaden's deep, gravelly growl spurred me on. My hips shifted against his as I straddled him. His hands gripped my hips, rocking and pushing me, lifting and pulling me.

I may have been on top, but he controlled every moment I made.

In the last eight months since I'd finally let my fears go, I'd surrendered to the fact that Jaden always had to be in control.

Especially in bed.

"Jaden." My head fell back and I moaned. His hand left my hip, fingers straight to my clit, and he rubbed. Hard. Just the way I liked it.

I exploded against him. My thighs shook. My head dropped down and my fingernails dug into his shoulders as he continued forcefully and frantically pushing inside of me like he couldn't get enough of me.

I loved it that I brought that out it him... his loss of self-control became my undoing every single time we were in bed. Or against a wall. Or in the shower. Or on the kitchen table.

Needless to say, sex with Jaden hadn't gotten boring.

And since we'd decided to stop using condoms, it'd gotten even better.

My body shivered again as he dragged his cock against me. The warm metal inside of me scraped against my G-spot and another miniature orgasm, short but just as intense as the first one, rolled through my body.

"Oh my God," I mumbled, losing all muscle control.

My chest collapsed against his. My pierced nipple dragged across his chest, and my nipples tightened with pleasure.

Jaden let out a groan of his own as he finished inside of me. His cock pulsed and twitched. His hands tightened on my hips as he held me against him while he finished.

Hell. I loved sex with Jaden.

"I love you," I breathed out on a shaky, completely sated exhale. Jaden had the ability to wring every last drop of pleasure and breath from my body. And he liked doing it daily. Multiple times. I hated working out, but because of sex with Jaden I was probably in the best shape of my life.

I could probably run a marathon.

Or maybe a mile without a breaking a sweat.

"Keeps getting better, babe." He pressed a kiss just below my ear. His hands slowly dragged up my ribs to my shoulders before clasping together behind my neck, leaving goose bumps along my sensitive flesh as the warmth from his hands sunk into my skin.

"Always will." I propped myself up onto my elbows, resting them on his chest, and faked a scowl. "But you've made me late."

"Shouldn't have worn that shit underneath your bridesmaid dress, then."

I pushed off him, rolled to the bed, and grabbed the offending black bra and garter set. "This?" I asked, a playful smirk on my lips. "You weren't supposed to see it until later."

He winked and sat up. "I'll pretend it's the first time all over again when I take it off of you."

I held up the thong, ripped in two. "I don't think that's going to happen."

He shrugged shamelessly. It was a move I had come to see often, and yet never tired of. Somehow, I lightened his anger and his guilt. Being together, we were both lighter than we'd possibly ever been.

But seeing him so carefree always hit a spark in my chest and left me feeling like I could conquer the world.

"Then go without," he said, pulling his jeans on. He looked up as he finished buttoning his jeans. "Didn't you say we were going to be late?"

I grinned, staring at his chest, when I saw the tattoo on the left side of his ribs: a completely cliché rose and thorns, but wrapped around them were my name, Scratch's, and Sophie's. He had said he'd wanted us close to his heart forever. It was a tattoo he'd had done by Jasper Bay's newest tattoo artist. I had gone with him to GetInked2, now owned by some guy named Skull, and had felt on pins and needles the whole time. I knew they didn't kill Gunner, but it didn't stop me from being paranoid for the entire trip that something dark and sinister was lurking in the corners of the old place.

"Crap," I quickly muttered, pulling my eyes off his sexy chest and ink. "I need to get going or Liv is going to kick my butt."

Jaden smacked my ass. "I'll kiss it and make it better if she does."

"I'm sure you would." I wrinkled my nose, making Jaden laugh softly. Then I rolled to my toes, pressed my lips to his cheek. "I'll see you soon?"

"I'll be at the front waiting for you."

It wasn't our wedding. It was Liv and Daemon's. But the thought of Jaden standing at the front of a wedding, waiting for me, had my pulse racing and crimson blooming on my cheeks.

As if he could read my mind, his hand snaked out, grabbed my waist, and pulled me flush against him. "Someday it'll be us."

I swallowed. My knees went wobbly and I licked my lips. "Sounds good." I barely recognized my lusty, hopeful voice.

"It's a promise."

Then it was his turn to lean down and plant a panty-gushing kiss to my lips before he sent me on my way. I was already twenty minutes late getting to the club for our hair and makeup, courtesy of Cassie, Callie, and Cammie.

"Married," I said to no one in particular. "Who would have thought?"

Next to me, Faith and Marie laughed softly and we clinked our drinks together. I quickly learned a biker wedding wasn't your typical wedding. There wasn't a dance. There wasn't a bouquet or garter toss.

What there was, was a lot cheers. A lot of alcohol. A night that had everyone swaying between tipsy and wasted. And dozens of men with their women, drinking it up and enjoying life.

The picture in front of me—the crowd, the laughter, the squealing of the few children that were running around—had my heart swelling to a size I never knew it could hold.

I loved this family.

It was becoming *my* family—a greater, louder, but no less loving extension than my parents, who had slowly come around to the idea of me and Jaden together. Not that it hadn't taken a lot of work on my part to smooth the way. My dad finally not re-running for Jasper Bay Mayor helped.

We'd never do weekly Sunday dinners at their place, but we saw them enough. It helped that Jaden now lived in my apartment with me and Sophie, so my parents were forced to spend time with him if they wanted to see Sophie.

Gradually, my dad stopped hating him and being wary of him. Wasn't to say he still didn't worry, but I figured since I was his only daughter, that was his right. As long as the men were respectful, I didn't push it further.

My mom, on the other hand, had slowly come around to welcoming Jaden, and now treated him like the son she never had.

At first I figured it was for Sophie's sake. But now she called Jaden on her own when she needed "man help" around the house and my dad wasn't there. And she brought her car to the Nordic Lords garage, insisting Jaden take care of it. It was her olive branch, and one he took.

I was enjoying the night and the crowd when I saw Sophie rushing across the lawn, red plastic cup in her hand, amber liquid sloshing out of the sides. Jaden strolled behind her, headed my way.

"Mommy!" she squealed.

I reached down, picked her up, and planted her on my hip. "What are you drinking?" I frowned into the slightly foamy cup.

Sophie looked at me, nodded once. "Beer."

My eyes flew open just as Jaden walked up. "Don't even," he started, shaking his head. "She asked for beer, we gave her apple cider."

I rolled my eyes. "Like I thought you'd actually give her beer." But a small part of me wondered. Jaden was incredible with Sophie, but sometimes the men didn't think the clearest with kids around. Add in them all being drunk, and anything was bound to happen.

Plus, Sophie had sunk her little pudgy fingers into everyone's heart and she was doted on hand and foot whenever she hit the club grounds.

"Daddy's going to teach me to ride a bike when I get big," she declared, her face serious and hopeful.

My heart skipped a beat. It did every time she called Jaden 'daddy.' After a few weeks, I'd stopped trying to correct her. She still loved her "picture daddy," and she still talked to the photos of Scratch, but if she needed a real dad in her life, I couldn't deny her giving Jaden that name.

And besides that, every time she said it to him, it was if I could see a small piece of his angry heart softening. The effect was instantaneous. And Jaden loved it so much that a few months ago he'd told me he wanted more kids to call him by that name—said it so adamantly and sincerely that we'd begun making love without any protection.

I could have waited until we'd done everything the "right" way and been married first, but Jaden was impatient.

And so was I. Because seeing Jaden run his fingers through Sophie's hair and press his lips to her temple as she laid her head on my shoulder, I couldn't hold back the surprise I'd been trying to hold onto until after the wedding.

"I'm pregnant," I blurted. I bit my lip as Jaden froze inches from Sophie's face.

His head snapped to mine, his eyes widened fractionally, and his grip on Sophie's hair tightened.

"What'd you say?"

I couldn't read his slow drawl—whether he was upset or surprised in a good way.

I shifted Sophie on my hip and watched as Jaden stood up, letting go of Sophie.

A light sparkled in his brown eyes. "You gonna repeat that?"

I swallowed. "You heard me."

"Yeah, but I want to hear you say it again." The edges of his lips twisted and twitched, fighting a grin.

All the nerves I'd been holding fell to my feet and disappeared into the grass. I pulled in a deep breath and smiled. "I'm pregnant."

"Fuck, yeah!" he shouted. In an instant, Sophie and I were wrapped in his arms, lifted off our feet, and Jaden shouted loud enough for the entire club to hear him. "My girl is fuckin' knocked up!"

Hoots and hollers and cheers and shouts of congratulations rang through the darkening night. I buried my head into the crook of Jaden's shoulder.

"You weren't supposed to tell them on Daemon's wedding

night," I scolded once he set me down on my feet. My smile and blushing cheeks made it completely worthless.

Jaden took Sophie from me, holding her on his hip, and cupped my cheek with his other hand. "You think I'm gonna fuckin' wait to share that shit?"

"Language," I reminded him pointlessly. At three, Sophie cursed like a sailor.

"Kiss me," he demanded.

I didn't wait before I leaned in, pressed my lips against his, and tasted him.

"I can't believe how much everything can change in a year," Olivia mused happily.

She and Faith had heard the cheering and rushed over to congratulate me. Wanting a quieter place for me to share the gossip, we headed inside the clubhouse, where we could warm up a bit and sit down.

I stretched my feet out onto the sticky coffee table in front of me.

"I know, right?" Faith took a sip of her beer and glanced at her engagement ring. It was amazing. A year ago, the three of us who had grown up friends had barely had contact with each other for five years.

Now, life was completely different. Better.

I shook my head. The shock of being pregnant wasn't huge, but it still filled me with awe knowing that in seven and a half months I was going to be having a baby. Jaden's baby.

By then, Faith and Ryker would be married.

"Hey," I said to Faith, remembering a phone call she'd gotten earlier, before Liv's wedding. "What did Meg want?"

Faith frowned into her beer cup and sighed. "I don't know, but she's headed this way."

"What?" My eyebrows flew up to my forehead. "Why?"

Faith just shrugged. "Said she needed to get away and she and Brayden are headed this way."

"Who's coming this way?" All three of our heads snapped to the masculine voice as Ryker rounded the corner into the club house.

I bit the inside of my lip.

Faith pressed her lips together.

Olivia looked at Ryker like she'd never seen him before in her life.

His hands went to his hips and he glared at all of us. "What's going on?"

"Nothing," Faith said quickly. Too quickly. She scrambled to her feet and wrapped a hand around Ryker's elbow, pulling him outside. "Let's go party."

A frown line appeared in between Ryker's eyes as he slowly perused Faith's body and then looked at all of us.

"What's going on?" he repeated.

I shrank into the couch. I had no clue, but the phone call had shaken Faith up earlier and she didn't seem eager to tell Ryker about it now.

Finally, she quietly whispered. "Meg called. She's coming here."

"What?" Ryker shouted. His eyes flew wide open and he twisted out of Faith's hold. "Why?"

"I don't know, but she didn't sound good."

"What do you mean, she didn't sound good?" he hissed at Faith. I'd rarely seen Ryker mad.

It wasn't a sight I wanted to see again anytime soon as he leaned over Faith, barely containing his concern for Meg and Brayden.

"Calm down. I don't know anything. She called, sounded scared, said she was coming, and I said okay." Faith shrugged. "She'll be here tomorrow, I figure."

"Fuck," Ryker muttered and reached for his phone. In seconds he was dialing her number, and then snapped the phone closed when

Meg apparently didn't answer. He pointed a scolding finger at Faith. "We'll talk about this at home."

Faith smiled but it was shaky and uncertain. We all watched as Ryker turned on his heels and stomped out of the clubhouse.

"You okay?" I asked her once the door slammed shut behind him.

Faith tossed back the rest of her drink and sat down. "It'll be fine. We'll go home, have hot make-up sex, and he'll get over it."

I laughed. "Thinking of hot make-up sex sort of makes me want to go piss off Jaden."

"Shouldn't be too hard," Liv said, standing up. "But I get to go have wedding night sex. So we'll see you next week when we get back."

The three of us laughed and drew each other into a hug.

"Have fun on your honeymoon," I told Liv as she waved goodbye to us. She and Daemon were taking off to Colorado the next morning and would be gone for a week. "That leaves just us," I said, turning to Faith.

Faith shook her head and grinned. "Nope. It leaves just you. I'm going to go get started on make-up sex."

"Got it," I said, following her out of the clubhouse to the yard, where the party was still going strong. The bass from the music vibrated the ground beneath my feet. "I'm gonna skip the angry sex and go straight for the 'you knocked me up, let's celebrate' sex."

"Ohhh," Faith laughed. "Baby sex. I haven't had that yet."

I bumped her hip with mine. "You will someday."

She threw her arm around me, and pulled me toward the men. One of my hands went to my belly, and I smiled when I saw Jaden take in my hand on my stomach.

His grin went wide. His eyes softened.

And I knew.

I had my man. I had Sophie. And I had a new baby on the way.

Nothing... *nothing*... could be better than this.

ACKNOWLEDGEMENTS

To my BadAss CP's – you ladies, as always, rock. I'm so thankful for all of you and absolutely adore the friendships we've made. Thank you for always being there to help keep me sane. I can't wait until the day where we can all meet.

To Heather Carver, Samien Newcomb, and Natalie Gerber. Thank you for being such amazing beta readers. Y'all rock!!!

Thank you to my editor, Amy Jackson. You're the absolute best!!! I'm so honored I had the pleasure of working with you on this book.

After almost two years of writing and publishing, I have met some incredibly amazing writers, readers, and bloggers on this crazy journey. Thank you to every single one of the blogs that have helped promote my books through reviews, release days, and blog tours. Most especially, thank you to: Love Between the Sheets for all your excellent promotional help. Thank you to Reviews by Tammy and Kim, Three Chicks and Their Books, Up All Night Book Addict, Carver's Book Cravings, Shanoff Reads, A Literary Perusal, and Wild Wordy Women. I know… I'm leaving off a ton… but please know that I truly appreciate all of you more than I can say.

To the readers: You're the BEST!!!! Thank you so much for cheering me on, for pushing me to get books out, and for loving my books when I finally finish them! I read every single review, every post, every message, and every e-mail. Thank you for taking the time to let me, and others, know how much you love this series.

And to my family. I couldn't do this without your support Thank you for giving me the time to get lost inside my head while these books are written.

To my God and Savior, Jesus Christ. All Glory and Honor is Yours.

ABOUT THE AUTHOR

Stacey Lynn currently lives in Minnesota with her husband and four children. When she's not conquering mountains of laundry and fighting a war against dust bunnies and cracker crumbs, you can find her playing with her children, curled up on the couch with a good book, or on the boat with her family enjoying Minnesota's beautiful, yet too short, summer.

She lives off her daily pot of coffee, can only write with a bowlful of Skittles nearby, and has been in love with romance novels since before she could drive herself to the library.

If you would like to know more about Stacey Lynn, follow her here:

Facebook: www.facebook.com/staceylynnbooks
Twitter: @staceylynnbooks
Blog: http://staceylynnbooks.blogspot.com

**If you enjoyed this book, please leave
a review on the site where it was purchased.
And don't forget to check out Stacey's other books:**

The Nordic Lords Series
Point of Return
Point of Redemption
Point of Freedom

Point of Surrender – coming 2015

<u>Other Books</u>
Just One Song
Just One Week
Remembering Us
Don't Lie To Me
Try Me – A *Don't Lie To Me* Novella

Printed in Great Britain
by Amazon